THE
DAMAGE
DONE

THE
DAMAGE
DONE

A NOVEL

MICHAEL LANDWEBER

CROOKED
LANE

NEW YORK

Published in the United States by Crooked Lane Books, an imprint of The Quick Brown Fox & Company LLC.

Crooked Lane Books and its logo are trademarks of The Quick Brown Fox & Company LLC.

Library of Congress Catalog-in-Publication data available upon request.

ISBN (hardcover): 978-1-64385-947-7
ISBN (ebook): 978-1-64385-948-4

Cover design by Patrick Sullivan

Printed in the United States.

www.crookedlanebooks.com

Crooked Lane Books
34 West 27th St., 10th Floor
New York, NY 10001

First Edition: March 2022

10 9 8 7 6 5 4 3 2 1

DAB

D A Y

1

JUST RUN.

Dab careened up the stranger's driveway, heading to the side of the house. He was going too fast, losing control. Looking over his shoulder to make sure they weren't behind him. The car surprised him, even though it was quite large and stationary, parked right in front of the garage door. Still, Dab came at it hard, holding his wrist out to push off of the unforgiving metal. He recoiled from the pain, a jolt up his arm that he knew would linger for a few days. It didn't take much to hurt Dab; he bruised easily.

Still, he ran. Not slowing until he was around the corner of the house out of sight of the street. Only then did he pause, trying and failing to catch his breath, feeling a bit light-headed, the world tilting gently around him while his vision blurred for a brief moment. Dab had never been able to keep up with the other kids. He always felt unsteady in his own small body when it came time to display the physical prowess that seemed to come so intuitively to his peers.

They sprinted in a straight line; he always felt himself lilting left, then overcorrecting right, never true to his goal. His mother had made him play soccer in elementary school on a team with all the other boys from his class. He would watch them gather the ball between their feet and move with it down the field, the rolling orb an extension of themselves, drifting away then pulled back as if on a tether. When the ball was in the air, it would appear to float softly toward a teammate, who'd let it bounce off his chest to the ground directly in front of him. When Dab had tried to do the same, it had hit him square in the face, knocking off his glasses and sending him sprawling to the turf. Now that he was in middle school, Dab's mother had given up on making him participate in organized sports. He knew his mother didn't really like sports; it was just something she'd believed she needed to make him do, part of playing the role of good parent.

Dab sucked in air, leaning against the stranger's house. There was no time for this. He had to get home before they found him. Once he got inside and locked the door behind him, he would be safe. For today. He could consider tomorrow tomorrow.

For most of sixth grade, he had managed to stay off everyone's radar, not an insignificant feat given his name, which only got worse when you said the whole thing—Dabney—and his small stature and his hopelessness at sports and awkwardness in social interactions and just generally everything. Jane always told him that those things would be his strength someday. She had a way of making him believe everything she said. But his sister was away at college now, and he only heard her voice from a distance and saw her face on the computer screen, which diminished her power.

The problem now was that Dab had gotten on the wrong side of Connor and his buddies. It was a big problem.

Just run.

The backyard of the stranger's house opened up into the backyards of many other strangers' homes. This block was unusual in this town, in any town really, in that the lawns were continuous and contiguous, bleeding into each other out into the distance. No fences, no dogs, no swimming pools. Just an expanse of green, even more lush in these early spring days. There must have been an agreement between neighbors to be contrarians living without walls. Dab ran straight down the middle of the backyard, unimpeded, past the houses on either side. The only thing that could stop him was an unseen hole in the ground or tripping over his own two feet. He avoided both. This was the home stretch. Once he cleared this block, he would be just one corner away from his own house and safety.

Dab veered toward the house on the end of the block, again feeling that unsteadiness of needing to make his body execute specific movements on short notice. But he didn't slow down, proud of himself for pushing through the discomfort. He was feeling confident, an unfamiliar sense of control, when he burst back out onto the sidewalk and nearly ran into the woman pushing a stroller.

Someone screamed. Dab thought it might be him. But he had other problems. The world was spinning out from under him. He had managed to will his momentum sharply to the right and barely avoided barreling full force into the stroller. Time slowed. He could see the toddler watching him from her perch in her chariot. His heavy backpack sped his rotation, spinning him like a top, until he finally landed with a hard thud on the grass between the sidewalk and street. He lay there for a moment, staring up at the cloudless sky, his backpack anchoring him to the earth. His wrist throbbed where it had hit the car.

"Be careful!" the young mom said, sounding like every mom. "You could have seriously hurt her."

The mom was pointing to her own child. The little girl looked up at her mother, expression indistinct as she determined whether she was being yelled at. When she realized Dab was the victim, she laughed. Dab couldn't help but smile at the joyous sound. But the mom was not amused.

"You think this is funny," she said. "You're just lucky you didn't cause an accident!"

"Sorry," Dab said, rolling himself over awkwardly and struggling to his feet. "Sorry."

Dab ran away from them. As always, he wanted to say more. To find words that were more eloquent. It was how he always felt at school. The answers to questions sounded great in his head and barely coherent when they came out of his mouth. His sister had assured him that would change too. *All kids sound like idiots*, she said.

Almost home. Dab ran into the street, checking for cars only at the last second. Luckily, the world was empty around him. No cars, no people save for the woman and her daughter, who were receding away into the distance. Just around the corner was his house, his refuge. Another day of not getting beaten up. Dab was eleven years old and had never been in a fight. He was looking forward to extending that streak.

The word *accident* hung in the air next to him as he turned the corner. Dab hated that word. His brother, ten years his senior, used to call him that. Jane would defend Dab but had never corrected the slight. In her mind, accident was the best-case scenario. Dab had never known his father. He didn't even know where he lived. The closest guess he had was somewhere north, gleaned from an overheard drunken conversation his mother had had with a friend where she also accused her ex of spending most of his time now smoking pot and sleeping with prostitutes. Dab had no idea what was true. All he knew was that his brother had said Dab was the reason his father had left. His parents hadn't expected to have three children. During another argument between his sister and brother, Jane had paused to explain to Dab what a vasectomy was before his siblings got back into debating exactly what the nature of the accident was.

Dab coasted around the corner, right up to the edge of his front lawn, lost in thoughts of arguments past—watching his siblings fight had always been his favorite spectator sport—before he realized that Connor and his three henchmen were waiting for him on his front steps.

Just run.

Connor stood up first. The other three boys leapt to their feet behind him, puppets on strings. Dab's quick breaths filled his head like claps of thunder, making it hard to think. He couldn't get past them to his door. He could run down the street, but he didn't know his neighbors very well. He couldn't guarantee they would take him in even if they were home. And he couldn't outrun the boys. He was already winded, having far exceeded his usual daily exercise.

Dab made a quick decision that turned out to be horribly wrong. He sprinted toward the side of his house. He would go in the back door before they could get to him. It was only when he got to the sliding glass door off the back patio that he remembered he didn't have that key. His only worked on the front door. And his family and their neighbors were not quite as neighborly as the folks on the other block. These yards were boxed in by high fences that were impossible to see over or through. They weren't soundproof. People could hear him scream. But would they care?

"Hey, Dibs," Connor said. "What are you running from?"

One thing about having the name Dabney was that it was hard to come up with derogatory nicknames worse than the real thing. Dab found himself admiring Connor for the effort. That was the problem. He had a wide variety of feelings about Connor. For example, at this moment he was scared. But he also couldn't help but look at his hair. It was Connor's hair that had gotten him into this situation.

Dab had been in class with Connor all year. But only recently had he found himself staring at the other boy's hair. All the time. Without even realizing it. It didn't look remarkable. Sandy blond, like so many other kids'. But it kind of swept over Connor's forehead in a wave that Dab felt was mysteriously appealing. And sometimes a strand would fall out of place, drifting down over Connor's blue eyes. Dab had an almost unbearable urge to move it back into place when it fell, letting his fingers brush the skin of Connor's forehead.

Today, in class, he had been caught staring at Connor by one of his henchmen, who had alerted his leader to the transgression. There must have been something in Dab's expression, something intrusive, an assumption made even though he had no idea he was making it. Whatever it was, Connor was caught off guard. It made him very angry. Dab had looked away and felt himself redden, certain that other kids had noticed. He figured their teacher would care. But something must have happened at lunch, because Mr. Kaufman came back distracted. He went through the motions of his lesson but kept glancing down at his phone, which he occasionally tapped to refresh. That would have been the most interesting thing of the day if Dab hadn't been preoccupied with not riling Connor.

But his attempts to pretend that he had not been watching Connor in class had failed. Dab had avoided looking at Connor for the rest of the day. But maybe that had been too obvious. Maybe that had made it worse. By the end of the day, when Dab finally did glance at Connor again, it was clear that the strategy had not worked. Connor had that familiar expression on his face, the one every kid in the school knew meant he was about to beat someone up. Dab hadn't lingered after the last bell, knowing he was the source of Connor's anger.

Now that was confirmed. Connor and his henchmen were standing on Dab's front lawn. Connor's expression hadn't changed. And there was no one else around to beat up.

*   *   *

"Why were you staring at me?" Connor said. "You want a problem?"

Dab found his voice, but only half a sentence. "I don't want."

The boys waited for more, then laughed when nothing came.

"He's a retard," one of the boys said, seeking approval from the others. He looked at his feet and clenched his fists as his insult fell flat.

"We're going to kick the shit out of you now," Connor said.

This was not how Dab had expected it to go. Too much talking, too much prelude. Maybe they didn't want to hurt him. He had a fleeting thought: maybe this was like the movies, where the bully was actually a sensitive, misunderstood soul. Maybe Connor had been watching him too.

But just in case he was wrong, Dab took off his backpack and set it on the patio table. Then he removed his glasses and also placed them on the round table, slowly, deliberately.

"Not the face," Dab said.

He didn't know why he said it. It sounded like something he had heard in a movie. He desperately wanted this to be like a movie. Dab backed off the patio onto the lawn. He somehow felt this would hurt less on the grass.

Connor rushed toward him. Enough talk. The other three followed. Surprised that this was actually happening, Dab backpedaled, stumbling over his own feet, falling to the ground. He had been right; it hurt less on the grass.

The boys surrounded him. Dab squinted up at them. In class, Dab had wanted to touch Connor. He didn't know why. Or how that would ever happen. But now, looking into the grimace on Connor's face, echoed in the eyes around him, Dab did not want to be touched. He tensed himself, ready for the blows.

"Kick him," Connor said.

Simple and declarative, an order easily followed. Dab closed his eyes and waited. He thought of Jane, wishing she were still here. These boys wouldn't stand a chance if she came storming out the back door right now.

Dab had once asked her how she knew which boys she liked. That was her junior year, and she was dating a real jerk.

"You can't choose who you're attracted to," Jane said.

"Even if he's an asshole," Dab said, repeating what Mom had called him.

Jane laughed and gave him a hug. "You can choose who you spend time with."

Something touched Dab's side. It felt like a foot, but not a kick. More like a nudge. The way you might poke a motionless animal to check if it was really dead. Another tap from his other side. Then another. Each one softer than the last. Dab opened his eyes. The boys' expressions had changed. They were deeply confused.

"What the hell are you doing?" Connor barked.

The boys shied away from Dab as if he had caused them to fail. But he was as confused as they were. Did they not want to kick him? It wasn't that they weren't capable. Dab had seen all of them throw kids into lockers and get into fights. Kicking someone on the ground was certainly in their skill set. But now they looked scared. Something had happened and they didn't understand what it was, didn't even have the words to make an excuse to Connor.

Dab was also baffled. He raised himself on one elbow, still a deferential posture, just to test the waters. Maybe this was over. No one was paying attention to him. Connor was staring down his crew, and they were exchanging accusatory glances among themselves. They continued to back away—from Dab, from each other. Enough space opened up that Dab got bolder, pulling himself up to his knees. He was going to get to his feet when Connor turned back to him.

"Did I say you could get up?"

Dab found himself shaking his head. He stayed low, in a crouch. It would be the perfect position to launch himself at Connor. If he decided to take the offensive. No one had ever taught him how to fight. The closest was when Jane had shown him how to hold his keys between his fingers to stab an attacker in the eye. Dab's keys were in his pocket. But he didn't want to hurt anyone. Connor's eyes narrowed, his lips curled in a sneer. He clearly didn't feel the same way.

Again, Dab closed his eyes as the fist came toward him. And again, there was no pain. He felt fingertips brush his cheek, nearly a caress. Then he was tumbling back to the grass, the full weight of Connor landing on top of him. Dab breathed in and out in quick short blasts, his chest pressing against Connor's with each inhalation. Dab had never felt this before, the sheer density of another person on top of him. It was scary and he didn't want it to end. For a long moment, neither of them moved.

Had Connor pulled his punch on purpose? There was no way he'd just whiffed it. Dab tried to understand how he had avoided first the kicks, now the punch. Had he done something to move out of the way? Instincts kicking in? Superspeed?

Connor raised himself off of Dab by pushing his hand hard into his chest. A different kind of pressure. More threatening. But still not causing pain. Just holding his breathing in check. Connor looked down on him, wild-eyed, teeth clenched. He rolled his fingers deliberately into another tight fist and cocked his arm back. Dab knew he couldn't avoid this one. He didn't close his eyes this time. He stared directly at that fist. It flew toward him full of deadly force. But it never made it to his face. About halfway to his chin, it unfolded, fingers unfurling like the petals of a flower at dawn. The open hand hung between them. Connor gazed at it in wonder as if it were an alien object that had just landed on the end of his arm.

For a moment, Dab thought maybe the hand was for him, just as the fist had been a second before. He reached up with his own and took it. But that was another misjudgment. Connor pulled his hand away as if he'd been stung. Then he was on his feet, looking at Dab with disgust. Dab was both relieved and saddened that the weight of the other boy had left him.

"You're not worth it," Connor said. "Faggot."

Connor stormed off first. The other boys lingered for a beat. Dab could see them attempting to puzzle out what had happened. But it was too much to process. So they just followed.

Dab lay back and stared up at the perfect blue sky, amazed that nothing hurt except his own hand from that encounter with the car. He laughed to himself. The world had changed. He could feel it. Soon he would go retrieve his glasses and backpack and go inside. He would call Jane. He wanted to tell her that her ideas about attraction were both right and wrong. But first he would stay here and enjoy the ticklish grass against the back of his neck, the warm spring air in his lungs, and marvel at his good fortune.

2

THERE WAS A brief period in fourth grade when Dab thought he had the greatest name in the world. Nearly every kid in his elementary school would celebrate every accomplishment with a dab, the ubiquitous motion of tucking their face into the elbow of one crooked arm while pointing the other arm off to the side and upward. It took a little while for his classmates to connect his name with their joy, but once they did, every single dab in his vicinity came with an acknowledgment of his presence. Some kids would dab and then give him a slight knowing nod. Others would dab and point their outstretched arm directly at him. Some of the outliers would actually yell his name every time they struck the pose. No one was making fun of him. The single syllable that represented who he was also had become a reverential rite of passage for an entire generation. But dabbing, like all fads, soon faded away.

Dab never dabbed. He found the motion silly and pointless, even though he enjoyed the attention it had brought him. He was happy when it was happening and not particularly sad when it was gone.

Approaching his school on Friday, the day after his near beating in his own backyard, Dab was nervous, half expecting Connor and his buddies to jump him from behind a bush along the walk. But it was a bright, sunny day and no one attacked him. As he got close to the front door, he thought it might be all right. Maybe whatever had happened the afternoon before would be forgotten. He still wasn't sure why Connor had failed to pummel him, but certain things were better off just being accepted happily and not analyzed.

He had talked to Jane the afternoon before, tearfully recounting his ordeal immediately after it happened. She was sympathetic but also sad about something else she wouldn't tell him. Still, just seeing her made him feel better. She couldn't talk long. She was leaving for a weekend camping trip in the mountains with new college friends. They were going to drive through the night to get there and would be off the grid until they returned on Sunday.

"I don't remember anything that happened to me in sixth grade," she said, meaning to comfort him with the knowledge that whatever he thought was bad really wasn't.

The principal was at the front door as he was every morning, greeting students.

"Good morning, Dabney," the principal said as he passed. "Running a little late today?"

Dab just nodded and hurried up. The halls were starting to thin out. The first bell rang, and the remaining students quickened their pace. Dab realized he wouldn't have time to go to his locker before first period. He would have to lug his backpack around until lunch. He sighed and resigned himself to the burden. He jumped when an unexpected voice came up behind him.

"Fag!"

Dab spun around, expecting Connor or one of his friends. But the boy standing behind him, grinning, was unfamiliar to him. Maybe vaguely familiar, a face without a name he had seen wandering the halls, one of the hundreds of kids he didn't know at this school. Dab looked at him, confused, not sure what he had heard. He thought it had been his name, but it didn't sound right.

The kid's grin became a sneer. He dabbed in front of Dab and spoke into his elbow, muffling his voice. "Fag!"

"What did you say, young man?"

Neither of them had seen the principal approaching, done with his morning sentry duty at the front door. The kid looked chastened for a moment, then forced a smile.

"Nothing," the boy said. "I just said Dab."

The principal looked to Dab for confirmation. It was clear on his face that he thought it was a lie, that he was reasonably sure he hadn't heard a friendly greeting. But Dab just shrugged, ending the conversation.

"You're both late for class. Get moving."

The kid ran away. Dab darted off in the other direction, leaving the principal behind.

Before he got to his class, Dab wondered if he had heard the right word. After all, his name did sound a lot like what he thought the kid had said. But why would a boy he didn't even know say that to him? It made no sense.

Connor had called him a faggot the day before, using the full word for extra effect. After talking to Jane, Dab had Googled a definition. He was pretty sure he knew what it meant, although kids usually used it as a general insult rather than a specific one. But something about the way he and Connor had ended their encounter, with a touch and not a punch, made Dab feel the word had been used very personally, almost defensively.

An epithet for a gay man. That was one of the definitions on one of the respectable dictionary sites. Right next to British slang for a cigarette. The Urban Dictionary was a lot less diplomatic, providing a wide range of equally unacceptable alternatives, each one more graphic than the last.

Was he gay? Dab didn't know. They were supposed to talk about sexuality in gym class, but his teacher had said they were too young to know anything about that, so he'd skipped it and talked about avoiding athlete's foot in the locker room instead. Dab had been hoping for some insight. All he got was a suggestion to wear flip-flops in the shower.

Math distracted him. When the bell rang and he walked into the bustling hallway, Dab tensed himself for another random encounter. But he walked to English without incident. He was widely ignored, a condition he had sometimes lamented in the past but was now grateful for. His seat in English was in the back. As he passed by the other students already seated, he figured he must have misunderstood what had happened earlier.

Until the girl two seats in front of him dabbed as he passed.

"Fag."

She said it so quietly he could barely hear her. But he knew what she'd said. He froze in the aisle and the girl held her pose, shifting uncomfortably in her chair. Dab felt his skin growing hot, his face turning red.

"What's going on?"

Their English teacher was staring at them. Her expression was one of shock and horror. Dab realized the girl had moved her arm forward. It looked like a Nazi salute instead of a dab. She dropped her arm quickly and shook her head. Dab continued to his seat. He was sweating under his shirt, hoping it wouldn't stain the armpits. He knew who this girl was, vaguely. She was in the girl clique that hung around with Connor's boy clique. Now he knew this was no accident. There was a movement afoot. It took most of class for his temperature and color to return to normal.

After class, he lingered in his seat, watching the rest of the students file out. He came up with an excuse to ask his teacher a question, ignoring her answer while he waited for the bell. She didn't have a class this period. No students came in. So once Dab heard the bell and knew the hallways were empty, he ran to his next class. He walked to his seat with his head down, making no eye contact with anyone. He barely heard a word during science, thinking mainly about the next period.

Lunch.

There was no escaping kids at lunch. In the movies, the misfits ate lunch in the bathroom stalls, but

Dab knew that was a stupid place to try to hide. Nowhere in the school was more isolated and dangerous than the bathroom. Dab considered the nurse, but she was not a kind woman. She was prone to making quick diagnoses that led to sending you either home or back to class. There was very little middle ground that resulted in a place to hide and nap. Besides, if he did successfully feign illness, they would require his mother to pick him up. She would have to leave work, something none of them could really afford her doing.

He would go to lunch.

The bell rang. Dab headed down to his locker for the first time that day. He deflated at the sight of it. Someone had scratched his name into the metal. Dab, which now he heard as a homonym for the other word. The same person, a budding artist, had etched a cartoon figure dabbing. Dab took a deep breath, opened his locker, threw his backpack inside, grabbed his lunch bag, and hurried to the lunchroom. He scurried to his usual place at a table in the back corner. He didn't see if anyone dabbed at him as he passed. The cacophony of the room masked any ability to hear anyone talking in his direction. There were other kids at his table, the usual friendless crowd. They should have talked to each other, but they rarely did, eating in silence yet finding some comfort in the numbers.

Many of the kids in the lunchroom ate quickly and headed outside. It was a beautiful day. Others lingered, talking and eating, though fewer than normal. Dab planned to run out the clock in the corner. But then he noticed his gym teacher, the same one who had chosen athlete's foot over a discussion of sexual preferences, rustling kids out of their seats and shooing them to the door. Some days, the staff decided that everyone had to go into the yard. It was capricious and random, and unfortunately it was happening today. Then the gym teacher was at his table.

"Everyone outside," he said. "Get some exercise."

That was all that needed to be said. No one at this table was going to argue. With a collective sigh, they rose and walked to the door, squinting against the sunlight.

Dab did not move. His gym teacher considered him. For a moment, Dab thought he might ask him what was wrong, give him an opening to escape his fate.

"Dabney," the gym teacher said, spitting it out like a command.

It was nice to hear his name this way, even if it wasn't said nicely. At least it didn't feel like a slur. No malice in the man's voice, merely an utter lack of sympathy.

Outside, Dab slunk along the wall to a seat on a ledge. He tried to stay small and inconspicuous, not much of a challenge for him. His other classmates were deep into their own intrigues and paid him no attention.

It didn't last. With only minutes before the next bell, Connor walked in his direction, leading a pack of kids, rats behind the Pied Piper. His smile widened as he approached. Putting himself in the corner had made Dab less visible but also gave him no means of escape. The children fanned out around him, giving him nowhere to go.

An endless minute passed. Dab thought about the previous day. Maybe they couldn't hurt him. But then a wordless signal from Connor led them all to dab simultaneously. Dab thought he heard some of them mutter the word under their breaths, whispering it into their biceps. But most of them said nothing. They knew they didn't need to. And they held their poses and stifled their laughter until the bell rang again and the yard emptied of students, including Dab's tormentors.

Dab wanted to leave. Just run home. But the yard was fenced in. The only way out was back through the cafeteria and the hallways to the front entrance. There, he would be confronted by a security guard asking for his pass to leave. The other options—the nurse or the front office—both led to phone calls to his mother. He could hide until the day was over, but he would be found and he didn't know by whom. Holding back tears, Dab resigned himself to going to his next class. History with Mr. Kaufman.

He walked into class late to a low rumble of snickers. He took his seat, fully aware that all eyes were on him. It was hard to stifle the tears, but he tamped them down. He would not cry. He would not give them that.

Mr. Kaufman didn't appear to notice his distress. He usually just launched into his lecture, letting them all zone out peacefully. He rarely asked questions or demanded any kind of participation. But today felt different.

"Do any of you have any idea what's going on?" Mr. Kaufman said.

The class returned a collective blank to his question. It felt like he was about to lecture them, but he sounded happy. Like he didn't believe what he was about to say. All eyes were on Mr. Kaufman, a rarity in his class. Dab was grateful for the distraction. Mr. Kaufman held up his phone.

"You carry these around all the time. Has anyone paid attention to the news today?"

The class sighed. It was a trick. A lecture was coming. No one responded.

"We were going to talk about the Great Depression today. Important history. But I think you need to know what's happening now. History is being made right outside your window. The world is changing. At least that's what they say. You can see it on your phones."

Some of the kids took out their phones, but Mr. Kaufman scowled at them. Phones were not allowed in class, so they put them away again, confused about why he kept mentioning them if he didn't want them to look at them.

"Yesterday, a man walked into a nursery school with an automatic rifle. That happened right here, just a couple of miles away. He wanted to kill as many children as possible. But he didn't. Or as some eyewitnesses are saying, he couldn't. The guns didn't work, the police said. But some people are saying the bullets bounced off the kids. Imagine that?"

He had the full attention of the class now. Dab didn't really understand what he was talking about but, like his classmates, was fascinated by the possibility that his teacher was having a mental breakdown in front of them.

"That man, the potential shooter, used to be a student in this school. I remember him. He was a quiet kid. Never would have imagined . . ."

Mr. Kaufman trailed off. The class was silent. Dab found his attention drifting back to Connor a few seats in front of him. He still was fascinated by his hair, but now he wondered if Mr. Kaufman would be talking about his evil ways ten years in the future.

"They say that people all around the world are unable to hurt each other. That violence has stopped completely. It may be the most elaborate hoax ever pulled. But if it's true . . . what if it was true? What would the world be like if we couldn't hurt each other?"

Mr. Kaufman looked expectantly at the class. It was clear that this was not a rhetorical question. He wanted to have a discussion. But the students weren't ready for it. They fidgeted in their seats and stared off into space, played with their pencils, twirled their hair.

Connor must have sensed Dab looking at him again. He turned before Dab could avert his gaze. They locked eyes. Connor's anger was red-hot. Yet he smiled. And subtly—not a full motion—gave Dab a dab.

The tears came. Dab couldn't help it. Even though he knew this was social suicide. Crying in class. Giving in to the sadness. Connor would win.

Dab didn't realize that Mr. Kaufman was next to him until he felt his teacher's hand on his shoulder.

"It's okay. I know this is all a little scary. Such unexplained change. But if it's true, it will also be wonderful."

In that moment, Dab knew the answer to Mr. Kaufman's question. *What if they couldn't hurt each other?*

The answer was that they would always be able to hurt each other.

EXCURSUS A:
THE PRESIDENT

THE PRESIDENT RAN his fingers along the edge of the Resolute desk, which had also been used by seven of his predecessors. Some of those presidents had considered themselves wartime leaders, though most had governed through times of peace. Yet all had led the armed forces as commander in chief; each had authorized military operations, whether it was peacetime or not.

The President's tenure in office had not been long. He had not been called upon to send soldiers into harm's way. And now, as he considered the two military orders on his desk, he wondered if he ever would.

The intelligence reports had seemed fantastical at first, the work of fevered brains hoping for a different world. But they were consistent, all using the same phrase—"a high degree of confidence." Clandestine speak for *we got this one right.* People were still trying to kill each other. But they couldn't. Not even in war zones. Not anywhere.

The President sat back in his chair and looked around the Oval Office. He had asked for some time alone to read the two orders and consider his decision. Abraham Lincoln stared past him from a canvas that had also attended many presidencies, serious within the darkness, contemplating a decision of great importance. That man's choices had led to the deaths of more American soldiers than any president's since. This president's decision, while still possibly a decision to kill, paled in comparison. He found comfort in that, though mainly in the realization that his choice might be irrelevant. He was, after all, merely testing whether he could authorize the military to engage in lethal force anymore. That power, so fundamental to his position, had perhaps become moot.

He wasn't relying only on the intelligence services for his information, of course. They had put out a call to police districts through the Justice Department, to hospitals through the CDC, looking for victims of violence. They had found none. "When's the last time no one was shot in New York, Chicago, or Los Angeles?" his chief of staff had joked. The President hadn't laughed.

If this was true—and the news reports were starting to confirm it, beginning to make an unsuspecting world aware of the change—then the President knew he would need a speech. He glanced at Lincoln again. This would be his Gettysburg Address, if done right. He would be the president who'd led the world at the moment that rewrote history. That changed the fundamental nature of humanity. Neither a wartime nor peacetime president, he would be the first to have been given the opportunity at another way. He would be judged by how he handled this charge. It was more than he could have hoped for, more than he'd ever dreamed of.

But first, the decision in front of him. His administration needed to know what their military capabilities currently were. The President pulled the two orders toward him. They differed in one crucial way: conventional versus nuclear. The target had been chosen for its remote location and small population—disputed territory that his advisers claimed belonged to no country, so the risk of being accused of an act of war was minimal. The operation would occur within twenty-four hours. It would tell them everything they needed to know.

The President picked up his pen and without another hesitation signed the order on the left. He buzzed for his chief of staff to let him know the decision had been made.

MARCUS

DAY

1

WHEN THE DOCTOR told them the choices, Marcus's mother broke down again. Marcus hated to see her cry. Normally, she was stoic and stern, like his grandmother, telling him that whatever problem he had would pass or wasn't as bad as someone else's. He had never seen his grandmother cry. Not even now, sitting here in this hospital room, watching over her grandson Malcolm from the uncomfortable chair in the corner, his brother's lifeless body connected to the machines that kept him breathing.

Malcolm, four years older than Marcus, was merely a shell of himself, an intermittent beep in the background the only indication that his heart was still beating. Marcus's grandmother's right eye stared beyond the bed. His mother said she saw floaters, a symptom of the diabetes. When Marcus had asked his grandmother what she was looking at, she'd said ghosts. She saw nothing out of her other eye, which had become milky white. No one knew why that had happened. It was hard for her to get an appointment with her doctors, let alone a diagnosis.

The doctor cleared his throat to regain Marcus's mother's attention.

"You understand that we do not think Malcolm will live without the machines. He is effectively brain-dead. His body could continue to persist, given the appropriate assistance. But he will never recover his cognitive functions. That is why it is our recommendation that he be removed from life support."

Marcus watched his mother take a deep breath. Her chest rose and fell, just as Malcolm's did in the hospital bed. This room was small and spare. The grimy window looked out on the darkened alley behind the hospital. With five people in the room, it felt particularly claustrophobic.

"If I decide to keep him on the machines—"

"Then he will be moved to another facility," the doctor said, cutting her off.

"Where?"

"I don't know. That's not my decision. It will depend on where there's space. At his age, the assumption would be that he would require a significant timeline of unresponsive care."

A significant timeline of unresponsive care. Marcus wanted to scream at the doctor's tone of voice. He was shrouding his meaning in a string of nearly meaning-less words, but what he meant was that Malcolm would be a drag on society forever. Better to let him die at twenty-one than keep him alive as a vegetable any longer.

At seventeen, Marcus had assumed Malcolm would always be there to take care of him. Marcus knew he had to be strong, but he felt small, weak, helpless in this hospital room.

"What if he lives?"

"I'm sorry," the doctor said. "I don't understand."

"What if you take him off the machines and he lives?"

The doctor sighed and rubbed the day-old stubble on his face. Marcus could read his mind. He was ready to move on. There were dozens of other patients in his care, some dying, some he might be able to save.

"That is always a possibility. If that happens, we will do everything in our power to keep him comfortable."

Marcus's mother started to cry again. The word *comfortable* felt like a dagger in all their hearts. This hospital was no longer trying to save his brother. That moment had passed. It was only a matter of time now.

The first time Marcus remembered seeing his mother cry had been in this same hospital the day his father was shot. That night they had never left the waiting area of the emergency room. Marcus had watched Malcolm put an arm around his mother and cry with her. His older brother was ten years old then, Marcus only six. But somehow, it seemed, those four years had given Malcolm the wisdom to understand how to behave in that place. In that situation. Marcus had just felt at sea. There was so much movement around him, rough waves threatening to pull him under. He remembered shivering until his grand-mother showed up with his jacket.

His father had died before he could be transferred to surgery that night. Four nights ago, when Malcolm was shot on the street half a block from their apartment building, the ambulance had arrived faster. The emergency room doctors had stabilized him and the surgeon had saved him. This time, everyone had done their job successfully. Malcolm had lived—for the time being, anyway.

When they'd arrived at the emergency room waiting area, Marcus had been overwhelmed by déjà vu. It looked exactly the same. It sounded exactly the same. It smelled exactly the same. His mother was crying. But he was seventeen now. And it was Malcolm bleeding out in triage.

"You don't have to decide right now," the doctor was saying. "It can wait until morning."

Marcus's mother nodded. The doctor put a hand on her arm. Maybe Marcus had misread him in thinking him callous.

"I'm sorry," the doctor said.

There were only two chairs in the room. Marcus got up to let his mother sit down after the doctor left. He wanted to perch on the edge of Malcolm's bed; he was sure that was where his brother would want him. But the last time he had touched the bed, his mother had snapped at him. So Marcus stood in front of the bathroom door, wondering what to do with his hands. He knew there was a right thing to do now. He knew that the only person he could ask about that would never talk to him again.

"Take your grandmother home," his mother said.

That was not what he thought he should do.

"What? I need to stay here."

Marcus's mother looked up at him. She had stopped crying. He knew that look. He had already lost the argument. But he suddenly felt a desperate emptiness in his stomach. They were going to take Malcolm away in the middle of the night while he was gone. His brother was going to die without him.

His mother seemed to be reading his mind now.

"Nothing is going to happen before tomorrow," she said.

Marcus's grandmother stood up. As always, she wobbled when she got to her feet. She complained that one leg hurt more than the other, but she never remembered which was which until the pain came.

"I need to sleep in my bed," his grandmother said.

"Don't forget your medicine," his mother said.

The older woman started toward the door with her unsteady steps. It always took her a few paces to regain her balance, then she was fine walking. She put a hand on her daughter's shoulder. It wasn't clear who was steadying whom.

"I don't forget anything," his grandmother said, before continuing on.

Marcus kept a hand near his grandmother's elbow as they walked. Together they glided down the hall, into the escalator, and out onto the street. They passed through the emergency room waiting area, which seemed unusually quiet tonight. After a hot day, the world had cooled. The night air was a relief after the stuffiness of Malcolm's room. Marcus chastised himself for being happy to be heading home.

"I'll get us a cab," Marcus said, motioning to a line in front of the hospital.

"Nonsense. The bus is still running fine."

She shuffled away down the street. The bus stop was a half block away. Marcus wasn't thrilled to be waiting out there at this time of night, scanning the area around them. He was pleasantly surprised when their bus pulled up just as they arrived.

There were only a few people on the bus. Other than one guy near the back who was speaking in urgent hushed tones to the empty seat next to him, everyone appeared to be on their way home from work. Marcus sat next to his grandmother in the seats reserved for seniors and the disabled. She took his hand and stared off into the distance at her ghosts.

The last conversation Marcus had had with his brother had taken place in the room they'd shared since Malcolm had gotten out of prison nearly a year earlier. Marcus was happiest when the two of them were there together. It was tight with the futon wedged in, particularly when it was pulled out into a bed and covered most of the floor. Marcus had to jump over his sleeping brother to get to the bathroom. But when it was configured as a couch, the room felt comfortable, like a freshman dorm. Malcolm's books strewn about amplified the feeling.

"Done!"

Marcus remembered swiveling in his chair to face the futon. Malcolm was holding up a flash drive triumphantly. Marcus shrugged.

"My sociology final paper! Done!"

Eighteen months in jail had changed Malcolm. He had always been a good student, passing his classes without trying. But he'd spent most of his free time hanging out with friends, drinking, and smoking weed. In high school, he had seldom met a bad idea he didn't like. It was the second time getting caught trying to steal a car that had gotten him locked up. And since both had followed his eighteenth birthday, he also had two strikes on his record. The judge sent him away knowing he was only a couple of months and a few requirements away from his high school diploma. None of that mattered. He was a poor kid from a bad neighborhood. The rest of it was irrelevant to the judge, despite the public defender's best efforts.

Malcolm had told Marcus on his last free night that he was sure he was going to die in jail. Instead, he found a program that helped him finish his high school diploma. He worked in the library. The non-profit that helped stock the library ran another program for former inmates that offered them admission to a local college with a generous scholarship. Malcolm walked out of jail and a week later back into the classroom. When Marcus's mother found out about the program, she said a little prayer under her breath and clutched her shirt over her heart. Sometimes Marcus would find her cooking or cleaning in their apartment, humming the name of the program, Down to Gown, over and over to herself like a protective mantra.

"Which of your boring classes is this?"

"International Voices of Protest. Professor Davis is awesome. And it isn't boring. Is Nelson Mandela boring?"

"No," Marcus said reluctantly.

"How about Gandhi and Václav Havel?"

"Yes. Definitely boring."

"You'd rather talk to your computer than think about people."

It was true. Marcus also did fine in school, and he didn't have Malcolm's rebellious streak. He had plenty of his own books to keep him company, titles like *C++*

for Engineers, Elegant Python, and *Java for Idiots.* Programming spoke to him in a way people didn't. Which suited his mother just fine. She liked knowing where her children were.

"People are assholes."

"That's what I wrote about! What happens when the protester takes power. Do they stick to their ideals? Or do they succumb to human nature? Take this woman in Burma, Aung San Suu Kyi. She was in prison for years while a military dictatorship ruled her country. She won a Nobel Peace Prize. Then when her party won an election, she worked with the military to continue an ethnic-cleansing campaign."

"But we're good with Mandela, right?"

"Yeah, we're good with Mandela. Wait, listen to this."

Malcolm dove into a pile of books. He held up a paperback with a plain cover titled *Collected Works of the Empty Shell.*

"Essays by a turtle?" Marcus said with a smile.

"Smartass. No. This guy—actually maybe a bunch of guys; no one knows who the writer really is—he's been writing for twenty years. People just find his writing randomly, and it gets passed on. It's the only way to protest in a place like that. The first pieces were found in spent bullet cases."

Malcolm opened the book, so excited that his brother had resigned himself to listening, even though Marcus was thoroughly uninterested.

Now, looking back, Marcus felt a pang of regret at how much he had just wanted Malcolm to shut up.

They will drop their bombs on you.

If you take away their bombs, they will shoot you.

If you take away their guns, they will stab you.
If you take away their knives, they will bite you.
If you pull out their teeth, they will scratch you.
If you pull out their fingernails, they will find another
way.
But we will always win.
For even if they cut out our tongues, our words will
live on.

Malcolm looked expectantly at his brother. Marcus
nodded and smiled. "And if you keep talking about
this shit, I'll kill myself."

"Doesn't matter. My words will live on. Because
my paper is done!"

Moments later, Malcolm realized he was late for
work. He had been taking shifts at a fast-food chicken
place a mile away. The tuition might have been free,
but the rent and the food weren't. Marcus barely
looked up as his brother threw on his uniform—that
puke-yellow polo shirt and paper hat—and sprinted
out of the room. In the distance, the front door
slammed. Malcolm was gone.

He'd been shot on the way back home that night.

"Baby, we're here," Marcus's grandmother said.

She was already getting up. The bus driver was
looking over his shoulder, waiting patiently for them
to get to the door. Marcus leapt up out of his seat,
startling his grandmother.

"No need to scare me like that," she said.

Out on the street, they walked slowly home.
Marcus eyed the path ahead warily. He preferred to be
in the apartment with the door locked at this hour.
His breath caught in his throat when he realized they
were passing the spot where Malcolm had been found

bleeding. There was no indication that something had happened there, no roadside memorial. If all the places anyone had been shot in this neighborhood were marked, it would all be buried in flowers. Marcus could tell that his grandmother also knew where they were. She whispered something to herself and kept walking.

The lookout across the street from their building saw them first. That was his job. He gave a slight nod of the head, then went back to his previous practiced nonchalant posture. Marcus was reasonably sure he'd had a class with the kid last year. But he kept his head down and opened the door for his grandmother. The lock had been broken since they'd begun living there. There was an inoperable buzzer system there too, two columns of buttons with apartment numbers and no names.

As they entered the small lobby, another kid, this one with sunken eyes and a grayish tinge to his skin, hurried past them, clutching something in his hand. He was biting his own lip hard enough to draw blood. He didn't acknowledge Marcus and his grandmother, merely shoving his way out the front door into the night.

The building was five stories, no elevator. They lived on the second floor, and it was still possible for his grandmother to make the climb, but Marcus didn't know for how much longer. They might have to move, which would be fine with Marcus. He couldn't imagine going back to living there without Malcolm.

As they began the ascent, each step required a pause, a chance for his grandmother to catch her breath.

The dealer had an apartment on the first floor, but he did business in the stairwell. Malcolm had said he didn't like junkies eyeing his stuff. Marcus wasn't sure why Malcolm knew the dealer. Probably had gone to school together. Marcus could hear the dealer laughing with a crowd as he and his grandmother neared the first landing. Step by step, carefully and slowly, his grandmother made her way up.

The dealer and his friends, three other guys, sprawled on the stairs between the landing and the first floor. The regarded Marcus and his grandmother with sleepy stoned eyes as they turned the corner. Only the dealer appeared to not have been sampling the product. He stared at Marcus with cold resolve. Marcus didn't return the attention, focusing on his grandmother's back as she began the next set of steps. The dealer's friends didn't move for the woman. They covered most of the staircase with their relaxed bodies, leaving a small corridor on the right side barely wide enough for his grandmother to stand straight up with her two feet next to each other, which was what she did on each step, seemingly unconcerned about the young men.

Marcus wanted to tell them to move. That was what Malcolm would have done. Marcus had always admired his brother's willingness to look the other kids in the neighborhood in the eye and tell them what was what. It felt brave to him. His mother said it was stupid.

"Hurry up," one of the guys said. "You're killing the vibe."

The others laughed. Except the dealer, who kept his eyes on Marcus. His grandmother did not pick up her pace. Steadily she made her way to the first floor. When they reached the top, hallways stretching out in both direction from the stairs, Marcus realized he had been holding his breath.

"Hey, how's chicken boy doing?" the dealer called after them.

Marcus turned. At first he didn't think the dealer was talking to him. But the dealer was standing up now, leaning against the wall, no indication that he was coming up the stairs but still somehow more threatening than before. His focus was clearly on Marcus, who didn't answer.

"Your brother. Chicken boy. He's in the hospital."

Marcus didn't say anything. It wasn't surprising that the dealer knew about Malcolm. The police presence, however brief it had been, must have interfered with business. Not that people in the neighborhood didn't know everything that happened here anyway. Yet Marcus was still confused.

"Keep moving, baby," his grandmother said. "Keep moving."

"Yeah, baby. Listen to the old lady. Keep moving. Don't be like chicken boy. Getting up in other people's faces. You'll get the same."

The dealer pointed his finger at Marcus, the shape of a gun, and made a *pop, pop, pop* sound. The others laughed. The message was clear. Marcus felt the bile in his throat, something clawing deep in his stomach. He saw only the dealer, holding a gun, shooting his brother. His breath disappeared again. He felt light-headed.

Then, out of the corner of his eye, he saw his grandmother slip as she continued up the stairs to the next landing. Just a tiny stumble, but enough to get him rushing after her. Any fall for her could be catastrophic. The slow climb continued. Marcus followed her, staring at her back between her shoulder blades, ignoring the dealer and his friends, who had returned to their own conversation as they waited for their next customer.

At their door, Marcus rustled in his pocket for his key. His hand was shaking as he tried to fit it into the lock. His grandmother took it from him, letting them inside the apartment.

"Get me some water," she said. "I need to take my pills."

Marcus went to the kitchen. He filled the glass from the sink. He tried not to think about it, but all he could see in his mind was the dealer and his finger. *Pop, pop, pop.*

His grandmother sat at the small table where they ate their meals. She had a plastic container, fourteen tiny boxes fused together, each labeled with a day of the week and time of day. At the beginning of the week, it was a kaleidoscope of colors; now it was mostly empty. She opened the tiny lid for Thursday PM and started to take the three pills out one by one. Marcus put the glass in front of her. When she had taken all three pills, one by one, deliberately, she reached out for her grandson, taking his hands.

"I want to pray," she said. "You don't have to say nothing. Just think it in your head."

Marcus watched his grandmother as she closed her eyes and lowered her head.

"Lord, bless those we have lost and those still living. Give us your strength."

And those in between, Marcus thought.

Marcus had spent his life going to church with his grandmother. She believed in that higher power fervently, but he didn't understand why. The bullets had taken her father and her son and would soon take her grandson. Her own grandfathers had not been taken by the gun, as far as she knew. One had just disappeared. The other had never been there to begin with. And yet she prayed.

After a minute, she opened her eyes and gave his hands a squeeze.

"We need to sleep," she said. "Tomorrow is going to be a long day."

Another in a long line of long days. His grandmother lifted herself from her chair and padded down the hall to her room. After she left, silence filled the apartment, leaving only the sounds in Marcus's head.

Pop, pop, pop.

There was a gun in their room. Malcolm had brought it home a couple of weeks ago. Marcus had been angry. His brother was on parole. He was supposed to stay away from weapons. But Malcolm had assured him he wasn't going back to his old ways. He just had reason to feel like they might need a little protection at home.

"If someone comes after my family, I'll do what I have to do," he said.

He showed Marcus how to take off the safety, how to aim, what to expect when it went off. Then he put it on the shelf in their closet, buried deep underneath a pile of winter clothes no one would wear for months. He told Marcus never to touch it, the unspoken caveat being unless he needed it.

Marcus went to his room and stood in front of the closet. He felt like he needed it now, but he thought Malcolm might disagree. His shoulders slumped forward as he considered tomorrow. His grandmother was right. He should go to sleep. Maybe they would experience a miracle tomorrow. Maybe her prayers had reached someone who could help. They would take Malcolm off the machines and he would live, astounding all the doctors. They had all been wrong. He would sit up and smile at Marcus and tell him he sure as goddamn well better have kept his hands off his stuff. They would laugh. Their mother would cry again, this time for the best of reasons.

But that wasn't going to happen. Marcus shook off the fantasy. He did what he always did when he didn't want to think about anything else. He booted up his computer and worked on his latest project.

Scrolling through the hundreds of lines of code, Marcus forgot the world around him. No one else in this apartment could understand the language in front of him. This belonged to him and him alone. And every line he wrote, every error he debugged, was creation. A world invented with each touch of the keyboard.

This program was a game. The graphics were primitive, based off an old Atari shooter called Asteroids. In that one, you were a small spaceship in an asteroid field. You shot the asteroids to survive. But Marcus's game was a twist on the classic. In this game, your goal was to miss. Instead of shooting things, you shot around them, aiming for the voids. You got points for every shot that left the screen unimpeded. The longer you didn't shoot anything, the better your score. He also turned the asteroids into adorable animals. As you progressed, more and more filled the screen until eventually it was impossible to miss. If you did make it all the way to the end, you were literally smothered within their cuteness.

When his phone buzzed next to his keyboard, Marcus realized that two hours had slipped away. He was fine with that. He didn't want them back. The phone vibrated again. It was his mother.

"Marcus." She was crying. His name sounded like a death knell. "He must have known. He didn't want me to have to decide. He just went."

Malcolm was dead.

Marcus listened to his mother, but he couldn't hear a word. After he hung up, he stumbled over to the futon, falling back into it, feeling the weight of Malcolm on the cushion next to him. His eyes wandered the room, taking in his brother's books and papers and clothes and all the things he would never need again. There was an orange clamshell of molded plastic on the floor next to the futon. Marcus picked it up. He remembered when Malcolm had brought it home the week before, having found it at one of the thrift shops in the neighborhood. His brother had smiled like a cat with a dead rat under its paw, then opened the clamshell, revealing its secrets. Inside, nestled together, were two plates, a bowl, a collapsible cup, and plastic silverware.

"I'm going camping," Malcolm had said.

And the grin on his brother's face had shifted slightly. Marcus knew that look too, the one Malcolm got whenever he was thinking about a girl.

But Malcolm wasn't going camping. Not now. Not ever. Marcus bit his lip to stop the tears. Instead of crying, he lifted himself off the futon and crossed the room. He reached up into the closet and retrieved the gun. He could barely feel it in his hand. Marcus floated through the apartment to the front door.

Outside in the hall, everything got heavier—the air around him, the gun in his hand, the thoughts in his head. He should go back inside. That's what Malcolm would tell him to do.

In the distance, Marcus heard the dealer and his friends laughing. And a vision flashed through his mind: the dealer laughing as he stood over Malcolm, who was bleeding out in the street.

Malcolm, who would never give Marcus advice again. Malcolm, dead in that hospital bed, his mother holding his cold hand and crying alone.

Malcolm, his brother no more.

The voices got louder as Marcus walked down the stairs. The dealer and his friends didn't notice him looking down on them from the landing. The gun was no longer too light or too heavy. The rage saturated Marcus, and the bile of it flowed into his trigger finger. He expected the dealer to look up at him, understanding what was about to happen. But he never did.

Marcus pulled the trigger three times. *Pop, pop, pop.* Then he ran back to his apartment and locked the door behind him.

DAY

2

As he had throughout the night, Marcus woke
with a start on the couch, staring in the direction
of the front door. In his dreams, the door had burst
open, again and again, stormed by cops or in a blaze
of gunfire from the dealer and his friends. But each
time he was jarred awake, Marcus had found himself
alone in the living room. All the lights were on, unlike
in his dreams, where the apartment was inevitably
dark. No one was trying to break down his door. As
his breathing slowed, the panic subsiding, he listened
for sirens, for any muffled sobs in the hallway, gruff
cops interrogating his neighbors on the stairs. But
each time the world was mostly silent, interrupted
only by the usual noises outside from his perpetually
restless neighborhood.

This last dream had been the worst. The air was
still, everything gray. Marcus found himself standing
in the middle of the room as the front door opened
slowly. It was not being forced open, not battered
down. This was the way someone who lived there

would open the door, comfortably, without much thought. But as it swung wide, revealing the empty hallway beyond, there was no one there. Marcus found himself calling out, only to be answered by a low gurgle of a voice saying his brother's name.

Marcus sat up on the couch, struggling to regain his composure. His heart pounded in his ears. It had been so real, his brother's ghost coming home. But now he could see clearly that the door was shut tight. No one was coming in. Marcus was alone.

He had lain down on the couch not intending to sleep but to keep vigil. But he had slept longer than he'd expected. The sun streamed in through half-closed blinds. He picked up the phone next to him to check the time, only realizing that it wasn't his when he saw the reminder that had popped up over the lock screen.

Hand in paper.

This was Malcolm's phone. Marcus had taken it the first night in the hospital to check for anything that might explain what had happened. His brother wasn't careful with his passwords, and Marcus had been able to scroll through texts and emails but had found nothing unusual. He had meant to take the phone back to the hospital so that Malcolm would have it when he woke up, but he never had. He'd just kept it with him whenever he was home. The picture on the lock screen was one he had taken of Malcolm and their mother.

Marcus put the phone in his pocket. He didn't want to look at that. He didn't want to think about anything.

He knew he didn't have a choice. Wandering toward the kitchen, he noticed a note on the table, scrawled in his grandmother's handwriting.

Gone to hospital. Come soon.

His hand went cold holding the note. Returning to the hospital would only bring the truth to him. He knew it would come to him soon enough. He felt the empty space in his soul. An absence that would never be filled again.

Marcus wanted to go into his room and disappear into his program. But he had slept on the couch for a reason. Waking up to the unopened futon would have been too devastating. He wondered how long everything in this apartment would be little more than a reminder of their loss.

Marcus sat heavily in the chair at the kitchen table. He didn't want to go to the hospital. He didn't want to stay here. Maybe what he had done last night, firing those shots down the stairwell, was a good enough excuse not to move. Someone must be looking for him. He had committed a crime, hadn't he? Although the lack of anyone knocking on the door suggested that real life had mimicked his computer game. He had taken his shots and he had missed every time. Or maybe it hadn't happened at all. It seemed no more real than his dreams from the previous night.

Taking out his brother's phone, intending to check for messages again, Marcus found himself staring at the reminder. The people at the college probably didn't know what had happened. They probably thought Malcolm was flaking on them, blowing off his finals, not handing in his paper. All of Marcus's sadness morphed into anger at those snooty professors who wouldn't give someone like Malcolm, someone like him, the benefit of the doubt. They would just assume failure had always been the most likely outcome and

congratulate themselves for trying to better the wayward child's situation. Then they would go back to
their lives and forget about Malcolm completely.

Marcus wasn't going to let that happen. He hurried down the hall, pausing only briefly to glance
through the open door into his mother's room. The
bed was made. She hadn't come home last night. Then
Marcus stopped short in the doorway of his room. For
a heartbeat he thought he saw Malcolm sitting on the
futon, but the room was empty. Just another ghost.
Steeled by a newfound purpose, grateful for the distraction, Marcus rifled through Malcolm's books and
papers until he found an assignment sheet for the project due today. He knew the professor's name—
Davis—because Malcolm hadn't been able to shut up
about him. But now he had the office number where
the paper was to be dropped off. He dug around some
more until he found the flash drive, which he intended
to slam down on the professor's desk with a scowl.
Don't judge my brother. He finished your damn paper.

The hallway outside their apartment was empty.
There was no activity in the stairwell. It was too early
for the dealer to be awake; he worked the night shift.
None of the other neighbors were lurking either. Still,
Marcus rushed down the stairs, pausing at the first
floor to confirm that no one was lying in wait on the
next landing. When he was certain he was alone, he
hustled to the next set of stairs.

Marcus stopped abruptly when he felt something
poke him in the face. He fell backward on the stairs,
surprised. Touching his cheek, he traced the tiny divot
where something had run into him. It had felt solid,
hard enough that his tooth ached at the point of

impact. He scanned the space above him for something flying, a bee maybe, and the stairs around him for something small that had been thrown. But there was no one around to toss something his way, and no pests buzzed around. Then it caught his eye, hanging directly above him.

The bullet was suspended in the air, a freeze-frame. Marcus stood up slowly, nervously. At full height, his cheek lined up perfectly with the stationary bullet on this particular stair. Gingerly, Marcus reached out to it. It didn't budge when he poked it. He pulled his hand away, worried for a moment it might explode, not sure if that was how bullets worked. But nothing happened, so he grabbed it and tugged. No movement at all. Looking at his palm, he saw the bullet-shaped indentation left behind.

Marcus forced himself to breathe. The bullet was too small, but he was sure that if he could get a strong enough grip, he could swing in midair from it. By tracing the bullet's path, it was clear that this was one of those he'd fired last night from the far side of the landing. A quick survey around him yielded the location of the other two bullets, also lodged above the stairs, as immobile as if they were encased in concrete. He descended two steps to the next one and tapped it, just to be sure. Then three more steps to the third, this one much closer to the ground but equally unwilling to be moved.

On the landing between floors, Marcus turned and considered the bullets from a different angle. Based on their trajectories, he decided that he probably wouldn't have missed. All three would likely have found a body in which to come to rest.

But that wasn't what had happened. Marcus had wanted to kill the dealer and his friends. He had tried. The bullets had refused.

Marcus ran down the rest of the stairs and out into the sunny morning. For a moment he considered the possibility that this was another dream, that he was still asleep on the couch in his apartment. That made far more sense than the stairwell suddenly becoming untethered to the laws of physics.

Across the street, there was a vacant lot wedged between two buildings, overgrown with weeds and strewn with trash. Marcus could see the brightly colored tarps that had been erected by the homeless residents, makeshift tents and lean-tos. One man was sleeping on the sidewalk directly across from Marcus. Another man stood over him with wild eyes and a scraggly beard. His clothes hung off his frame in tattered layers. He stared down at the man on the ground and lifted a knife over his head, holding on to it by the blade. Marcus backed up toward his own building as the man threw the knife hard toward the sleeping man's chest.

Marcus gasped, fumbling in his pocket for his phone, wondering whether he would call the cops or hit record. Neither option seemed quite right, particularly when the knife abruptly changed its course rather than embedding itself in the sleeping man, taking a sharp turn and crashing harmlessly into the wall of the building. The standing man swore loudly. Marcus was surprised the man on the ground didn't wake up. The aggressor, getting angrier by the minute, retrieved the blade, assumed the same posture from a different angle, and threw it again. He achieved the same result.

As the man went to pick up his knife, Marcus wondered how long he had been doing this. Best to leave him to it.

But just as Marcus was ready to pull himself away from the homeless man's gravity-defying circus act, the man looked directly at him, pointing the knife in his direction. Whatever was happening, it didn't seem life threatening to the man on the ground. Still, Marcus didn't want to become the knife thrower's next target. The blade wasn't actually pointed at him, though. The man seemed focused on something over Marcus's head.

"Watch out," the man shouted in a surprisingly clear and rich voice.

Marcus looked up just in time to see a large object falling toward him. Gravity seemed to be working fine now. The object was rapidly getting bigger. Marcus had enough time to see it was a couch but not enough to get out of the way. Instinctively, he fell into a crouch, holding his hands over his head.

Marcus felt the rush of air as the couch approached. He braced himself for the blow, but it never came. The couch rolled away from him as if bouncing off a force field, coming to a stop a few feet away, upright and intact. Marcus recognized it as one of the pieces of furniture that had collected on the roof, turning it into a shabby outdoor living room. How it had fallen off was as much a mystery as how it hadn't hit him. Marcus glanced up but didn't see anyone peering over the edge of the roof. He didn't wait for any more furniture to fall to earth. He ran and didn't stop until he was at the bus that would take him to Malcolm's campus.

On the bus, rolling away from his neighborhood, Marcus tried to process what he had seen. As the world passed by outside the window, he convinced himself that the couch had been thrown by a junkie or two having fun, maliciously or not; it probably hadn't even been aimed at him. It was also possible that the homeless man had terrible aim, that it wasn't the knife redirecting itself. But the frozen bullets—no matter how hard he tried, he could come up with no reasonable explanation for those.

Marcus watched the scenery change. He expected to see other marvels. Cars flying by, people levitating into the air. Entire city blocks folding in on themselves. Buildings melting into puddles of jelly. Anything seemed possible. But nothing happened. The people that flitted by went about their days. The people on the bus were all distracted by their own devices.

The neighborhood around the college had gentrified in recent years, the buildings and houses having been bought up by both the school and millennials who liked the idea of living in the city. It meshed well with their world view and their liberal values, even as they ignored the fact that their property values pushed so many further out to the edges. By the time the bus pulled to a stop outside one of the college's storied gates, Marcus felt he had entered another world and hated how relaxed it made him.

That feeling only intensified once he passed through the gate onto the sequestered campus, which had long been a fixture of the city even if it had never felt truly part of it. Marcus had never been here. He wandered to the middle of the central quad, surrounded by majestic buildings, each looking like a misplaced castle. Students littered the grassy expanse, sprawled out on top of each other, reveling in the sunny day. A Frisbee whizzed by. The smell of pot wafted past Marcus. It smelled sweet here, not like the sour stench that lingered in pockets near his building. He understood why Malcolm liked it here. He'd said it calmed him. But Marcus also felt observed, like they all knew he didn't belong. Not under surveillance, the way he felt every time a cop car prowled his neighborhood, but watched just the same.

"Are you lost?"

The voice surprised him. Marcus turned to find a woman wearing a bright-yellow shirt and a ponytail standing behind him. He clenched up. This was what he'd expected. Someone asking if he belonged here, not believing he did. But then she smiled at him and pointed at the buttons pinned to her shirt. One said *Tour Guide*, the other *Ask me anything!*

"Prospective student?" she said, upping the perkiness of her voice. "Where are you headed?"

"No," Marcus stammered. "My brother . . ."

He didn't think he could explain. He didn't want to. Marcus imagined how Malcolm would have reacted. His brother would have smiled back at this girl and said he was indeed a prospective student. Charming conversation would have followed.

"Your brother goes here? Are you meeting him?"

The woman's voice wavered a bit. She suddenly seemed much younger, maybe only finishing up her own freshman year. Marcus fumbled for the paper in his pocket, searching for the name of the building where Professor Davis had an office.

"Marvin Hall," Marcus said. "That's where I need to go."

"Perfect!" she said, and actually clapped her hands. "It's right there behind you. The big red building. Folks around here call it Clifford. Like the big red dog."

Marcus sensed that she had defaulted to her tour guide patter. He nodded.

"Thanks," he said, walking away.

The inside of the building was far less majestic than the outside. Long hallways, classrooms and offices. He checked the paper again. Professor Davis was on the third floor. Marcus jogged up the stairs, grateful for the exercise, the rush of blood to his head reminding him he was alive.

There was already someone in Professor Davis's office, standing in front of the desk, fiddling with a stack of papers. It was a young man with skin only slightly lighter than Marcus's. Marcus assumed he was a student dropping off a paper.

"Can I help you?"

"I'm looking for Professor Davis," Marcus said, pushing each word out slowly, still slightly winded from the jog up the stairs.

"You've found him. What can I do for you?" Professor Davis walked to the other side of the desk and sat down. The office was small and felt even smaller, given the sheer number of books crammed into every available space. "Forgive the mess," he said. "I just moved in here. Believe it or not, this is bigger than my last office."

He laughed, deep and rich. Marcus felt himself drawn to this man and understood why Malcolm had liked him so much. His brother had never described Professor Davis to him. Marcus had assumed he was looking for an old white man with a beard and tweed jacket. Professor Davis was the exact opposite of his expectations, although he was in fact wearing a tweed jacket that even had patches on the elbows.

"I'd offer you a seat, but . . ."

Professor Davis motioned at the two chairs, which were both piled high with books. He laughed again.

"Sorry. I'm in a good mood. So rare to have a good-news day. But one like this? Imagine the possibilities. The end of police brutality."

Professor Davis peered over his shoulder out the window, as if he expected to see cops out there waiting for him. But his smile only widened when he turned back to Marcus, who had no idea what he was talking about.

"And you are?"

Marcus held out the flash drive. Professor Davis just stared at it.

"He finished his paper. This is it."

"Who finished his paper?"

"Malcolm. My brother. I didn't want you to think he didn't do it."

Marcus thrust the drive forward again. This time Professor Davis took it.

"Malcolm's brother? Very nice to meet you. He talks about you all the time. Sounds like you're a very talented programmer. Great skill to have. And we need more representation in that field."

Professor Davis tapped a pile of papers with the flash drive.

"I am a bit old-fashioned, though. I was pretty clear that I wanted the papers printed out."

Marcus's face fell. "We don't have a printer."

"And tell Malcolm I may have to grade down for not showing up himself. I'm a little insulted after all we discussed about this project. I figured he'd at least have the decency to show up after all I've done for him. So what happened? Too much partying after classes ended? What did he pay you to be his messenger? Or does he have dirt on you? Of course he does. Brothers."

Marcus hadn't been sure Professor Davis was joking until the end there. The professor's smile faded when Marcus didn't laugh. Marcus had forgotten that not everyone knew about Malcolm. In the conversations that had played in his mind, he hadn't thought about having to give that news.

"Malcolm's dead," Marcus blurted out, regretting it instantly.

Professor Davis fell back in his chair, sucker-punched.

"That's not funny."

Marcus said nothing, watching Professor Davis slowly realize it wasn't a joke.

"When? I just saw him a few days ago."

"He died yesterday."

"What happened?"

"He was shot."

Marcus felt like he was in one of those crime shows on TV. He was just an actor saying his lines, playing his part.

"Shot? Yesterday? That's not possible. The news . . ."

Marcus was getting annoyed. Did this guy think he was lying?

"He was shot four days ago. He died yesterday."

Crestfallen, Professor Davis drifted off.

"Oh god. Four days ago." He seemed to be doing the math in his head. "Two days too soon."

Suddenly, Marcus knew he was in the wrong place. That paper didn't matter. It wasn't Malcolm. Handing it in didn't prove anything. It didn't make anything better. He needed to be at the hospital with his mom and grandmother. If they were even still there. Maybe they were already home. He wondered where Malcolm's body was. He didn't want to see his brother on a slab, lifeless. Or in a coffin. He wanted to tell this professor that it was all a joke. Malcolm was sleeping off a night of drinking. He had paid Marcus five bucks to deliver the paper. The professor would tell him he should charge more.

But none of that was true. The truth was that his brother would never attend another class, never write another paper. And the tragedy of that was written all over the professor's face.

Marcus ran from the office. He couldn't stand to be there anymore, soaking in someone else's sudden grief. He didn't pause, even as Professor Davis called after him to wait.

EXCURSUS B:
THE POPE

T HE POPE WONDERED whether the Ten Commandments would need to be amended. Whether
only nine commandments should remain. It didn't
have the same ring: the Nine Commandments. More
likely, they would leave it as is. The Bible did not get
amended, even though it was endlessly being reinter-
preted. The words didn't change—although that
wasn't true either, since they had changed with every
new translation. Besides, the sixth commandment
would always be a reminder, if no longer a necessary
prohibition.

The Pope wondered if *Thou shalt not kill* really no
longer mattered. Or if it was just unnecessary. Like an
eleventh commandment decreeing *Thou shalt not fly.*

There were thoughts that the Pope had, every day,
that he didn't share with anyone. They were things
that a pope should not consider. But he believed that

part of his job was to allow himself to wonder, even if saying aloud the things he wondered might shake the faith of millions or, more likely, just get him excommunicated.

When it was clear that the change was real, the cardinals had drafted an apostolic letter for the Pope to issue. It seemed inadequate, given the circumstances. Still, the cardinals thought his voice needed to be heard but that they should reserve any longer theological arguments for when they'd had an opportunity to provide a more nuanced proclamation.

Reading the letter again, the Pope wondered if they would ever be able to adequately address the change. The cardinals wrote of the hand and will of God. It was a miracle. They encouraged believers to take this as an opportunity to reaffirm their faith.

The Pope wondered if it was a miracle. Of course it was. How else could it be explained? But the Pope had thought about miracles frequently throughout his life, mostly in the context of modern-day saints, who each needed two to be canonized. It took a great amount of work to attribute a miracle to a specific human being. They had to bend over backward to make it work. For example, an unknown woman had been inexplicably healed of an inoperable tumor and Mother Teresa had borne witness and prayed, so therefore the miracle was hers. One miracle toward sainthood. Because of her love and prayer. The Pope had no doubt that Mother Teresa deserved sainthood, but her miracles, like those of anyone else, had to be found, rationalized, and ultimately taken on faith.

So was something that was demonstrably and undeniably true a miracle? Miraculous, yes, but a miracle?

The Pope wondered about faith. In this letter, he was asking people to have faith that the change was the hand and will of God. But they didn't need faith to believe it. It was an incontrovertible fact. They could experience it all around them. It would scare them and thrill them. But it was hard to doubt it. And without doubt, did you need faith? There were still "mysterious ways" to be considered; the *how* and the *why* were unknown. But the *what*, always the first question, had been answered. That was not the way anyone had ever said God worked.

The Pope wondered.

ANN

D A Y

1

DINNER HAD BEEN ready for over an hour. Jake must have gone to the bar, probably with the guys from the warehouse. Ann didn't know on any given night when he would come home, but it was usually around eight thirty if he went out with his coworkers. If he didn't go to the bar, he would be home around six thirty. On the nights he went to the bar alone —just to take the edge off a long day with a couple of quick ones, he'd say—he would show up around seven thirty. Those were the worst nights, usually.

There were the few nights when he didn't come home at all.

Ann had gotten pretty good at making sure dinner was ready whenever he arrived home. Tonight the oven was on low, keeping the casserole warm. That usually worked for about an hour. Any longer than that and Jake could usually tell it had been sitting for a while. It was a guessing game for Ann, played nightly, based on his mood when he'd left in the morning and any other clues he might have given as to when he would be home. Early in their marriage, she had made the mistake of asking him to call her when he was on the way. She could still see the scar under her eye where the glass had hit her. A little concealer and you could hardly see it, though, not if you didn't know where to look. That night, after he'd hit her with the glass, she had sat up in bed with his head in her lap as he cried and apologized.

I didn't mean to hurt you. I love you.

And she had believed him. Ann believed that he believed it too.

Jake rarely threw things at her anymore. When he did, they were rarely breakable. He didn't like spending the money to replace things.

Ann had also made a salad this evening. Very simple: kale, some cucumbers, carrots, sunflower seeds for protein. It sat on the small counter next to the sink. She would put it on the table after the casserole, once she'd cracked open a beer for Jake. He hated to come into the house and see her "rabbit food." He snorted when he said it. Ann was used to his comments about her eating, his little jokes. She had always seesawed with her weight, though lately it felt like she was always on the up end of the seesaw, never coming down.

She had started a new diet a few weeks earlier after a trip to the doctor to talk about her sore ankles. She liked her doctor. He was honest but not cruel like so many other people, even with his eyes, which didn't judge her or linger on the bulk underneath her clothes. His eyes and his words correlated nicely, neither of them lying to her. The doctor had put the number she should lose at twenty pounds. Ann knew that was low, but not a lie. He was giving her a goal. And she had made progress. As of this morning, there was three pounds less of her than there had been two weeks before.

"And stay off your feet," the doctor had said. "Let your husband do some of the cooking."

They had both laughed, for different reasons.

Sometimes Ann tried to figure out when their relationship had changed. Her friends had cautioned her from the beginning about how he criticized her. They'd chastised her for calling his comments jokes that showed he loved her. Ann had just told them she had a tougher skin than they gave her credit for.

She also sometimes tried to pinpoint when she and Jake had stopped going out with her friends.

But Jake really did love her. She knew it. There was true passion between them. Jake rarely let it get out of hand, only occasionally grabbing her throat or bruising her wrists during sex. He almost never hit her, and when he did, he was truly sorry.

The small table in the small kitchen was already set. On the other side of the sink, dripping on the towels she had laid out, were the dishes she had already done.

Ann was nervous. She didn't want to sit down. So she went back into the refrigerator and came out with a red pepper, something else for her salad. She'd have to wash the cutting board and knife again, but she needed to do something while she waited. Ann circled the top of the pepper with the knife, pulling out the stem and seeds.

Jake could stand to lose a few pounds too. But Ann would never say that. He had packed on some weight after breaking his leg in the accident.

It had happened when Jake was driving the fork-lift at work. He said the collision wasn't his fault, but his coworkers said otherwise. He'd fractured his femur falling onto the concrete floor. The other guy involved was worse off, knocked unconscious and forced onto disability. Jake was reassigned to a desk off the floor—not a promotion, but he kept his job. When Ann told him in the hospital that at least they hadn't fired him, Jake swung at her from his bed. It was a weak and impotent shot that she easily stepped back away from. She blamed the drugs and the pain. But maybe that was when everything had changed. After that, his "jokes" had taken on a sharper edge until any hint of humor disappeared.

That had been three years ago.

They had wedged a little flat-screen into the cor-ner on the kitchen counter. Jake had brought it home the day after he told her she couldn't replace the dish-washer, which he said had broken because she used it too much. He'd presented the TV as a gift. Ann did like having it in the kitchen. It provided some com-pany while she waited.

It was currently tuned to CNN. Not much news. A slow day. She had ignored most of the long piece about prisons in North Korea and paid more attention to the shorter piece about how new U.S. policies were making the trek north more dangerous for immigrants seeking asylum in the States. That was more likely to affect her work.

Ann was starting to chop up the pepper when some-thing else on the TV caught her eye. A familiar build-ing. One of the synagogues in town. She passed it every day on her way home from work, but today she'd had to take a detour. Something had happened there. She had been a little annoyed because it added ten minutes to her commute, which was already nearly an hour.

She'd gotten her facts wrong, but only slightly. Something had *almost* happened.

Knife in one hand, Ann reached for the remote. She turned up the volume just in time to hear that a mass shooting had been averted. She wondered how they could call it a mass shooting when no one had been killed. The anchor—the one with blonde hair and sparkly eyes—patiently explained that they had recovered a number of guns and plenty of spare ammunition at the site. The shooter had walked into the nursery school. The anchor speculated that his gun had jammed and he had panicked.

Authorities hadn't caught the man yet. They were seeking help from the community. Ann continued to chop the pepper, the knife slicing up and down, up and down. But she focused on the TV. They didn't have much information on the almost shooter, only that he was a white male in his twenties with a short haircut. Pretty standard description for this kind of thing. But Ann watched closely. She was twenty-nine. Her birthday was next week. That description matched every guy she had gone to high school with. And all of their younger brothers. With a mixture of anticipation and dread, she waited for a police sketch, nearly certain she would recognize the face. The boys around here shared a certain aimlessness and anger with the kids she worked with in the city that made them capable of being stupid and dangerous.

A sharp pain in her hand grabbed her attention. The knife had sliced her index finger. Hand shaking, she looked at her finger and saw only blood. The pain was intense. For a moment, Ann felt light-headed and thought she might faint. But she breathed through it until she felt steady.

She held her hand under the water. The blood washed away. Ann put pressure on the cut with her thumb, hoping to stop the flow, but blood continued to rise to the surface, then flow away with the water.

Ann pulled her hand out from under the water. She tugged on the roll of paper towels, ripping some jaggedly free. She pressed her intact hand hard on the cut, the towels rapidly becoming soaked. She squeezed the towels tighter around her finger. They were already slick and needed to be switched out. She could tell the bleeding hadn't stopped.

Ann turned off the water with her elbow and checked the clock. She had to get this under control before Jake got home. She hurried down the hall past the two bedrooms to the bathroom. With a dexterity that surprised even herself, she gathered supplies— gauze, Band-Aids, antiseptic spray—and turned on the water. Gritting her teeth, she sprayed the wound and let the sting mix with the dulling pain of the cut to wake her up. She wrapped the finger tightly in gauze and secured it under a latticework of Band-Aids.

"What the hell is going on here?"

She was too late. Jake's voice bellowed down the hallway from the kitchen. He sounded amused and in a drunken haze, though she knew that was often a prelude to anger. Her shoulders slumped, and she carried herself slowly out of the bathroom and down the hall, toward the kitchen. It was only when she was almost there, too late to go back, after he had already seen her, that she realized there were bloodstains splotched down the front of her shirt.

"Did you get attacked?" Jake said.

"I had an accident," Ann said. "I'll clean it up."

Jake scoffed, "Where's dinner?"

Ann felt the rush of heat on her face as she opened the oven. The tomato and garlic from the meat sauce soaked into her. She loved that smell, and she knew Jake did too. Ann could always sense him near her. He still walked with a slight limp from the accident. She felt him smile as he sat down. Grabbing one oven mitt and a dishrag, Ann took out the casserole, using the rag with her injured hand and carefully balancing the baking dish on her good fingers, the heat radiating through the thin fabric.

Jake waited to be served. Ann obliged, then took a small portion for herself.

"I'm starving," Jake said, digging in.

Crumbles of meat and a glaze of sauce immediately coated his goatee. Jake didn't care. Ann watched him eat and thought about the almost shooting on the news. Jake could never be mistaken for a young twentysomething anymore, even though he had just turned thirty a few months earlier. An eyewitness would be more likely to peg him as early forties, if not older. The sauce dyed the premature gray in his facial hair like henna.

"There was this girl at the bar. She was all over me. I swear, I don't know what her deal was. The guys won't ever let that go. Just a horny bitch, I guess."

Jake licked at a strand of cheese in his moustache, which just drove it in deeper.

"Don't worry. I told her I was married. Besides, she was a fat one. Definitely not my type. Why aren't you eating?"

Ann realized she had been staring at the wall, where there was a water stain they hadn't been able to source. Her finger was throbbing, maybe jarred by carrying the casserole. Picking up her fork, she stabbed a noodle, but a wave of nausea kept her from raising it to her mouth.

"What's the problem? Something wrong with the casserole? You trying to poison me?"

Ann found herself shaking her head, even though she knew he was joking. Jake grinned widely at her. His face was flushed. It was rare that he was drunk and happy. She hardly recognized him. There was a hint of his old self, the man she'd once known. The one she'd defended to her friends. He shoveled the food into his mouth.

"At least have some of your goddamn salad," Jake said.

The edge returned to his voice. That was a command, not a suggestion. Until that moment, she hadn't realized she had forgotten her own dinner. Ann reached over to the counter and retrieved the salad bowl with her good hand. She left the partially cut pepper on the cutting board. Jake smiled and returned to his own food.

Jake ate and talked and laughed. He was enjoying his own company and seemed unoffended by hers. He told stories about his coworkers, each one more derogatory and vulgar than the last. Each one brought him more joy.

Pushing her food around her plate, Ann found herself feeling hopeful—not about anything in particular, just generally. Her finger stopped throbbing. In fact, she couldn't feel much under the bandages at all. She considered that a step in the right direction.

So when Jake leaned back in his chair, hands on his stomach, after his third helping, Ann thought this might be her best chance to bring something up she had been avoiding. She stood up and carried both of their plates in to the sink. Her back to him, she took a deep breath and let it out slowly.

"It's my birthday next week," she said.

When he didn't answer, she wondered whether she had said it out loud. Her voice had been soft, even in her own head. She turned around. Jake was giving her a quizzical look. He seemed sleepy and sated.

"That time again already," he said. "Don't expect me to be planning anything."

Ann forced a smile.

"That's not what . . . it's just some of the people at work . . . we kind of have a list of everyone's birthday."

Jake kept his eyes on her, not hiding his boredom. He shrugged at her.

"So some of the girls want to take me out. There's a place near the office. But I'd be home late."

The metal ends of the chair legs screeched along the floor as Jake stood up suddenly. Whatever good mood he'd been in had disappeared in an instant.

"You want to go out on your birthday without me?"

He had gone out on his birthday without her. But that wasn't relevant. Not to him.

Ann shrank back into the counter. The edge dug into her back. Jake strode over to stand in front of her, his face inches from her own. She remembered the days when she longed to be that close to him. Now she tried to look away but couldn't.

"I can tell them no," Ann said.

"Damn right you can."

Ann braced herself for the first punch. Jake almost always hit her in the torso, body blows like he was a boxer in a clinch. The jabs usually came in rapid succession: *left, right; left, right.* Once he had told her that hitting her was like pounding a sack of dough. It barely bruised his knuckles at all. Some of his punches hurt more than others, depending on whether they landed on her stomach or up around her ribs. There were always bruises that no one else could see.

The first shot never came. Jake took a step away from her. He was looking at his own fist. Then he glared at her with more anger than she had seen in him recently. He threw his arm forward toward her breast. But the fist never got there. With half the distance crossed, Jake's hand drooped limply at the wrist, fingers dangling below. Momentum brought his arm into her body, where it landed softly against her. The back of his hand lay on her breast, and as he pulled back, it brushed lightly across her nipple. Even through her shirt and bra, she felt it. He hadn't touched her that way in so long—tenderly, even if it was unintended. Ann couldn't help but let out a sigh at the unexpected pleasurable sensation. But what she felt wasn't the truth. The fear on his face was. He had momentarily lost control of his arm and had no idea why. It fell away from her to hang limply by his side.

After a moment, Jake regained his bearings. The muscles in his arm reacted when he lifted it, holding it out in front of him, flexing his fingers. The fear faded. With renewed purpose, he balled up his left hand and struck again, this time going for her side. But the result was the same. He atrophied before her eyes, his hand opening, his arm losing its power. His palm caressed her side, less pleasurably this time.

Jake backed away, scared. It was his left arm hanging limply by his side now. Ann didn't understand what was happening. Maybe he was having a heart attack. Or a stroke. Jake said nothing, his mouth hanging open slightly. Ann didn't move, half expecting him to keel over to the floor. She resisted the urge to reach out to him, to steady him.

Jake stood there, a statue. Then he was flexing again, rolling his wrist, wiggling his fingers. He squeezed his bicep with his other hand and seemed satisfied. He looked at Ann with a mixture of disgust and dread. She could feel him blaming her for whatever had just happened. It was always her fault.

"Clean up this fucking mess," he said.

His voice was different. Almost a question. Almost a request. Not quite. But almost.

Ann had always known that Jake needed her. Watching him now, she could see a desperation in his eyes. Things had changed. She saw something break across his face, a pain, a loss.

Jake left the kitchen. Ann heard him in the living room. She had a lot to do in the kitchen. But first she had to check her finger. Assess the damage. Consider the future. As she walked softly down the hallway back to the bathroom, she felt that maybe the bleeding had stopped.

DAY

2

FRIDAY AFTERNOONS WERE usually quiet at the office. Ann spent much of her time reviewing the week, checking her files. The foundation had seventeen different active programs, each one the brainchild of the tech billionaire who funded them. Most of the foundation employees were located in the suburbs close to the headquarters of his company. But Ann and the other engagement officers were based here in the city, in an office building that was affectionately known as Bleeding Heart Tower because it housed the public defenders and a raft of do-gooder nonprofits. The foundation occupied the top floor, and Ann's office, while small, had a great view of the courthouse on the other side of the park. It was particularly easy to get distracted at this time of year with the flowers in full bloom and all the trees returning to life. The annual rebirth of the park, which never went fully dormant in this part of the world but turned gray and lifeless during the wet winter months, gave Ann hope for all her clients.

Her previous job had been as a social worker for the city. All her clients in that job had been mandated by the court to interact with her. She'd spent too much of her time explaining to people that the threat to losing this benefit or that was real if they didn't do what the state demanded. She was never the one to enforce the law, but every time a case file was taken away from her and transferred back to a less friendly agency, she felt as if she had been the arresting officer. It felt like the system was designed to help people fail rather than succeed.

Ann had said that in her interview for the foundation. It had probably gotten her the job. The tech billionaire believed strongly in helping people succeed, and armed with a bottomless well of funds and no need to be accountable to the public, he was able to achieve that goal to some extent. She still wished he saw the clients as people rather than statistics, but she had to settle for providing that personal connection herself. That was why he'd bought himself an entire floor of engagement officers—so that the clients would be more than merely a number to at least one person in the foundation.

The foundation gave small grants for housing assistance and food security, transportation and childcare. The amounts were minuscule to the billionaire but life changing for the recipients. As a child, Ann had frequently been a half step above the poverty line herself, so she understood how important the money was to the clients, even if her boss didn't. Not that she or anyone else in the office ever saw the billionaire. Aside from giving the occasional directive or starting a new program now and then, he was busy multiplying his billions through his company.

Her favorite program was Down to Gown, which provided full tuition to a local college for prison inmates who had completed a series of academic requirements while serving their time. Of all her clients, Ann found that these men and women were the most likely to thrive. It was almost graduation time again. This year she had four clients receiving diplomas.

Down to Gown participants were required to check in with her every two weeks. She picked up her pile of folders to confirm that everyone had done so this week. Only after reviewing her list did she realize that one person hadn't been in touch. He was in his first year in the program, which was typically when any backsliding occurred. But this kid was so smart that she had never considered him to be in danger. She loved chatting with Malcolm. He was truly passionate about his classes, more so than she had ever been in college. It was refreshing for her to be reminded of what true enthusiasm looked like.

Ann flipped through Malcolm's file for a phone number and gave him a call. Straight to voice mail.

"Hey, Malcolm. Ann here from Down to Gown. Missed you this week. Hope everything is all right. Check in as soon as you can."

Hanging up, Ann was sure she would hear from him by the beginning of next week. The college tuition grants were far and away the largest awards given to individuals. The effect was not quite as immediate as picking up a mother's day care tab or covering the down payment on a car, but Ann believed it paid more dividends than anything else the foundation did, making it worth the price tag.

"Ann! Come see this!"

Her friend Barbara sat in the office next door. Ann had been avoiding her most of the day, staying in her own office, working, feeling guilty about lying to her earlier. Barbara was spearheading the effort to take Ann out for her birthday. She had asked about it again that morning. Ann had told her that she couldn't because Jake was planning something special for her, something romantic for just the two of them. Barbara had believed her, which made the lie worse. Ann didn't talk much about Jake at work, but when she did, she always lied. None of her coworkers had ever met her husband.

But she couldn't avoid Barbara all day. She didn't want to, either. They spent most of the day, when clients weren't around, bantering back and forth with diet tips and gossip. Ann craved the interaction and had been feeling the absence of it. She poked her head into Barbara's office.

"What's up?"

Barbara waved her over to her computer, where a video was paused. It was from one of the local news stations. The freeze-frame showed a woman holding a destroyed tambourine in front of her. Barbara hit play.

"It was a miracle," the woman said to an offscreen reporter. "Look at this. I could feel the bullets ripping through it. But then they bounced off me. They felt like little pinpricks."

The woman on the screen started laughing and crying at the same time. The reporter started talking over footage of the synagogue where the almost shooting had occurred.

"Isn't this right near where you live?" Barbara said.

"Yeah, messed up my commute yesterday," Ann said.

"Wow, that's cold," Barbara said with a laugh.

Ann felt the bottom drop out from under her. She hadn't even thought about those kids.

"Whoa, honey, I'm just joking," Barbara said. "It's not like anyone died."

"Yeah," Ann said, unconvinced.

"And might not ever again," Barbara said with another laugh, more nervous this time.

"What do you mean?"

Barbara turned to Ann in disbelief. "Haven't you been watching the news?"

Ann hadn't been watching anything. She had been working and not eating and avoiding everyone. Doing her best disappearing act.

Before Barbara could elaborate, another coworker ran by the office, heading toward the break room. They heard someone swear down the hall. Then another person ran by. That was all the incentive Barbara and Ann needed to follow.

The break room had big windows that looked out over the courthouse. This was where the tech world bled fully into the foundation. The billionaire had it tricked out with foosball and Ping-Pong tables, ridiculously comfortable couches, and cabinets overflowing with snacks. Ann tried to stay out of the break room except during birthday celebrations and mandatory team-building events. Those cabinets held too many temptations.

Near the door, two of Ann's coworkers were in the middle of a heated discussion.

"It can't be real. Seriously. The whole thing is a hoax."

"You think everything is a conspiracy theory."

"You think this is true? I wouldn't put it past this administration to make the whole thing up."

"Why would they do that?"

"Why wouldn't they?"

Barbara grabbed Ann's arm and pulled her deeper into the break room. Neither of them wanted to get caught in that conversation.

The TVs on the walls were all tuned to news channels. One of them had a headline underneath the field reporter that read *The End of Violence?* Ann wondered about the question mark. But the TVs weren't holding the attention of the rapidly filling room. Everyone was looking out the windows at the park below.

Ann had noticed that there seemed to be more people in the park than usual. She had attributed that to the beautiful day. But now it was clear that it was something else. It looked more like a political rally, people standing elbow to elbow. They were milling around, mostly focused on the courthouse. It was a restless crowd. When she had glanced out the window earlier, the park had been more sparsely populated, those gathered seemingly in a festive mood. But now it looked tense, like a nest of snakes about to uncoil. As Ann glanced around the periphery of the park, it became clear why. Police vans had pulled up at most of the intersections, unloading officers in full riot gear, holding their shields and batons in front of them, heads obscured by helmets and face masks. More vans skidded into place in the empty spaces.

"I talked to someone from the PD office down-stairs," Tom said. He was the director of client engage-ment, the ranking voice of authority. "It started in the courthouse. A defendant got belligerent with a judge, just starting ranting about aliens or something. When the officers tried to restrain him, they . . . couldn't."

Everyone was looking at Tom now. Ann held her breath. *Couldn't.* She thought of Jake the night before with his open hands, his unintended caresses.

"People in the room said that two cops attempted to grab the man, but every time it looked like they were going to wrestle him to the ground, they lost their grip," Tom continued. "Or they let go. No one was quite sure. And the man was throwing punches at them. But not a single one landed. The PD said it became comical—these three men unable to lay a hand on each other, unable to do more than give each other hugs. The moment anyone got aggressive, they just stopped, unable to follow through."

Tom stopped talking. He seemed confused by his own words, as if they didn't make any sense. The silence in the room was broken by the sound of a heli-copter overhead. Ann assumed it was the police until one of the TVs suddenly cut to an aerial shot of the park. The break room became a surreal panopticon as half the people watched the scene on TV while the other half continued to look out the windows.

"I was in the courthouse right after that," said Julie, another coworker whose proximity to the events gave her instant credibility. "Word spread fast. Another guy got in the face of a police officer in the hall. Same result. Neither one of them could do more than pos-ture. After that, people started streaming out of the building, leaving their hearings, ignoring orders to stop. Out in the park, people were making videos and calling friends. Telling the world that the cops couldn't do anything to stop them."

"Oh god," another coworker said, though Ann couldn't tell who. "Looks like they're going to test that theory."

The police were fanning out now. The crowd shrank away from the streets, toward the middle of the park, as the cops formed a long semicircle between them and the courthouse. The officers stood shoulder to shoulder, shields in front forming a continuous wall. Ann thought there must be at least fifty cops and more than twice that many in the crowd. If this wasn't a protest before, it would certainly become one now. More people were approaching the park from every direction. And a protest could easily become a riot.

Ann looked at the time in the corner of one of the TV screens. It was already four o'clock. If she didn't leave soon, she'd get home late.

"I need to go," she said to no one in particular.

"No such luck," Barbara said, holding up her phone. "Just got a notice that they're closing the garage and putting the building on lockdown. No one's going anywhere for a while."

Ann felt her throat close up, her airway constrict. She felt Jake's hands on her. She flinched, unable to help herself. Barbara touched her forearm lightly, calming her. Together they watched the scene unfold outside.

The crowd turned in the direction of an officer with a bullhorn, who stood behind the line and barked orders. The foundation employees couldn't hear him, but it wasn't hard to tell that the crowd was being told to disperse. It seemed to make them angry. Ann could see countless fists punching upward into the air. The roar of complaints sounded like a gentle buzzing from up here. But there was still a healthy distance between the cops and the crowd, which had naturally backed away from the threat.

All the riot police raised their batons and smacked them against their shields. The noise must have been crisp and startling down below, because a ripple went through the crowd. Then, like a synchronized drill team, the entire line of cops took one step forward. When the crowd didn't move back, the police repeated the action. Baton slap, step forward. It was undeniably threatening, but to Ann it seemed more like a small animal puffing itself up to seem dangerous to a predator.

Then someone came out of the crowd, hands over his head. It looked like he was surrendering. He walked up to the nearest officer and stood directly in front of him, close but not quite touching his shield. He turned his back to the cop and looked at the crowd. The police raised their batons again, but the officer with the man in front of him couldn't hit his shield without hitting the man. When the others pounded their shields, his baton remained over his head. When his colleagues stepped forward, he was stuck in place. Ann smiled. He couldn't move without shoving the man.

Others in the crowd noticed the break in the line. The man in front of the cop raised his arms again, this time in victory. Within moments, people broke from the crowd, each picking a cop to stand in front of until the entire line was covered. The cops all raised their batons again.

"They're going to beat the crap out of them," one of Ann's coworkers said.

"No," Ann said. "They can't."

"How could you know that?' someone else asked.

Ann understood the skepticism. It had been reflected in the question mark on the TV news chyron. How could this be possible? But Ann had seen it up close the night before with Jake. It was possible.

And she was right. The batons stayed raised for a long moment, followed by another. Finally, one cop here, another there, brought their weapons down, back behind their shields. The crowd cheered the standoff. Their enthusiasm swept through Ann. It was more than the joy of momentary victory. It was a deeper feeling. A relief that grew within her. The understanding that she was safe. That they all were.

"We should be down there," Ann said.

"I don't think anyone should go anywhere," Tom said.

"We shouldn't be hiding," Ann said. "We should be participating."

That was what they told their clients every day: Show up for your own life. Take control of your own destiny. Participate. Yet they were all going to stay up here on the top floor and just watch life unfold below them. Ann was gripped with the need to be in the crowd, to be deafened and buffeted by it.

"This is a volatile situation," Tom said. "The best thing is for all employees of the foundation to shelter in place until the threat has passed."

Ann realized that was exactly what she had been doing. Sheltering in place. Waiting for the threat to pass. More than anything right now, she needed to leave this building.

"I'm going," Ann said.

She realized that her coworkers were staring at her in stunned silence. Ann was usually the quietest person in any room, the most compliant, the last to question. Not today.

Ann walked past Tom and left the break room. In the hallway, on the way to the elevators, she realized a handful of coworkers, including Barbara, had followed her. In a last-second decision, she walked past the elevators to the stairs. Together they jogged down. Winded and exhilarated, Ann led her coworkers through the lobby and out onto the street.

Whatever tension had been in the air had dissipated. The festive mood had returned. Ann could see that the police had started to fall back at the far end of the park, taking up positions in front of the government buildings in groups of three and four. Most of them dropped their shields, letting them rest on the ground or against the nearest wall. Ann took Barbara's hand and pulled her into the crowd. They waded through the people celebrating. There was no jostling in the crowd; the slightest touch of a hand and people made room. In the distance, a group had started singing, a happy song, a song of triumph. Ann and Barbara made their way into the song's growing periphery.

Ann knew that it was probably naïve to believe that this was the reality of the new world. But at this moment, it was. She closed her eyes to appreciate the voices and let hers join in.

They sang and swayed until the sun started to go down. The park darkened and the streetlights began to glow. Only then did Ann and Barbara head back to their building. And as they said good-bye, wishing each other a good weekend, Ann told her friend that she would like to go out for her birthday next week.

Driving home, Ann turned up the radio loud and sang the whole way. Until she pulled into her driveway. The front porch light was off, but the kitchen light was on. It was almost eight o'clock. In the back of her mind, though she might have said it didn't matter anymore, she had assumed Jake would be out drinking on a Friday night. It appeared that he was home.

Inside, she slipped off her shoes and flipped on the outside light.

"Jake?"

No answer. Ann found him in the kitchen sitting at the table. There were three empty beer bottles in front of him, a fourth in his hand. No food.

"Hey," Ann said, warily circling the table on her way to the refrigerator. "You been home a while?"

"Yeah," Jake said. "A while."

His voice was oddly subdued. Maybe he'd had a couple before he got home. If he was really six deep, he might be more sleepy than angry. But he was staring at her intently.

"Where were you?" Jake said.

"There was some excitement around my office. They weren't letting cars out of the garage."

Jake grunted. Maybe that explanation would suffice. Ann didn't feel like getting into a fight with him. The residual elation of the afternoon was still keeping her warm, but the glow was fading.

"Are you hungry?" Ann said. "I can heat up last night's leftovers."

"I made myself dinner."

Jake raised the beer bottle to her, then drained it. Very carefully, he lined it up next to the others. Ann backed up into the counter, keeping her eyes on him. She felt the palpitations, the fear. But he couldn't hurt her anymore. She repeated that to herself but wasn't convinced.

"You hear what happened at that synagogue yesterday?" Jake said. "Know whose kid that was? The shooter, I mean."

"He didn't manage to shoot anyone."

Jake laughed. "I know. Who manages to screw up a school shooting? Point and shoot. How hard is that?"

Jake made a gun out of his thumb and forefinger and pointed it at Ann. She pushed herself farther into the counter.

"I'll tell you who screws that up. My perfect supervisor's kid. That's who. Not so perfect, I guess. Raised a fucking Nazi."

"They caught him?" Ann said.

"Not yet. But cops came by the warehouse to talk to Daddy Hitler. His dumb-fuck son might as well have smiled for the cameras. They got good pics of him."

Jake went silent again, staring at the bottles in front of him. When he looked back up at her, he seemed completely sober. It chilled her.

"You been watching the news today?" he said.

Ann couldn't find her voice. She managed a nod.

"You believe it?" he said.

He can't hurt you, she thought. *Not anymore.*

Jake stared through her, then picked up a beer bottle. He stood up. Ann held her breath.

"I do," he said.

Then, without warning, he threw the beer bottle. Not at her. He chucked it at the floor in front of her. It shattered. Through her stockings, she felt the pieces of glass bounce off her legs. Ann froze. She looked at the floor for a clear path out of the kitchen. Then he threw the second bottle to her left and the third to the right. Ann jumped at each crash. Jake's smile was malicious. He seemed to be going for full coverage of the floor with glass shards. Seemingly satisfied with his work, he twirled the fourth bottle high in the air, letting it crash to the middle of the floor.

There was definitely no safe path out for Ann now. Jake walked out toward the living room. He had been wearing his shoes all along.

"Clean up this mess," he said before disappearing.

Ann took a deep breath. She was already formulating an escape plan. If she crouched and used oven mitts, she thought she could clear a path to the front door without shredding her feet. Once she had her shoes, everything would be fine.

She heard her own voice in her head. *Everything will be fine.* Except that her husband had just trapped her in the kitchen amid a sea of broken glass. It had been only hours since she'd thought everything had changed. But nothing had changed.

EXCURSUS C: THE DICTATOR

THE DICTATOR'S OFFICE, which covered most of the top floor of the Main Presidential Palace, was filled with birds in cages. Macaws, parrots, mostly tropical birds from around the world, none of them native to his country. The birds had learned to be silent, suppressing their natural calls and songs; those that hadn't learned had been killed.

The Dictator was alone in his office with the birds. He stood in front of the "bald" eagle, and it looked back at him from its perch. When his country had first been sanctioned by the Americans so many years ago, near the beginning of his rule, the Dictator had demanded that a bald eagle be added to his aviary. When it arrived, it did not have the characteristic plumage, the purest of white heads that the Americans imagined symbolized their policies. The man who procured the bird swore it was the right species, that the youngster had not yet grown into its full majestic plumage. But others, more knowledgeable, had informed the Dictator that this was a golden eagle, a close relative but not the same.

The man who'd brought him the bird, as well as those who'd told him the truth, had now all been executed. This was a bald eagle now, and no one would contradict him.

The Dictator looked across the room at the dead body of his eldest son. Twenty, maybe thirty years from now when the Dictator was too old and tired to rule, his son would have taken over. A long apprenticeship, for sure, but his son had seemed more than happy to wait, enjoying the rewards of this life. The Dictator's own rise had been rapid, a coup accomplished over the course of a single night. Now he knew that the end had come equally fast, another eternal night.

His son had a halo of blood around his head, at the spot where he had fallen, from the bullet in his skull. His son, twenty-seven but still childlike sometimes, had been playing around with the gun while the three men he had just failed to shoot still cowered on their knees in front of him. The Dictator's eldest, his favorite, had pressed the muzzle to his temple, then crossed his eyes and pursed his lips, mimicking the expression Jerry Lewis made in all those ancient films they used to watch and love together. He pulled the trigger, never expecting it to fire. Why would it? He had just pulled the trigger three times with the gun aimed at the backs of the heads of three men, trying to test the new reality of the world. The gun had not gone off. It had seemed to be jammed. But pointed at his own head with his own finger, it worked just fine. The Dictator's son was dead by his own hand, unintentional suicide.

The Dictator knew that all his advisers had already fled. His wife, this fourth one that he admired the most, was also gone with the other children. He didn't know where she would go. Maybe to Cyprus, where they had friends still, a refuge. He hoped they would make it there safely. After a moment, working through the situation, he realized he need not worry. No one could harm them.

The gun was still in his son's hand. The Dictator pulled it from his fingers, lingering over the touch of his son's rapidly cooling skin. He closed his eyes and said good-bye. He was not a sentimental man, but a wave of nostalgia for what he was about to lose did pass through him. The Dictator shook it off, striding across the room to the balcony doors. Shoving them open, he presented himself in the cool night air to the throngs of people below.

Hundreds had squeezed onto the palace grounds to look up at him. They were calm and silent. He had been told there had been no rioting, no looting, though he expected at least the latter would come within days as the rules of the new world were learned. These were the people who'd been forced to listen to his endless speeches in the past, the ones who'd been rounded up and threatened, those who pretended to love him given no other choice. These were the people who were compelled to applaud. They were here to see what he would do now that he could no longer send his police to beat them, his soldiers to maim and rape them. They were here merely to witness.

The Dictator returned their gaze. He raised his arms, as he always did before he spoke. To the extent that there had been any murmuring, it silenced them. The Dictator had never been one to delay a decision. He was known for acting quickly, impulsively.

The gun, somehow still warm from its last use, tickled his cheekbone. The end was sudden. The Dictator never heard the applause.

RICHARD

DAY

1

OLIVIA HAD BOUGHT Richard the tweed jacket
with the patches on the elbows as a joke. A gently ironic one in honor of him becoming the youngest
tenured professor in the Sociology Department at the
college. She'd unveiled it at a party at the beginning of
the school year, making him hold his arms out behind
him so he could slip it on. Richard felt the same elec-
tric shudder through his body when she fixed his collar that he did every time she touched him. The
assembled crowd, a mix of friends from their old
neighborhood and neighbors from this new one, colleagues from the college and all the people they'd collected through many years, clapped as he bowed
majestically.

That should have been the end of the jacket. It
should have disappeared into the closet, never to be
seen again, except maybe trotted out for a far-in-the-
future retirement party, where equally friendly fun
could be made of his inability to fit into it anymore.
But by the end of the night, a long one that would be

fuzzy the next morning, Richard realized he was still wearing it. It fit him perfectly. So comfortable he forgot about it completely until he and Olivia were alone, the kids long since gone to bed, and she helped him slip out of it.

Now the second semester was almost over. Just a few days until summer. He wore the tweed jacket at least twice a week. Richard needed to wear a jacket every day. He had found that when he didn't have a jacket on, he was mistaken for a student. Not even a grad student but one of his undergrads, those wide-eyed, confused kids. Growing facial hair didn't help—it just made him look like he was trying too hard. Olivia put her perfect hand on his cheek and called him Babyface whenever he complained about it.

Richard topped off his coffee and considered the front page of the *Chronicle*. He stood at the island in their kitchen and sipped himself awake, bored by the previous day's news. Olivia read everything online, but he preferred paper to digital. Books, newspapers, magazines. He even made his students print out their work to hand in. Old-school, or in their eyes, just old.

It was a beautiful sunny day. From his perch in the kitchen, Richard could see through the living room and out the windows to their front yard. Someone walked by slowly on the distant sidewalk, leading a very reluctant old dog. Over his shoulder, Richard could look out into the backyard, where a newly installed playset awaited the boys. Later, after school.

Richard glanced at the clock. Soon he and the boys would head out to walk the few blocks to their school. On cue, footsteps thundered down the stairs, a herd of elephants or two elementary school kids chasing each other. They burst into the kitchen, Elijah and Theo, seven and five respectively, each wielding a giant fluorescent Nerf gun, their thumping feet accompanied by loud shouts, prepubescent war cries as the two of them charged some unseen enemy.

"Teeth brushed?" Richard shouted at them as they passed.

The boys ignored him, flying past into the family room and out of sight, though their screams still filled the kitchen. More noise on the stairs, the clicking of Olivia's heels. She appeared in the doorway. Richard grabbed her travel mug, filled it with coffee, and slid it across the island toward her. Olivia was dressed for court, her suit impeccably tailored. She was running a lint brush over her lapels even as she reached for the mug. She pressed her lips together, evening out her lipstick. Richard wanted to take her back to bed.

"Lunches?" Olivia said.

She smiled at Richard. He pivoted to the refrigerator and retrieved the two lunch boxes, each adorned with cartoon superheroes.

"Elijah! Theo!"

The house fell silent at the sound of their mother's voice. Richard recognized that obedience. The boys would grow out of it, but for now there was no sound that meant more to them. It was the only thing that could stop them in their tracks. Richard felt that power echoed in his own past. When he was the boys' age, it had been the voice of his grandmother, his aunts and cousins, the various women who raised him. There was also the faintest trace of his own mother, before she went away to prison, before the man she said was his father died.

Elijah and Theo slumped into the kitchen, Nerf guns hanging by their sides. Olivia pointed to their lunch boxes.

"Time to pack up," she said. "Then take that commotion outside until it's time for school."

The boys grabbed their lunches and ran to the front hall. Richard heard them unzipping and stuffing their backpacks full before crashing through the front door. Outside, they were shouting at each other again. Richard envied his sons, the lightness in their bodies, their unchecked exuberance. So unlike him as a child. Richard had been quiet, reluctant, skittish. The boys darted back and forth on the front lawn.

"You don't have to watch them," Olivia said. "They're fine."

"I know," Richard said, forcing his eyes away from the window and onto her. "I just don't like the guns, that's all."

"I don't either. But if we take them away now, they'll want them more. Give it a few days. They'll get bored and move on to something else."

Richard knew she was right. Neither he nor Olivia would ever have bought the boys any kind of toy gun. Too much history, too much experience. But at Elijah's birthday party the week before, they had made the mistake of having him unwrap the presents in front of all the kids. The Nerf guns were a gift from one of the boys in his class.

Olivia was by his side, leaning forward and kissing him on the cheek. In her heels, she was slightly taller than Richard. She wiped the lipstick off his skin with her thumb. He drank her in, every contour of her face. He leaned forward for another kiss, this one on the lips, but was met with a finger on his mouth. *Not now. Later.*

"You look beautiful," he said. "No earrings today?"

Olivia reached for her earlobes, surprised to find them empty.

"Damn, I knew I forgot something," she said, already walking away. "Thanks."

Richard watched her go. He listened to the *tick, tick, tick* as she returned upstairs. Then he returned his attention to the boys. He circumnavigated the island and passed through the living room to stand in front of the window and monitor them. They were rolling around on the grass, wrestling, their guns still in their hands, the occasional bright-orange projectile firing into the sky, like dud fireworks that never exploded.

Richard rubbed the patch on his elbow, a habit he had developed when he was nervous. He wished the boys had gone out to the backyard instead. He chided himself for wanting to limit them and rubbed his elbow harder.

In their old neighborhood they had been the only Black family for a few blocks. Here, in this area around the college, things were much more transitional. Unlike Olivia, Richard had grown up in this city. She was a transplant, having arrived here for law school and never left. They had met as stressed-out, sleepless grad students, Richard in the fourth year of his PhD. So she didn't understand the history of this neighborhood, didn't feel it the way he did. Growing up, this had been one of the middle-class Black neighborhoods that was purely aspirational to the families that lived around him. With its big houses and wide lawns, its quiet streets and relative safety, this area was a dream realized, an oasis in a struggling world. About half of his neighbors here were Black, many of them the same occupants he'd envied as a child. But more and more of them were being pushed out as the home prices sky-rocketed and houses were scooped up by millennials seeking an urban environment. In his old neighbor-hood, the people around him were not racist, but he knew exactly how they saw him. Here, it was more complicated. He and Olivia were the invaders. They were the ones gentrifying the neighborhood, even if their neighbors, new and old, Black and white, couldn't be sure at first glance that that was the case.

Outside, Theo stood up and loomed over his brother. The only time he was taller than Elijah was when his older brother was on the ground. He laughed and fired round after round at Elijah, who blocked them with his forearms. Richard tensed and watched them. He wanted to stop them. He found himself worrying about what the neighbors might see—two Black boys running around with guns. Bright-orange plastic toys, but still guns. Only a few more minutes and they would head to school. Maybe he could hide the guns later. Maybe the boys would forget about them, just like Olivia said.

A police car rolled down the street. Richard saw it out of the corner of his eye and stopped breathing, an old habit never shed. Expecting it to drive past, he was surprised when it pulled up to the curb across the street. The boys didn't notice, didn't care.

Richard watched the cop focus on something near his dashboard, maybe a touch screen. It was hard to see in the distance, but the officer seemed to be

talking to someone. Maybe he was checking to see if
he was in the right place. After a moment, the cop
leaned back in his seat and stretched out his arms,
flexing before opening his door. Richard told himself
to relax. Whatever the cop was doing here didn't have
him worked up, so Richard should calm down too.
But he couldn't quite shake the feeling that he should
run or hide, another learned response to a distant past.

The cop got out of his car. He stood in the street,
considering the houses around him, checking
addresses.

Elijah let out a victory cry. Richard spun his attention toward his sons. The tables had turned. Theo was
now flat on his back on the lawn, his brother's foot on
his chest holding him there. Elijah had a huge grin on
his face. He pointed the Nerf gun at his brother, ready
to exact a youthful revenge.

Richard swiveled back to the cop, who had also
had his gaze drawn to the noise in front of the house.
He was staring in the direction of the boys. Richard
couldn't tell if his expression was confused or concerned. Suddenly, the whole scene washed over Richard. There were cars parked on the street, trees in the
median strips, various objects blocking sight lines.
What did the cop see? Could he see that the object in
Elijah's hand was a technicolor plaything? Could he
see it at all? Or did he see only a kid standing over
someone else, pointing something downward and
screaming? Richard swore the cop's hand was hover-
ing near his own gun, which was not plastic, not
bright orange, not a toy. Elijah yelled something else.
Richard couldn't quite make it out, but it sounded
threatening. If that was how it sounded to him, that

was how it would have sounded to the cop. Elijah was tall for his age, but not that tall. Did he look like the seven-year-old he was? Or was the cop seeing only Black kid, possible weapon?

Richard stopped breathing again. He sprinted toward the front door.

"Richard, what. . . ."

Vaguely aware of Olivia's voice behind him, he didn't stop. Richard exploded out onto the porch. Elijah turned toward him, and when he saw his father's face, his own face froze in a fearful mask. Theo also looked up, grinning broadly. It was the cop who looked most worried now, peering across the street at him. His hand was definitely on his still-holstered gun now.

Richard felt his chest rise and fall quickly, rapid breaths returning air to his lungs. He felt sweat glisten on his forehead, a heat rising into the skin of his cheeks. Every muscle in his body was taut. He felt them ache. Richard stared at the cop, who looked back. He should wave. He should smile. He could do neither. Then Olivia was standing next to him on the porch, her hand on his back.

"Elijah, Theo, go grab your stuff. Time for school."

Richard calmed at her voice. His wife smiled and waved at the cop across the way. He returned both gestures. Richard watched as Olivia strode away from him, down the slight incline of their walkway to the sidewalk, into the street and over to the police officer. The boys were back on the porch as she started talking to him. As a prosecutor, Olivia spent much of her day with the police. She had an ease with the uniform that he couldn't understand.

Richard shook off the last of his panic and went through the checklist with the kids, their daily call-and-response ritual.

"Backpacks?"

"Yes!"

"Lunches?"

"Yes!"

"Homework?"

"Yes!"

"Winning attitude?"

"Yes!"

"Then I guess we're ready."

Olivia was now pointing at their neighbor's house across the street. The cop nodded, and Richard could read his lips. *Thanks.* Then she was walking toward Richard and the cop was walking away. She kissed Elijah and Theo on the head as they moved past her to the sidewalk. Richard waited for her on the porch.

"What happened there?" she asked.

"I don't know."

But Olivia knew. She could read his mind. "Not all cops are racist," she said.

"But enough are," Richard said. "Can't tell from a distance."

"So we agree," Olivia said. This time she gave him a real kiss on the lips. "Have a good day. I'll see you later."

"Come on, Dad!" Elijah yelled. "We're late!"

One more quick peck and Olivia brushed past him into the house. Richard hurried toward his boys and, with one small hand in each of his, led them off to school.

D A Y

2

THANKFULLY, ALL OF his students had turned in
their papers early. People were leaving the campus in droves, heading home to their families, their
friends. When Richard had first begun to understand the magnitude of the news, the changes in the
world, earlier in the day, he had been giddy. But after
hearing about Malcolm, meeting his brother, he had
grown anxious. Expecting the worst even though the
world seemed to be signaling that the worst was no
longer possible. Richard wanted to go home. He
wanted to have his kids within his control. Whatever
this new world was, he suddenly felt agitated at the
thought of them out there in it alone. His hope was
that the schools would close, that he would be forced
to pick them up and spend the afternoon with them.
But that didn't happen. Whoever made those decisions for the city didn't think this was an emergency—the kids were better off in school, even
though there were only days until the end of the year.
Parents needed to work. The world continued to spin

on its axis. Nothing had changed and everything had changed.

The last paper was turned in by a student who had slept through most of his class in the back row. Richard was already packed up and ready to go. He arrived home a few minutes after the boys. They were sitting at the island, having their afternoon snack, the nanny cleaning out their lunch boxes. Richard could see the relief on her face when she realized he was home early. She had her own kids to get home to. At the front door, paying her for the week, Richard paused.

"What do they know?" Richard whispered.

"Not much, I think," the nanny said. "Theo nothing. Elijah said some kids were talking about people not hurting each other anymore. I don't think they understand."

"I don't think any of us do," Richard said.

The nanny smiled at him before she left. She had such kind eyes, Richard thought. He and Olivia had discussed how that was one of the irrational reasons they'd decided to hire her. She had been with them since the boys were babies.

Back in the kitchen, Richard hugged Elijah, then Theo, too long and too hard. They both squirmed away after a few seconds, returning to their carrot sticks and cheese slices.

"Why are you home?" Elijah said.

His tone was firm, probing. A little prosecutor like his mother.

"I wanted to be with you guys," Richard said.

"But you have a job."

"I do."

"Did you get fired?"

"What? No, of course not."

"A girl in my class, her dad got fired."

Theo stared at Richard, wide-eyed.

"I didn't get fired. My class is over. All my students handed in their final papers. Their homework. So I didn't have any reason to be at work. And I have two very good reasons to be at home."

"Us!" Theo shouted triumphantly.

Elijah looked at his brother scornfully.

"You can play war with us," Elijah said. "You can have Theo's gun. He can be our prisoner."

"No! It's my gun."

"It's my gun," Elijah said. "It was my birthday present."

Richard felt a sinking in the pit of his stomach. He didn't want them to play with the guns. Not now. He realized he was surprised they even still existed. In the new world, shouldn't all guns have disappeared, toys and real alike?

Elijah ran into the entryway by the front door and returned with the two Nerf guns. He put one on the island in front of himself and slid the other one across to Richard. Theo was about to cry over the loss of his weapon when he grabbed Elijah's. But he wasn't fast enough. Elijah had a death grip on the other end of the gun. The boys yanked it back and forth in a game of tug-of-war. Both were now shouting at each other, on the verge of tears.

"Stop!"

Even Richard was surprised by the sharp tone in his voice. The boys stopped pulling, but neither let go of the gun. Richard took a deep breath before coming around the island to take the gun from them. He collected the second one and took them both into the family room. He placed them on a high shelf of the built-ins that surrounded the TV. When he returned to the kitchen, the boys regarded him silently. He was rarely the enforcer. He never raised his voice. The boys waited to see if there had been a shift in the universe of far greater importance to them than anything happening in the world outside. But with a grin and a wink, Richard assured them that nothing had changed.

"How about we play a game instead?" Richard said.

"Candy Land!"

"That's a baby game," Elijah said. "Monopoly."

Theo's lips drooped again. He was always the more sensitive of the boys, but he seemed closer to the edge than usual. Maybe he was aware of what was going on in the world.

"We can play both," Richard said.

"Monopoly first," Elijah said.

"Candy Land first," Richard said, before Theo could issue another wounded complaint. "Then we won't be rushed with Monopoly."

That satisfied both boys. Candy Land did go fast, and in a stroke of luck Theo won, which put him in a better mood for Monopoly, which he didn't really understand. He liked moving the pieces, but the buying of properties and the manipulation was lost on him. He did enjoy watching Elijah and Richard do battle.

After two hours, they had settled into a draw. Everyone was losing interest. When Theo asked if they could go outside, Richard felt his chest tighten again. Everything seemed so normal in the house, sequestered from the events outside. Monopoly hadn't changed. Candy Land hadn't changed. But Richard said yes, happy when the boys charged out the back door to the playset rather than going out the front. They didn't ask for the guns back.

Richard sat at the island and watched them out the back window, Elijah swinging and giving orders to Theo, who had installed himself on the platform at the top of the slide. Richard checked his phone. No new texts from Olivia. He'd let her know he was home. She'd seemed relieved. She'd said her day was crazy. A lot going on at the courthouse.

A lot going on everywhere, Richard thought.

Richard checked the news feed on his phone. It was overwhelming. He didn't know where to start. Every article, no matter what part of the world it came from, was more baffling than the last. It all seemed like a hoax, missives from a satirical website that had lost its sense of humor. It was too cruel a joke to try to convince the world that the worst of human nature had suddenly been overcome if in fact it hadn't. He tapped his way over to local stories. There was video from outside the courthouse—people swarming outside in the park, confronting police. It looked like the beginning of a riot. It was the kind of footage that usually ended in tear gas and beatings and death. Except not today.

Richard dialed Olivia's cell.

"Richard? Everything okay?"

Richard exhaled, nourished by the sound of her voice.

"Yeah. I just saw what's happening outside the courthouse. Are you okay?"

"I'm fine."

"It looks dangerous."

"It's not. Everyone is safe. It's just . . . there's a lot going on."

"I know."

"They've got us on lockdown here. As soon as they let us out, I need to spend some time at the office. There's a lot to figure out. I'm going to be late."

Richard wanted to tell her to come home. He didn't want her to be away from the kids, away from him. He couldn't wrap his brain around how an angry mob and hyped-up police could result in anything but violence. Anything but tragedy.

"I feel like I should be doing something," Richard said.

"You're doing exactly what you need to be doing," Olivia said. "Taking care of Elijah and Theo."

Richard glanced out the window. Both boys were now on the platform, dizzyingly high off the ground. They appeared to be yelling at birds in the trees.

"Come home soon, okay?" Richard said.

"You know I will," Olivia said. "Sorry. Gotta go."

Richard felt her absence as soon as she hung up.

He made dinner. The boys ate at the island, Elijah seated, Theo up on his knees. Richard ate with them, sharing their mac and cheese, slices of kohlrabi from the farmers' market, tall glasses of milk. There was no homework tonight, not for the boys. Richard had papers he could start reading. So after dinner, he sent Elijah and Theo to the family room to watch a movie. He did the dishes, then spread the students' papers out on the island. He had weeks to get these graded, but he needed a distraction. He picked one from a junior who always had intelligent things to say in class but put it down after a couple of paragraphs. Richard dug for another one, this time from a sophomore who was already getting an A. But again he had trouble reading beyond a few sentences. It wasn't the papers them-selves. They were well written, the theses laid out clearly from the start. It was just that they felt dated, relics from another time. The class, about voices of protest, had become almost anachronistic overnight. Everything these kids were writing about was grounded in violence, the threat and the reality of it. None of these figures, freedom fighters and orators, rebels and disrupters, would have existed without an unjust political structure propped up by violence. Without violence, could there be the subjugation of colonial-ism, of slavery? Would there be no Gandhi, no Martin Luther King? What did the history of the world look like without war?

Richard put down the paper. Everything he had ever studied, everything he had ever written, was transmogrifying in front of him. For the first time, he felt the thrill of it. The discovery of something truly new. The chance to analyze the complete unknown. He would have to grade the papers based on the old world. But not tonight.

Outside, the world was starting to darken, dusk into night. He longed for Olivia to be home. But the worry had lifted. He knew she would be fine.

The flash drive that Malcolm's brother had brought him rested at the edge of the island, in danger of being accidentally knocked off to the floor. Regret flooded over him. He searched his memories for the last few times he had seen Malcolm, seeking any moment that he might have handled differently, anything he could have said that would have altered the trajectory of his life just enough to nudge him away from the circumstances that got him shot. Richard didn't know exactly what had happened, but he'd grown up in Malcolm's world and could imagine the possibilities.

The sound of cartoon characters doing cartoonish things emanated from the family room. He heard the boys laughing. They were safe and secure. Richard's desktop computer was in his office on the other side of the house, the only place he could use a flash drive until Olivia brought the laptop home.

Richard felt his anxiety return as he moved farther from the boys. But he could still hear the TV in the distance. And he needed to at least open Malcolm's paper on the screen, confirm its existence, if not read it. As he inserted the flash drive, he considered the possibility of a virus, but he quickly decided he didn't care. He opened the menu, then the paper.

Richard had spent his entire life reading the posthumous work of famous people, but never that of one of his students. Never someone he knew. Never someone he wouldn't get to know. As he read, he heard Malcolm's voice, in class, chatting over coffee during office hours. He missed that voice, though he had barely known it. A voice that had already survived a harsher truth than any of his classmates. A voice that would never graduate or grow old. Richard realized he had already been writing a recommendation for Malcolm to get into grad school or find his first job.

Two days, Richard thought. If only Malcolm had stayed inside for two days. If only he hadn't gotten in a fight or crossed the wrong person or been in the wrong place, whatever the circumstances of his death were. Two days in quarantine. Two days laying low. Two days the difference between living and dying.

There was a sentence in the conclusion that stopped Richard.

If you give someone a gun, expect them to shoot you.

It broke from the scholarly tenor of the paper, the only place Malcolm had taken narrative liberty in the otherwise impeccably researched and footnoted work.

Expect them to shoot you.

As if it were the cue for the prop master offstage, there was a loud clap outside, somewhere in the distance. Richard flinched and swiveled toward the window. It sounded like a gunshot to him. It felt like a bullet fired. There were other explanations: Cars misfiring. Large deliveries dropped off trucks. Fireworks—people were celebrating tonight.

Another loud noise. This time much closer. A crash. Inside the house.

Richard froze for a moment. He felt the air strain against his lungs. His vision blurred, then focused. He heard someone crying. He was out of his chair. Running from the office, through the living room, to the door of the family room.

Theo sat on the couch in tears. The TV still blared. Books were scattered all over the floor. Elijah stood in the middle of the room, one of the Nerf guns in his hand, the other on the floor. Richard glanced toward the window. No sign of a bullet hole, no broken glass.

"I wanted my present," Elijah said.

He wasn't crying, but he was on the verge.

"Are you hurt?" Richard said.

Elijah just shook his head. Richard looked to Theo, who was mimicking his brother. It was clear what had happened. Elijah had climbed the built-ins to get to the guns. He had succeeded but brought down a whole shelf of books in the process.

But Richard saw only a seven-year-old boy with a gun in his hand. He had only a couple of pictures of himself at that age. Olivia had told him it was remarkable how much Elijah looked like him. And now Richard saw it too.

And he remembered that day thirty years ago when he had stood in the living room of his mother's apartment with a gun in his hand. When he pulled the trigger, it wrenched his wrist. The pain was excruciating, but he didn't let go of the gun that his father, the man his mother said was his father, had brought into the apartment. Richard's mother and this stranger had argued. She had convinced the man to put the gun down. But when he hit her, Richard picked it up. He had never shot a gun—he was only seven. But he had seen boys and men in the neighborhood carrying them around, flashing them at each other. He had watched people shoot guns on TV and in video games. He had heard people on the street brag about killing their enemies. He knew, even at that age, what the gun was for: protecting yourself and those you loved. So when this man, this intruder, his father, went for his mother again, Richard pulled the trigger.

How often over the years had he wondered how the bullet had found its target? Richard just pulled the trigger. He didn't aim. He wasn't trying to hit this man in the head or the heart or any other body part. How lucky, how unlikely, was it that the bullet hit flesh? A child firing a gun randomly, with the kickback and the inexperience, the lack of intent or understanding— that bullet should have hit the ceiling or the wall, flown harmlessly out the window. But instead the man who was his father, the man Richard had never known, was on the floor of their apartment, his blood soaking the rug his mother had scavenged off the street.

"Dad? Are you mad?"

Richard returned his attention to Elijah, who dropped the Nerf gun guiltily. All Richard could do was shake his own head this time and hold out his arms. They were all crying now as they fell back onto the couch. Theo and Elijah each nestled under one of Richard's arms. They ignored the mess. It could wait.

As they watched the movie together, the tears gradually dried up, the laughter returned.

But Richard was lost in his own thoughts. Two days too late for Malcolm. Had it been thirty years too late for him? In this world, today, that bullet would have missed. His mother would never have had to take the gun out of his small hand and tell him it would be all right. She would never have told the police that she'd shot his father in self-defense. She would never have had a jury convict her anyway. *Thirty years too late.*

The movie was just ending as Olivia came into the family room. She had had a difficult day, a compli- cated day, and Richard could see on her face that she was ready to share it. But her expression changed when she saw the dried tears on their faces. Instead of telling her story or listening to theirs, she simply helped Rich- ard put the boys to bed.

EXCURSUS D: THE MURDERER

THE MURDERER'S NEXT parole hearing was sched-
uled to happen in three days. Given the state of
the world at the moment, he wasn't sure it would take
place. There was a lot of other shit to take care of out
there right now. Still, he decided to spend some time
in the library and review his materials just in case. He
had been turned down three times. Unless he was
ready to lose hope entirely, he figured the fourth time
must be the charm.

He hadn't believed the assholes on the block who
said he couldn't threaten no one no more. That his
time as enforcer was over. Not that he saw himself
that way. He was just a big guy with a knack for picking appropriate people to do favors for at appropriate
times. And he had been greasing the wheels with the
guards and the staff for years. They needed favors too.
Not a lot of write-ups for him. To a parole board, he

looked squeaky clean, with the necessary classes and skills training under his belt for taking on the challenges of readjusting to the outside world. No recidivism for him. He had even had one of the white-collar guys teach him how to pronounce *recidivism*, quickly and smoothly, in case he had to say it at the hearing.

The Murderer did believe the world had changed; he'd seen it for himself. He'd made it a point not to get into any of it this week, not right before the hearing. No favors for no one—even when the guys told him he couldn't hurt them, tried to goad him into throwing that punch, to get him in trouble. But then he saw the two guys in the yard attempting to go at it. These weren't no lightweights. He'd seen them both fight before. No problem landing a punch. Out in the yard, though, whatever had gotten them heated wasn't enough to overcome the new reality. They looked like they were having a pillow fight without the pillows. They weren't even tapping each other.

He'd watched TV, like everyone else, for a while. It seemed real. And here in the library, the Murderer figured it must change his situation, every killer's situation, in a parole hearing. There were lots of criteria in the parole regulations, but those decisions boiled down to mainly two things: were you sorry about what you did, and were you likely to do it again. (There was an unwritten criterion, of course, which was how much pull the victim's people had to keep you inside. Luckily for the Murderer, nobody gave a shit about the guy they'd collared him for.)

The Murderer had been practicing sounding sorry for years. But he had trouble convincing parole board members he wouldn't do it again. He had the hands and face of a killer—dead eyes and meat-hook fists. He couldn't help that. All the apologies in the world couldn't change the fact that he looked like someone you didn't want to fuck with.

The words in the parole handbook, provided by a do-gooder nonprofit, blurred before his eyes. He had been reading it over and over, trying to identify the way out. The universe had provided the loophole—for him, for everyone in for murder. He was sorry for the past, and now, whether he wanted to or not, he couldn't repeat his crime. There was no possibility he was a danger to society.

It didn't matter that he was guilty. It didn't matter that he knew he'd kill again if he could. It didn't matter that he'd known it was a lie when he told them at the last parole hearing that he would be a different person if given another chance. It didn't matter how much he'd enjoyed killing the guy they'd caught him for, and the ones they didn't know about. None of that mattered. The Murderer couldn't murder. Not anymore. Now he just had to find the words that proved that meant they had to let him out.

JULIAN

1

S SJUDENHATER MET RYANHOPE88 online, the same way he found most people who agreed with him. They were in a chat room on one of the social media platforms that still allowed them to speak freely, to tell the truth about the world and how to fix it. The difference was that unlike most of the people he interacted with, he and Ryanhope88 had managed to make a connection in real life as well. True, SSjudenhater had attended that rally near Berkeley that had turned into a near riot. They had been seriously outnumbered. It wasn't a fair fight, so they had retreated. That's what the organizers called it—a strategic retreat to regroup. The next time would be different. They would be better armed. Ready to do some real damage.

Before Antifa showed up, SSjudenhater had enjoyed hanging out in the park with his fellow believers. He didn't usually have contact with anyone he could be his true self around. It was liberating, a genuine moment of peace in his angry soul. Then the others had come, with their brown faces and black faces and checkered bandannas, and ruined it. Just like they ruined everything.

But somehow in all the noise of the chat rooms and the memes and the bluster, Ryanhope88 had singled him out, inviting him into a private conversation. She said she was a girl, which he doubted. It was a common troll move, pretending to be a woman who understood the movement. Who understood the threats and the need for action. After hours of intimate conversations, she said she wanted to meet. He was even more skeptical, but agreed. In the back of his mind, he wondered if she might turn out to be a cop. Other than attending that rally, however, he had done nothing they could peg on him. No criminal record. Hadn't even thrown his first punch yet. So he went.

She was exactly who she'd said she was. A believer, a woman, and not a cop. She was also the most beautiful woman he had ever seen, and she seemed to like him as well. At first, he wasn't sure, but then she came back to his parents' house and fucked him in his room. His parents had been in their room when they got home that night, and he knew they'd heard them. He resisted the urge to pound on the wall their rooms shared; that was the only urge he resisted. Ryanhope88 was eager to indulge as well. She drank him in. They had hardly been apart a day since then.

Together they had planned what would happen today.

"I didn't realize you would be up early. I would have made you something more."

"The eggs and toast were great, Mrs. James."

"Pass me your plate, Tanya."

"No, I'll do the dishes. You're late for work."

He had been a little surprised to find out that her name was Tanya. He had assumed it was Ryan. *That's what everyone thinks,* she'd said. *But you have to sound out the first letter. R-Yan. Aryan.* That was the moment he'd realized she was also the smartest person he knew.

"Julian, what are you doing today?"

His mother looked at him. It had been a few weeks since he had moved out of the house and into the room above the garage with Tanya. Julian's father had been disapproving, but Tanya had won his mother over. She thought her son was finally putting his life together, or at least taking the tiniest step in that direction. It was true, in a way. Tanya did help him focus.

She'd persuaded him to fight less with his parents. *They're not the real enemy, even though they can't see how wrong they are. The key with them, the key with everyone, is to make them think you aren't a problem. Better yet, convince them you're on their side.* Julian had read the same thing from the leaders online. Out with the shaved heads and swastikas tattooed on knuckles. So much more could be accomplished wearing polo shirts and khakis. Never underestimate the element of surprise.

Tanya and Julian sat at the kitchen table. His mom lingered by the sink. It was shocking that after all these years, she still thought he was likely to answer her questions. But Tanya took his hand and smiled.

"Julian has a job interview today," Tanya said.

Julian watched his mother light up. He surged red-hot at her hope, her misplaced belief that she knew what constituted a successful life. Still, he forced himself to speak.

"Yeah, Mom." That word choked him, but Tanya encouraged him to use it. "I think it might be a good day."

His mother put her hand over her heart. She didn't even realize that she did it. Had no idea how infuriating and clichéd she was. Julian looked at her, wearing her bright-pink scrubs, and hated her. She reminded him of a Sour Patch Kid come to life, but there was nothing funny about what she did for a living. *Helping people live and die with dignity*, she would say. But where was the dignity in a white woman wiping the asses of all the blacks and Mexicans and who knows what who came to that facility? It wasn't right. Those people should be groveling at her feet, not getting sponge baths from her. Yet she thought it was righteous work. She had no real conception of the meaning of that word.

"A very good day," Tanya said.

"Well, I'll look forward to hearing all about it at dinner," his mother said, grabbing her keys and leaving them alone in the kitchen.

Tanya narrowed her eyes, and her grin turned mischievous. Sometimes Julian was convinced he could hear her thoughts.

Your mother has no idea what she'll be hearing about at dinner.

Julian's dad had left the house at six AM as usual. He was a foreman at a warehouse. Growing up, Julian remembered him always complaining about lazy coworkers, the ones who called in sick on short notice or lingered during breaks. His world was divided into good and bad employees. And though he never described them, Julian knew exactly what each type looked like. A couple of years earlier, after Julian realized he was done with school for good, his dad had gotten him a job in the warehouse. It had lasted a few months. Julian seethed all day listening to the chattering in Spanish and watching the black guys take the best picnic tables outside for lunch. When someone etched the words *The Monkey Cage* into the central table, he was accused, but no one could prove it. Still, Julian had been fired a few weeks later when he showed up stoned. He tried to argue that it was legal, but his dad pointed out, with infuriating logic, that alcohol was legal and you still couldn't show up to work drunk. Both Julian and his father were relieved the next day when they didn't have to drive in to work together.

His dad was more deluded than his mom. He thought the men he supervised worked for him, but they just played him. He might as well be wiping their asses. And, of course, he was merely a puppet for the Jews who owned the warehouse and everything else.

The front door closed behind his mother. Julian heard the car pull out of the driveway. Living in the garage had been useful for their planning. No one poking around in their business.

Tanya took his cheek in her hand and turned his face toward him, freeing him from his reverie.

"Today's the day everyone will know your name, Julian James."

Then she pushed his chair away from the table and undid his pants, pulling them down around his ankles. She got down on her knees until he got hard enough, then stood up and took her panties off from under her skirt.

When they finished, Tanya did the dishes. Then they went to the garage together to finish the preparations. They checked the guns and the ammo. They loaded up the duffel bag. They discussed the route to the synagogue, the steps he would take once inside.

Where he would park the car, how he would get away. This was not a suicide mission. That was not the plan.

Julian repeated the conversation in his head as he drove. He thought of the taste of Tanya on his lips. Through clenched teeth, he remembered why he was doing this. The world had turned upside down, the traditional order of things inverted. Perverted by a class of people who had stolen what belonged to his people. The strong had been turned into the weak through decades of government intervention on behalf of the minorities and the foreigners. Only the real Americans realized that this manipulation had been going on for centuries. The patterns were obvious once you looked. The Jews always tried to destroy the true rulers, never in direct ways, always underhandedly and in the shadows. But others had taken a stand, and today was his turn to inspire the world. To show them his strength.

The decision to take action had been made before he met Tanya. He had already started collecting the guns before she moved into his life. But she helped him focus. Originally he'd planned to go back to his middle school. There had been articles about how public schools had been helping the latest wave of undocumented children assimilate. Invade was more like it. These political leaders had declared his town a sanctuary city. They might as well have signed an executive order authorizing their own genocide. Julian had considered taking down a government building instead of the school. He had also thought about the warehouse. He wouldn't kill his dad, but imagining the look on his face as his employees fell in a spray of bullets made him smile.

Julian dreamed of the bodies hitting the ground, the blood splattering the windows. He heard the screams while he was awake. The tears nourished him.

One night in bed, naked with Tanya, he'd told her of the failed jobs his parents had forced him into. She'd laughed at the vandalism of the picnic table, the impotent rage of the politically correct owners of the warehouse. But it was the job that followed that made her sit up. Julian's father had gotten him a position with an HVAC company his friend owned. It had lasted only two weeks. They had a big installation upgrade for a large building. Julian was there as just an extra pair of hands. They thought they were giving him an apprenticeship, a chance to learn an honest trade. Instead, he pitied these men who spent their lives in the crawl spaces and attics and basements. Their sweat did little but make the rich more comfortable. Julian quit before the job was done, but not before he had spent ten days in that building seething.

"That's the place," Tanya had said. "They paid you to case that goddamn synagogue."

She was right. He knew how many people were in the building during the day. The ebb and flow. It was crowded and noisy in the morning when the nursery school was in session. He knew when the teachers and dirty little Jews were in their classrooms, when they jostled like animals in the hallways. Julian knew that the parents started lining up in their expensive cars around a quarter to twelve to collect their spawn.

While he'd been there, they had done an active-shooter drill, sugarcoating it so the kids would think it was a game. He knew their procedures. He knew the layout of the classrooms. He knew that even if they locked the door to the hall, the classrooms along one hallway were all connected by interior doors that didn't lock. When they weren't drilling, he knew the daily routines of two security guards.

And the guards knew him. By name and face. Julian had forced himself to exchange greetings with these black men who were too stupid to know they were worked as slaves to the Jews in that place. Somehow, even before Tanya crystallized it for him, he'd known his destiny would bring him back.

Julian had left that job and stolen the shirt with the HVAC company's logo on it. As he pulled up to the designated spot two blocks from the synagogue, he ran his fingers over the raised embroidery on his chest with satisfaction. It was as good as a key to the kingdom.

The synagogue was a series of low-slung buildings connected by a series of glass hallways. Julian hurried around to the back. He walked past the playground, empty for the moment, to the back door that led to the nursery school. That door was always locked, but one of the guards was sitting just inside, as expected. Julian tried to slow his breathing. There was nothing he could do about the pounding of his heart, which was driving so hard he couldn't believe it wasn't visible through his chest. He took a deep breath and tapped on the glass.

The guard saw him and looked confused. Julian thought for a moment he hadn't been recognized. He tapped the logo on his chest and shrugged. Then he saw the memory bubble up in the guard's mind. The guard opened the door. Julian was in. He scanned the guard's body and around the small desk he had been sitting at to confirm something else he already knew. The guard was unarmed.

"They didn't tell me there was work happening today," the guard said, checking a piece of paper on the desk.

"Kind of an emergency thing," Julian said. "They turned on the AC and got a weird smell in one of the classrooms. Probably nothing, but they wanted us to check it out."

It was the first hot day of the year. Julian forced a smile, hoping the story worked. He was looking forward to killing the black guards, assuming they would rush toward the gunfire, but the plan was to get most of the Jew children first. Gunfire now would just put everyone on alert.

"Okay. You gotta go around to the front and check in."

"I was up there already. They sent me down here."

"They didn't give you a badge?"

"Oh, shit. Forgot about those. You're not gonna make me go back up there."

"Nah. I'm sure you're good. Just let me call up to confirm."

The guard reached for a walkie-talkie. Julian couldn't let that happen. The guard froze when Julian pulled one of the AR15s out of his duffel bag.

"Fuck!"

The guard surprised Julian by rushing directly at him. The plan was out the window. Nothing but instinct to go on now. Julian pulled his finger back into the trigger, but it must have slipped in his haste. No recoil. No concussive blast. No bullet tearing through the guard. Julian stepped back. The guard had made up the distance with shocking speed. Julian was going to have to fight him off. There was a handgun in the duffel along with another AR15. In a split second, Julian considered how to get to it in case he couldn't get the muzzle of the AR15 pointed in the right direction.

The guard lowered his shoulder. Julian braced for the initial blow. It never came. The guard fell forward, veering just to the right, missing Julian completely and crumbling heavily onto the duffel bag. Without thinking, Julian stepped backward, leaving the rest of his weapons to the guard. They both considered each other for a moment before the guard also realized that he had a bag of guns at his disposal. He shuffled away across the tiled floor, reaching into the duffel. His hand emerged with the handgun.

Julian again tried to pull the trigger, aiming for the man's chest. But his finger didn't move. Was he freezing up? That couldn't be. He thought of Tanya. She would never forgive him if he lost his nerve. The guard also seemed to be having trouble with his gun. He looked at it, confused, flipping the safety on and back off again before pointing it back at Julian.

One shot would end this, one way or another. Julian ducked and ran, expecting the gunshot that never came. He sprinted into the nursery school. Behind him he heard the desperate guard on the walkie-talkie.

"Active shooter! Lockdown! This is not a drill!"

Julian reached the first door of the hallway. He had only a few seconds before there was an announcement over the speakers. But the room was dark, empty. He heard singing coming from the next room. He saw them gathered around a woman with a guitar, twelve kids and two other adults, sitting cross-legged on a carpet in the far corner of the room. Their screechy voices grated on him as they vomited out the words of a song in their Jew language that he couldn't understand.

The door slammed behind him. Julian reached down and locked it. The tables were covered with arts-and-crafts supplies, dried macaroni and beads of various sizes, rows of string ready to become necklaces. Another table was covered with paper and finger paints.

Everyone in the room turned to him. The song ended abruptly. The children considered him with various levels of interest. One of the boys waved at him, his fingers stained red. The paint looked like blood to Julian. One of the teachers gasped when he raised his gun. The three women in the room moved in front of their four-year-old students. Julian smiled as they held their instruments out—a guitar, a tambourine, a pair of maracas—as if they would shield anyone from the bullets.

Three sharp blasts sounded over the PA system, followed immediately by three more.

"This is not a drill. Lockdown! This is not a drill!"

The woman's disembodied voice trembled through the halls. In an instant, fear permeated the building. Julian could hear screams and barked commands up and down the hallway. In the room next door, children were already crying. But in here, there was only silence. Everyone stared at the gun.

Julian knew he didn't have much time. He cursed himself for giving up his duffel bag. But he still had nearly one hundred rounds in his cartridge. He pulled the trigger. It didn't budge.

The teacher with the guitar slowly raised the strap over her head. Julian thought she might try to hit him with it. Instead, she put it down carefully. She and the teacher with the maracas shrank back toward the children, gathering them beneath their protective shield. The kids were still mostly quietly, only a few whimpering to themselves. The third teacher, a short plump woman with jet-black hair that ran straight down her back, stepped in his direction. She held the tambourine out to him, more of a peace offering than a weapon.

"You don't have to do this," she said. "You don't want to do this."

But she was wrong. He did want to do this. Her presumption angered him. She must have seen that in his expression, because she stopped, pulling the tambourine back, clutching it to her chest, about to cry. Julian wanted her to cry. He wanted to hurt her. He wanted to kill everyone.

He had never believed some of the things that the believers said on the boards. That the Jews knew magic. That the women in particular could put a spell on you, make you do things, paralyze you, enchant you with their wickedness. That must be what was happening. These three sorceresses were bewitching him.

But I am strong, Julian thought. He would not be made weak. He would not be neutered, castrated, like the rest of them. The strong had been made weak. He would show them who was strong again.

His finger moved, freed from whatever had held it. The trigger moved. Julian braced himself against the glorious recoil. Again and again. The explosions echoed in the room, deafening all. Three rounds directly into the chest of this evil Jew.

The room filled with screams and cries, reverberating through the entire building. Julian was filled with a joy he had never experienced before. This was it. He was a hero. A liberator of his people. A name everyone would remember. Just as Tanya had predicted.

Then he looked for the blood. He expected the woman's body to fall, giving him a clear shot at the rest of the Jews in the room. But she stood fast, looking as surprised as he was. The tambourine in front of her was shredded, as was her blouse. But her flesh was unbroken. There were three spent shells on the ground and none in her body. She finally did collapse to the floor, not in agony or death, but weeping in relief.

Julian screamed. They couldn't all be bulletproof. He took small steps toward the mass of bodies on the carpet, unloading the cartridge in their direction. Bullet after bullet after bullet, a steady stream, each one exiting the barrel with a satisfying kick to his shoulder. His finger palpitated on the trigger. His body swayed back and forth to maximize the area of damage. And there was damage. The window behind them shattered. Pages flew out of books in bursts of confetti. Divots pockmarked the walls and floors. Clothing was rent.

But every time a bullet found skin, it bounced off harmlessly, as if they were made out of foam, their true nature revealed again when they clinked on the floor. It must have tickled the children, for they laughed.

Julian stopped shooting. He dropped the gun and backed toward the door. The last part of the plan was to leave by an emergency exit that led to an overgrown area at the side of the synagogue. He just had to jump a fence to be in a wooded park where he could easily disappear. Julian unlocked the door. Before he ran into the hall, he looked at the children, who were gleefully scurrying around the room, gathering the spent bullets with their tiny fingers, juggling them in their palms while the metal rapidly cooled.

DAY

2

JULIAN HAD FALLEN asleep to the sound of gunfire
somewhere far below him. The blacks were killing
themselves again. He marveled at their willingness to
kill their own people but knew that was one of the
things that would always keep them from winning.
When the war came, they were as likely to shoot
themselves as they were to put a bullet in his head. But
he also envied the person who had fired that gun,
assuming its bullet had found its target. He wanted to
kill, and he had failed. Jealousy flowed through him at
the thought of someone else succeeding. Julian didn't
care who or what or why it happened, just that one
person had watched another die. That was what he
wanted, and he had drifted off after a long afternoon
and evening alone waiting for Tanya.

He woke up after a night of unsatisfying dreams
in which he was taunted by black faces and Jewish
children and beautiful women as he attempted to
attack them, with knives, with guns, with his fists,
and failed again and again and again.

Julian opened his eyes to a bright sun. Before he left on his mission, Tanya had taken his phone away and given him a wristwatch. He had never worn a watch in his life, but she said they could track the phone and he needed to tell time. Like everything she said, her logic seemed unimpeachable to him. Julian still had a little trouble deciphering the time from the tiny hands and tiny numbers on the tiny face of the watch, but he knew it was morning and too early to be awake.

And Tanya still wasn't here.

Julian was starting to doubt that she was going to come at all. Maybe she didn't want him anymore now that he was a failure, to himself and to the cause. He had neither killed nor been killed. He was neither a hero nor a martyr.

He sat up on the anachronistic couch that Tanya had known he would find on the roof of this building in the middle of the city. She had picked the place. She had said no one would ever look for him here, no one except her. She'd promised she would be here as soon as she could. Then they were going to make their escape together, probably drive north to Idaho, where they would find sympathetic shelter and be hailed for their deeds.

So Julian had executed the plan faithfully, sticking to it to the letter after his guns and bullets betrayed him at the synagogue. At least this he could do right. He circled around through the park and back to the car. He heard the sirens just as Tanya had said he would, but he didn't panic because the roads he drove were all clear, just as she'd said they would be. Once he arrived in the city, he stowed the car in an overgrown abandoned lot four blocks from his destination. Then he hoofed it to the address Tanya had given him. It was midafternoon and there were few people on the streets, but every face he saw was black. Every pair of eyes that judged him as he passed lacked a soul. Anger permeated him with every step. They had no right to consider him anything but their master.

But he kept his head down and found the building. Tanya had said they wouldn't bother him, and she was right. She'd said white faces in that neighborhood were looking to score drugs. And he knew this was true too. He felt it in the pity of those who watched him pass by.

The building was exactly as she described it. The door was unlocked. The stairwells were empty. Julian went directly to the roof, two steps at a time, and he had been there ever since. Tanya had been right about everything, right down to the mismatched ratty couch and chairs on the roof.

When Julian had asked Tanya how she knew about this place, she hadn't wanted to tell him. But he had pressed her, and she'd relented. Before she found the cause, before she became a true believer, she had been lost in a world of sin and drugs. Julian had known that she had been living on the streets for a while, kicked out of the house after her mother accused her of sleeping with her mom's boyfriend, which Tanya denied. She told Julian that the building was where one of her drug dealers did business. That had been enough for Julian. He didn't want to know why she knew about the roof and the couch. He never asked what she'd done up here, though he'd been thinking about that throughout the night and into this morning.

Julian hadn't judged Tanya for her past life, but he couldn't help but wonder if her absence now was her way of judging him for his current failures. He couldn't let himself think that way. After all, she had found him a place to hide. And the backpack she had promised him was up on the roof, where she'd hidden it the day before. In it, he'd found his favorite sandwich—a spicy Italian hoagie—for dinner and plenty of water to get him through to the next day. Now he opened the backpack and pulled out the box of Pop-Tarts she had left him for breakfast. As he ate one, he forced all his doubts about Tanya aside. She loved him and he loved her, and they both knew what was right and wrong in the world.

Without his phone, he had no access to news. No one could contact him. That was the point. But he also wouldn't know if the police had figured out that Tanya was involved. Maybe they had picked her up and were holding her, waiting for him to surface. She had said that would be a possibility, although she'd sworn she was going to sweep any sign of their plans from the garage. He was supposed to sit tight, at least for the rest of today, and wait for her.

Pop-Tart in hand, Julian wandered to the edge of the roof. He looked down at a space between the buildings across the street that housed a makeshift homeless camp. They were pathetic and filthy, these wretched people emerging from their tents and from under their tarps, stretching in their ratty clothes that they'd been wearing for days or months. He wanted to burn the whole lot of them to the ground. He suspected all their belongings were highly flammable. Julian smiled at the thought of the inferno.

Then two men on the sidewalk near the lot caught his attention. One was on the ground, either asleep or passed out or maybe dead. The other one stood over him holding a knife. Julian smiled at the expected outcome—these animals continuing to kill each other. And he was not disappointed when the standing man threw the knife at the prone one. But before the blade found its target, the knife swerved and landed harmlessly on the sidewalk. The thrower picked it up and looked at it, as baffled as Julian. He tried to lodge the knife into the other man again, to the same effect. Julian leaned over the edge of the roof, surveying the entire street to see if anyone else was seeing this.

Five stories below, someone came out through the front door of the building. He stopped dead on the sidewalk to watch the man try and fail repeatedly to kill the other man. Julian looked down on the tight black curls of the hair on the kid's head, and it suddenly called to him like a target. A nice fat bull's-eye waiting for something to be dropped on it.

Without thinking, Julian ran over to the couch and grabbed one of the arms. It was heavier than it looked, which made him happy. It would do more damage. He dragged it to the edge of the roof. Julian propped its feet up on the small wall ringing the building and peered back over. The target was still there, ready to be crushed. This was his chance to be redeemed.

Then Julian noticed that the man across the street, the guy with the knife, was looking up at him. It was now or never. Julian gave the couch one hard shove and it went over the edge. He ducked down, back against the short wall, and waited for the scream. Only then did he think about where he would go if neighborhood do-gooders came to the roof looking for the culprit. He wondered if there were two stairways down. Or maybe a fire escape on the back of the building.

But it didn't matter. There was no scream, from either the victim or horrified bystanders. Julian thought he heard a low thud, but that was it. Cautiously, he peeked over the edge. The couch was sitting on the sidewalk, as if someone had put it out for the trash. The kid was running away down the street. The man with the knife had returned to his failed attempts at murdering the guy on the ground.

Julian lay back on the top of the wall. It was just wide enough to hold his body. But if he fell asleep, if he rolled, just the slightest shifting of his body weight could cause him to fall back onto the roof proper. Or go the other way, off the edge of the roof, and plummet to the street below. He considered both possibilities while staring up into the bright blue sky for a long time.

After a while, he closed his eyes. *All I have to do is lean*, he thought. *Just lean.*

"Hey, baby, did you throw the couch off the roof?"

Julian sat up quickly. Almost too fast, worrying for a moment that he had swung his legs the wrong way and was going over the edge. Instead, after the world spun for a moment, he saw Tanya standing in front of him, smiling. He didn't even realize he was holding his arms out to her until she came and embraced him, pulling his head into her chest.

"Oh, baby, did you think I wasn't coming?"

Julian said nothing. For a long moment, he just breathed her in.

"The cops came by your house this morning. They ID'd you from some surveillance video. Your mother was shocked. She told them she couldn't believe you would do such a thing. I repeated every word she said. Matched her tear for tear. Apparently they went to your dad's work too. Your parents really were clueless. When the cops left, I told your mom I was going to go look for you. That hopefully I could talk some sense into you. She looked so grateful. It was kind of sad, actually."

Tanya pulled away from Julian. She took his face in her hands.

"They showed me some of the video. You looked totally badass."

"I don't know what happened," Julian said. "I shot right at them. I thought I hit them."

Tanya was nodding. "I know you did. Weird things are happening everywhere."

Julian didn't know what she meant. She didn't elaborate, instead tossing another backpack at his feet.

"New clothes and a baseball cap. Put them on and we'll go find lunch."

"I thought the cops were looking for me," Julian said.

"Yeah, but you didn't kill anyone, and they've got bigger fish to fry today. I think we'll be fine. Never underestimate the baseball hat disguise."

"Did you bring my phone?"

"Don't get cocky. I'm not sure anyone will be looking for us, but if we're stupid, they'll still find us."

Julian knew she was right. He changed into the new clothes and pulled the hat down low over his face. They gathered all their stuff and headed for the stairs.

They recovered the car, and Tanya drove them to a hole-in-the-wall diner near a college campus. No one cared who they were, and they settled into a booth for a long afternoon. As they kept a steady stream of food and coffee coming, Tanya surfed the web on her phone, showing Julian what he had missed during his night and morning on the roof. She was right. It was a lot. And she kept discovering new developments that the two of them devoured together, side by side on the same bench of the booth. Tanya put her hand between his thighs while they watched and ate.

"I don't understand," Julian said. "How is this possible?"

"See, though," Tanya answered, not really answering. "It wasn't you. You're a victim of circumstance."

Julian didn't want to be a victim of anything. That was the whole point. So while he felt better about his failure, the circumstances of the day merely added to the growing ball of rage inside him. There had to be a way. They had to find a way.

As the afternoon wore on, Tanya connected with their network. Julian knew that she had promised them a major event yesterday. Everyone would know what he had almost accomplished at the synagogue. He wasn't sure how much credit he would get, but Tanya assured him that everyone she chatted with was as frustrated as they were.

Then, suddenly, Tanya's face lit up.

"They're working on a plan," she said. "We're going to prove that everyone is wrong."

Julian didn't understand. Instead of elaborating, Tanya took his hand and yanked him to his feet. Without paying, she pulled him to the door and out onto the street, ignoring the waitress yelling after them. Tanya was skipping as they returned to the car. Julian had never seen her quite this happy. He got in the driver's seat and turned on the car.

"Where are we going?"

"Doesn't matter," Tanya said. "Just drive."

And that was what he did. They toured the city, block by block, waiting for further instructions. Tanya kept one eye on her phone and the other on the people on the street. She started the game, pointing at a woman with a giant purple sun hat.

"Douse that hat in gasoline and set it on fire. Make her wear it while it burns."

Julian laughed. He nodded in the direction of a homeless man leaning against a building.

"Strip him naked from the waist down and strangle him with his own shit-stained pants."

"Nice!" Tanya said.

So they drove and played the game, passing the time while their internet friends formulated a plan. They took turns picking out a pedestrian or someone in a nearby car and deciding how they should die. Extra points for making it personal to their circumstances. The hours passed like minutes. Julian's favorite moments were between deaths when he stole glances at Tanya as she scanned the street and let her mind wander through her homicidal options, each one more macabre and wonderful than the last. He wanted to take up residence in her imagination and never leave.

Night fell. Darkness gathered at the boundaries of the city's streetlamps and neon storefronts. Tanya steered them into neighborhoods that were poorly lit, relishing the cover. Julian was starting to wonder whether the plan would come together tonight or take more time, whether they might need to find shelter, a place to sleep. Tanya's enthusiasm for the game, which had waned only after a couple of hours, had gotten him horny. The anticipation of getting his hands on her was almost as tantalizing as the act itself would be. He was considering suggesting pulling over for a quickie when Tanya squealed.

"They figured it out," Tanya said. She looked at Julian with eyes that burned through his soul. "We are the strength."

Tanya called up the directions on her phone and filled Julian in as he drove. It was a block party. Something had happened earlier in the day that had them popping up all over the city. Tanya said with a smirk that the ghetto was celebrating.

"They won't be for long," she said.

This party had been chosen for a few reasons. Someone on the message chain knew a cop who'd said they wouldn't be patrolling around there. Actually, the cop had said they were hanging back from most residential areas, focusing on the commercial strips, where they were expecting looting and rioting that hadn't materialized. The partyers, about a hundred or so, were all on a single block.

The plan was simple. They would join the other believers, twenty-five strong by Tanya's count, and surround them, half stationed at each end of the street. Then do as much damage as possible.

Julian and Tanya were the last ones to arrive. They pulled up to the curb across the street from two white box vans. About a dozen young men, some in khakis, others with shaved heads, the old and the new, lurked by the vans. Julian wondered if they had all come together. Tanya was already halfway across the street, skipping again, by the time Julian opened his door. She was the only woman there. He felt the others watching her approach, the bounce of her, eating her alive. Julian hurried after her.

"Hey, man, didn't expect to see you here," one of the guys said to Julian as he approached. "Saw you on TV. Thought you'd be laying low."

The guy nodded at him, respect in his voice. Julian recognized a couple of the other guys from the Berkeley protest. They also seemed to be approving of his presence and his actions of the previous day. The jealousy and fear that had been pooling inside Julian dissipated. These were his people.

"Look what they brought us," Tanya said, bounding back over to Julian from the open back of one of the vans.

She handed him a bottle. At first he thought it was a forty. He wasn't feeling like drinking, but it probably wasn't a bad idea. Help loosen him up a little. But the bottle was clear, and he realized there was a rag sticking out of the top of it. The liquid inside was clear too. He had noticed the smell of gasoline but hadn't realized it was coming from the van. There were nearly a dozen more Molotov cocktails lined up there, as if the believers were caterers delivering wine to an explosive wedding reception.

"Toys!" Tanya said.

When she kissed him, Julian felt the envy from all the other men. He had what they wanted. He had tried to do what they hadn't at the synagogue. Julian was ready to set the world on fire.

He was not alone. They emptied out the back, each man taking one or two bottles. Someone had a box of lighters. They each took one. Tanya whispered to Julian that the rest of them were already at the other end of the street. They marched together shoulder to shoulder toward the growing sounds of the block party—music, laughter, the murmur of a hundred voices. The aroma of barbecue wafted their way. When they got to the end of the block, Julian was reminded of why this place had been chosen. Every face he saw—men, women, and children—was black. He wanted to melt them all.

The believers fanned out into a line. In the distance, at the other end of the block, they could see the faint figures of their fellow believers, also forming a line. They didn't need a signal. They all knew what to do. They lit the rags. As they burned, they held them above their heads like torches. Across the way, another line of fire mirrored theirs. They hadn't discussed something to yell, so one by one they all joined together to let loose a guttural yowl of pure rage.

Most of the partyers didn't notice them at first. But those who did looked panicked. They desperately shook the shoulders and grabbed the arms of their loved ones, drawing their attention as well. Mothers and fathers and grandparents searched the crowd for their children. The panic was starting, spreading fast, at the sight of the righteous flames.

Tanya threw her Molotov cocktail first. It flew in a perfect arc above the heads of the revelers. The light trailed behind it, leaving a phantom streak across Julian's retina. It was beautiful, and even the scared people who were its target stared up at the sky as more missiles hurtled their way. Soon the night was full of the glow of the projectiles reaching their pinnacles and starting to descend. It was a glorious sight, and Julian braced for the explosions, which would be even more so. The screams from the crowd only added to his joy.

Tanya's bottle was the first to reverse course. Instead of continuing its path back to earth, it shot upward into the sky, flying higher than it had at the apogee of its previous trajectory. It was followed quickly by the others, as if it were a magnet drawing all the fire away from the people below. An unseen ceiling covered the street and each bottle bounced off it, a trampoline sending them all heavenward, where they exploded in a burst of yellow and orange. One after the other, blast after blast, harmlessly in midair, like so many fireworks.

After the bottles exploded, after the fire burned itself out, after the glass shards blew away on the winds instead of showering the people below, there was silence, broken only by a child's voice here and there, asking if there would be more. Julian exchanged glances with the men in his line, knowing the same thing was happening on the other end of the street. He felt Tanya's fingers interlacing themselves with his own.

A line of young men emerged from the crowd opposite them, clenched fists and determined expressions. Julian braced himself for the fight. As those around him rushed toward each other, Julian was held back by Tanya, her hand tightening around his. They watched as the melee started and didn't start. Every punch thrown missed its target. Men latched on to each other ineffectually. They lifted each other up and put each other down gently. They kicked and thrashed and did no damage at all—a highly choreographed ballet of the illusion of violence.

Julian was speechless. It was true. It had not been his failure in the synagogue. It was the world's.

"Do you trust me?" Tanya said.

"I do," Julian said.

Tanya dragged him away from the unfolding scene of confusion and foiled determination. Back to their car. She motioned him toward the driver's seat.

"Where are we going?" he said.

"Back there," she said, gesturing toward the block party.

Julian turned the car around, pointed it toward the street party. They could see the fighting already slowing down in the distance. The music had never stopped throughout it all. Julian looked at Tanya and shrugged.

"I want you to mow them all down," Tanya said. "Floor it. As fast as you can. And right when we get there, close your eyes."

"Close my eyes? How will I know who I'm aiming for?"

"You won't. That's the point. There are so many of them, you'll hit plenty. But if you're not looking, it can't stop you."

It. Whatever it was.

"We can win," Tanya said.

Her smile infused him with courage. He felt that she was right. She usually was. And he loved her. He wanted to please her. This was the best gift he could ever give her. He would close his eyes, and she would keep hers open.

Julian gunned the engine and popped the car into drive. They shot off like a rocket toward the party. He never let up on the accelerator. Getting closer, closer. And then when they were about to hit the first person, Julian closed his eyes.

He felt like he was flying. Shooting at hypersonic speed through the universe, stars and planets and all manner of possibilities whizzing by him. He kept his eyes shut tight. His foot pressed the pedal into the floor. More screams, a sweet, satisfying sound. It was working.

Julian expected the car to be buffeted by the impacts of body after body. He expected to rise and fall as the tires crushed limbs and heads below them. There should have been obstacles forcing him to hold the wheel tightly in order to keep it straight. But there was none of that. All was smooth, even as they sped up to the limit of the car, as if they were on a closed track that had been greased to reduce any sign of friction.

People must be dying. People must be dead. He wanted to open his eyes and see the windshield smeared with blood.

But he kept them closed, just as Tanya had instructed, and drove. So he didn't see the dozens of people in his way, each one yanked to safety as if by an invisible bungee cord and set down without a scratch.

When the impact came, it was sudden and jarring, the front wheels hitting a curb and going airborne. Julian opened his eyes just in time to see the front of the car smash into a giant oak tree and crumple. The tree barely moved.

Glass shattered around them as both he and Tanya flew through the front windshield. Neither of them had put on a seat belt. Julian felt an excruciating pain in every part of his body, and then he felt nothing at all. He had made it only halfway out the window, and now he hung there, impaled, unable to move, locked in on what he saw in front of him. Tanya had catapulted onto someone's front lawn. She wasn't moving, her body bent at odd angles, broken beyond repair.

Julian wanted to scream, but he had no voice. He wanted to run to her, to cradle her in his arms, to kiss her, to carry her away to safety. But he had no body, at least not any physical sensation of one. He was breathing. He could blink. Nothing else. He was helpless to do anything but watch as the crowd surrounded them and poked at Tanya to check if she was dead, the last thing he saw before going under.

EXCURSUS E: THE REVOLUTIONARY

THE REVOLUTIONARY LAID his guns on his cot. The handgun he always had holstered on his hip, the one he used when it was necessary to kill a person by his own hand; the AK-47 that he used in combat situations, when there was a military assault on one of the many bases he and his comrades had established in the jungle, mobile tent cities that had become his home over the past twenty years; and the old rifle, simple and efficient, that had been his grandfather's, the weapon his father's father had used to try to hold off the government when they successfully took his land from him. It was the rifle that he would hold up over his head when he made speeches, to new recruits and the old faithful alike, in which he told his grandfather's story, a parable about never yielding to tyranny.

Most of his soldiers had left already, along with all his lieutenants. The camp was empty, tents hollowed out of anything of value, the rest of the supplies abandoned. The Revolutionary looked around his own tent. It was identical to every other tent in the camp, to every other tent throughout the movement. They all slept in the same accommodations. They were all equal. Though, admittedly, the Revolutionary had a tent to himself, save when he chose to invite in company. The others generally had an occupancy of three or four.

When the news arrived of the change, the end of violence, it was met with incredulity. Another attempt at government propaganda, and a truly bizarre one at that. They were losing their minds. It was a sign that the revolution was succeeding. *We are driving them mad!*

But soon the sources expanded well beyond the government-controlled media. Foreign broadcasts, firsthand sources, personal experience—all pointed to the same truth.

The Revolutionary had not been the first commander, but he had been there at the beginning. He thought of those who'd died and wondered what they would think of this moment. They had started this fight because of violence committed against them, the need to avenge those who had been wronged, and their revenge had led others to seek vengeance on them. So much blood, so much loss. The Revolutionary, in his middle age, had begun to think the cycle might be endless.

And then it had been broken, in a day, in a moment, without explanation.

Everyone was gone. They had all walked out of the jungle, alone, in pairs or groups. Back to the cities, back to their families, back to other lives. The Revolutionary would follow them soon. There was still a question about power in his country. But with the usual levers of control dissipated, there were only discussions to be had. Raised voices and threats would certainly continue, but they would be impotent. Reason, persuasion, logic: these things might be possible again. And the Revolutionary knew that he needed to be in the capital to engage. No longer would his disembodied voice from the jungle be enough.

The Revolutionary gripped his single blanket between his fingers. The coarse wool scratched his skin, just as it had for two decades, reminding him of the suffering that drove his cause. Now he pulled it up over his cot, covering the guns. It was time to start walking.

GABRIELA

DAY

1

THE SMELL OF the manure stung Gabriela's nostrils, making her eyes water. In this confined space, the stench of it was like a mist that coated her and the others. Gabriela pulled Cristela more firmly against her chest. She was reclined in the middle of the trailer, leaning back against a sack of manure, arms around her little sister, who was cradled between her legs. There were nine other women and children making this journey north with them, but Gabriela couldn't see any of them. The trailer was a maze of shelves and piles optimized to hide as many people as possible. The wretched smell was part of the camouflage.

The only other person Gabriela could see was Oscar, crouching behind a low wall of manure sacks, cradling his gun. He was their main protection in case someone opened the back of the trailer and saw them. In case they weren't hidden well enough. In case the smell didn't drive the bandits away. Oscar and his gun were the last resort. Gabriela supposed the Lion and the Vulture might also help in a fight—they were driving and sitting up front in the cab, away from them and the reeking heaps. But it was Oscar whom Gabriela had grown to count on these past three days, just as Cristela was counting on her.

Oscar glanced her way. He winked, then put a finger to his lips when she laughed. He'd said he was twenty, but Gabriela thought he was maybe a year or two younger. He clearly had the least seniority in this crew. That might explain why he was the only one of the three men who was kind to the women, who played with the children. Or he might be the only one who was a good person. Gabriela suspected that was the case.

Cristela opened her eyes and cocked her head back to look at her sister. The short, stifled laugh had woken her up.

"It still stinks," Cristela whined.

Gabriela put her finger to her lips, like Oscar had to her, and shushed her sister. Cristela closed her eyes again, but only after a snort of disapproval. She was still only eleven years old, more likely to gravitate to the little kids at a party than to the grown-ups. Gabriela, at age fifteen, had only recently started to hang around the adults herself.

After they crossed their second-to-last border into Mexico, the Lion and the Vulture and Oscar had grown more wary. Oscar had told her they were traveling through the most dangerous part of their journey. More than crossing into the United States? she had asked. Yes, he said, much more so. There were gangs around here searching for women to steal. And children for the same purpose. Everything Oscar said sounded charming to Gabriela, so coming from him, this had the feel of a bedtime ghost story. But she knew it was real.

On this trip, she was certainly one of the women, not a child. At home, it had been less clear. Her mother and abuela had no doubts about her status. But the men around her had grown confused after the summer when she grew into her body. It was a rapid and uncomfortable transition that required her mother to refit her entire wardrobe in a matter of weeks. Those comfortable shorts and shirts that had been accommodating to the active little girl now clung and stretched in ways that made the men stare. Even after her wardrobe shifted to outfits that were deemed modest enough by her mother, the men paid her more attention than before. The ones she knew started to call her by new nicknames, little flower or hummingbird, Gabita, all of which sounded more menacing on their lips than flattering. Men on the street would sometimes call after her or whistle, though that was cut short when they realized she was being trailed by Tio Isaac's boys. Those who didn't notice had an up-close encounter that left no misunderstanding. But most people knew that Gabriela and Cristela, along with their mother and abuela, were under Tio Isaac's protection. For while most people called the local gang boss Tio, he actually was Gabriela's uncle. There was no confusion there.

The confusion about whether Gabriela should be treated as a woman or a girl was part of the reason she and Cristela had been forced on this journey away from home, toward a foreign land.

Not the main reason, however. The main reason was death.

The truck had been rumbling along steadily for a couple of hours, lulling them all into as much peace as possible in this manure vault. Suddenly, the brakes engaged, bringing them to an abrupt stop. Gabriela felt the cargo vibrate and shudder around her. Somewhere in the labyrinth behind her, she heard a child's voice, probably their youngest companion, only five, traveling with his mother and sister. He asked a question Gabriela couldn't quite make out, though it was still too loud. Oscar swiveled around. The child was quieted by his mother. Then there was only silence in the trailer, amplified by the lack of other noise outside, particularly when the engine shut off.

Maybe they had reached their destination. But Oscar's demeanor suggested otherwise.

Death had always brought change in Gabriela's life. The death of her father, Isaac's brother, had brought them under Tio's wing. One boy at school had said her dad had died to teach Tio Isaac a lesson, though she didn't know what exactly. Another boy, larger and crueler, described how the bullets had mangled his body and left his face unrecognizable, sending Gabriela fleeing to the bathroom to cry alone. She knew it was true. She had not been allowed to see her father's body after he died. After her mother was widowed, they'd moved into one of Tio's compounds. The death of her grandfather had brought her abuela from her mother's village to live with them. Her grandfather had died of natural causes, old and sick, and without him her abuela needed care, having become mostly hobbled and blind herself. Reluctantly, and not without much consternation, her abuela had joined them in the city.

The latest death in Gabriela's life had led to this long journey and banishment.

Three days ago, someone had killed Tio Isaac.

It wasn't a surprise. Tio Isaac had many enemies. What was a surprise to Gabriela was being woken up by her mother in the middle of the night. A backpack filled with essentials for her and Cristela was thrust into her arms. She and her sister were rushed to a waiting car. As her mother explained the plan, Gabriela realized that this escape had been formulated long ago, possibly from the day they moved into the compound.

"Why aren't you coming with us?"

"I have to take care of your abuela. I will take her back to her village."

"Why can't we go there with you?"

"The wolves have been watching you. If they find you . . ."

Her mother's face answered too many questions about what they would do.

"But they'll find you."

"They don't care about me. They want you."

Gabriela and Cristela had been told to lie on the floor between the back and front seats of the sedan, out of sight. The driver was a trusted friend of the family. Her mother had said he would get them to America, where her mother's cousin would take them in. She was partially right. The man had taken them to the first border, where he gave the girls and the money and a stern warning to the Lion, who'd said solemnly that he would care for the girls as if they were his own.

There was a loud noise at the back of the trailer, metal scraping metal as the doors were unlatched. Gabriela flinched, waking Cristela. They couldn't see the back door by design. If they couldn't see it, they couldn't be seen. But when it opened, the interior flooded with light and the promise of fresh air. Oscar tensed across the way, gun at the ready. Gabriela held her breath and put a hand over Cristela's mouth.

"Damn, you weren't kidding!"

"I told you you didn't want to open that."

The first voice was unfamiliar. The second belonged to the Lion. He always spoke with a swagger, more confidence than was warranted given his station in life.

"Yeah, but damn!"

A third voice, also unknown. "You don't have anything else in there?"

"Nope. Just shit."

"We might just check that out."

"Help yourself," the Lion said. "But I'll tell you what you'll find. Shit, shit, and more shit."

Gabriela heard someone climb up into the trailer. She could see his shadow on the wall.

"Whoa! I am not going in there!"

"Yes, you are. Check it out."

Instead, the shadow disappeared as the man jumped back to the ground.

"You go check it out."

The Lion intervened. "Why don't you trust me? And here's a little something for your trouble."

There was a long silence. Then the doors closed with a loud clack. Whatever fresh air had arrived instantly became stale and fetid. Gabriela didn't breathe again until the engine fired back up and the thrum of the road surrounded them. Only then did Oscar put down his gun and fall back onto a sack of manure, spent.

Two hours later, the truck ground to another halt. This time Oscar stood up nonchalantly, signaling to everyone to emerge from hiding. The back doors opened. The Lion and the Vulture waited there to help everyone out into the fading light. Cristela crinkled her nose at the sights outside. They were parked in the middle of a garbage dump. Mountains of trash loomed in all directions. If anything, it smelled worse than the inside of the truck.

The Lion and the Vulture could not have been more different men. Although short in stature, the Lion was blandly handsome, with a full head of hair that resembled a jet-black mane. The Vulture was tall and lanky, hard to look at, with a beak of a nose that came to a point and shifty eyes that followed you everywhere. The Lion was gregarious and loud; the Vulture rarely said a word, and then only terse commands.

"If everyone will gather over here, we will find our evening accommodations once I finish the day's business," the Lion roared.

Oscar herded the women and children toward a small shack. Gabriela noticed another man lingering by the truck. The Vulture gave him the keys in exchange for a large envelope. Oscar noticed her watching them.

"The manure is both good cover and a nice side business," Oscar said, laughing. "Everyone needs shit."

Cristela looked at him with a grin when he swore. Gabriela hit him playfully on the arm.

"Language, please," she said. "Why are you so happy?"

"Because I don't have to sleep at the dump," Oscar said, then hurriedly, "Not that it won't be fine for you.

But my abuela lives close by. This is my only night off. She makes the best rellenos."

Oscar saw Gabriela's face drop. He stammered quickly, "I wish I could take you with me . . ." And for a moment, he considered the possibility, but the moment soon passed. "But I can't."

A loud double blast startled them, the horn from the truck as the unfamiliar man got into the cab. He was looking at Oscar.

"That's my ride. You'll be fine here. Just stay close to the others."

Instinctively, Gabriela pulled Cristela closer to her. In three days, she had never been more than an arm's length away from her sister. What she hadn't realized until now was how close Oscar had stayed to them as well, a constant companion. The first night, they had slept in a clearing outside, Gabriela, Cristela, and Oscar in a row. The next, in an abandoned house, Oscar on the floor outside their room. But not tonight. He would be eating rellenos with his abuela. She would be sleeping in a dump. A surge of jealous anger coursed through her. She could tell Oscar wanted to say more, but the horn blasted again. He ran off to the truck without another word.

As the truck rumbled off, popping over the gravel and strewn garbage, the Lion beckoned for his charges to follow him. The group did as instructed. The place where they had disembarked from the truck was a clearing in an otherwise claustrophobic landscape. There were trails, bulldozed and maintained, canyons between the mounds of garbage that loomed two stories high. The Lion walked confidently ahead, the Vulture in the rear, ready to corral stragglers. Gabriela noticed patterns in the hills. One side was an escarpment of appliances—washing machines, stoves, refrigerators—piled atop each other and melding together. Around another corner, the front bumpers of cars poked out their noses, like newly hatched turtles emerging from the sand on the beach before heading to the sea. Atop another hill, perched like a sentry, was the abandoned carcass of a fishing boat. Cristela pointed with unbridled glee at a field of bicycles.

They turned corner after corner. There was no way Gabriela could lead Cristela back to the entrance to this wasteland on her own. The better to hide them, Gabriela thought. Or prevent them from running off. Cristela must have felt her sister shudder, for she moved closer. Gabriela took her hand.

When they reached their destination, the sun was low in the sky, behind the garbage hills. The shadows made it clear it would be a dark night.

The Lion stopped and pointed at what appeared to be an opening in one of the hills. Were they going to sleep in caves tonight? But on a closer look, it became clear that it was an abandoned shipping container, open to the path, nestled among the garbage but not buried by it. Gabriela looked ahead of them and saw another one in the distance. The Lion motioned to one of the families—two women and two preteens. He ushered them inside and came back out alone. The Vulture nudged the rest of them forward to the next container, where another woman and her child were left behind.

Around another corner was another shipping container, and the Vulture motioned the last mother and her two young children inside. She paused at the doorway. This woman reminded Gabriela of a teacher she'd once had, with her kind eyes and sad face. She looked at Cristela and then at the Lion.

"They can stay with us tonight," she said. "There is plenty of room."

"No," the Lion said. "We must spread out. Not to be found."

Now the mother looked at Gabriela, moving closer to her. The night before, this woman had brought her children—the five-year-old boy and the seven-year-old girl—to Gabriela's room and asked if she could watch them for her. Oscar had looked away. Gabriela had said yes but couldn't bring herself to ask why. From the look on the mother's face, it had seemed any questions might make her cry. So the children stayed with them. And later that night Gabriela, nestled in with three other children on a large mattress, heard noises from nearby, the kind she remembered coming from her parents' room years before when her father was still alive. In the morning, the children were gone, collected by their mother in the dark while Gabriela and Cristela slept.

The night before that, out in the clearing, Gabriela had awoken to different sounds, like restless animals grunting and whimpering, somewhere close by in the woods. She had considered waking Oscar but abruptly put her head back down when the Lion and Vulture emerged, leading one of the other mothers back to the group.

Gabriela could tell that the young mother was also thinking of such moments now as she turned back to the Lion.

"It is no problem. We can be quiet."

"I said no!"

The woman shrank back, instinctively putting an arm around Gabriela. But the breath caught in her throat when the Vulture took a step toward her own children. She whispered hastily in Gabriela's ear. "Remember your steps," she said. "Remember where we are."

"Please take your children inside," the Vulture said.

He seldom spoke, but when he did, it sounded like the groaning of the land before an earthquake. The woman ushered her children into the container.

Gabriela and Cristela followed the Lion and the Vulture deeper into the dump until they came upon another container, this one rusted gray with Chinese characters on the side. It was less buried than the others, and that made Gabriela feel better.

"Go on in," the Lion said. "There's a mattress in the back. Comfortable and clean enough. We'll be back with some food later. Don't come out unless we tell you to."

Cristela had gone inside and immediately come back out. "It's dark in there." She meant to whisper to Gabriela but was too loud.

"There's a small light on the wall. But make sure the doors are pulled shut when you use it."

Only then did Gabriela realize that the shipping container's opening could be closed. She put on her most solemn face and nodded at the Lion, who seemed pleased by her gesture.

"Good girls," he said. "We'll see you later."

Gabriela led Cristela back inside the container. There was a mattress at the back that was comfortable and unstained. Gabriela felt along the wall until she found the light, a small circle that blazed alive with a click when pressed. It gave a soft white glow to the space that was not unpleasant. The rest of the container was bare, an empty space intended to be filled with other things.

"Gabi?"

Cristela had been quiet for most of the past three days, which was unusual for her. Her sister was an annoying chatterbox at times.

"Yes?"

"Will Mommy and Abuela visit us in America?"

Gabriela hugged her sister. Together they sat down on the mattress, leaning against the cold metal of the container wall. Gabriela had already concluded that she would never see her abuela again. She was old and not in great health. If she couldn't make this trip, how could she possibly ever come to America to see them? But Gabriela had not considered the possibility that they would never see their mother again. She took a deep breath to compose herself, steadying her emotions so that the lie would be convincing.

"Of course they will," Gabriela said.

She felt Cristela relax next to her. The lie had been successful.

About an hour later, the Vulture appeared in the doorway. He handed them two takeout containers. The way he looked at them before he left reminded Gabriela of something else she needed to do before they went to sleep. But first they ate their dinner: rice and beans and—a pleasant surprise—a handful of fried plantains. It made Gabriela feel better to find such familiar food in this place. They were not alone, abandoned on a strange alien planet. There must be people close by, a village, maybe even a city. Somewhere that people cooked and sold food, somewhere that other people lived. People like Oscar's abuela.

They finished eating. Gabriela spit on the plastic knives and forks and wiped them off before putting them in her backpack. She had been trying to save anything that might be useful later. Then she took the cardboard containers and stood up.

"Where are you going?"

"Just to throw these in the garbage."

"We are in the garbage can."

Cristela laughed at her own joke. Gabriela smiled at the small reminder of who her sister had been three days ago and would be again.

Outside, she tossed the boxes on the nearest heap, then started to look around on the ground for what she needed. The sky was dark, but there was light in the junkyard, though she couldn't tell exactly where it was coming from. Not much, but enough to see by.

When they had first been handed off to the Lion, he had searched their backpacks. Gabriela had thought he was going to rob them, but he took nothing. Oscar later explained that he didn't allow anyone to have weapons, nothing sharp, nothing dangerous. But thinking about the young mother's fear, her words, Gabriela had decided that was exactly what she needed.

She almost stepped on the glass shard before she saw it. It looked like a teardrop, oval with a tapered point. It was almost as big as her palm, just the right size to conceal in her hand, perfect for grasping and stabbing. Her cousin Moy, Tio Isaac's oldest son, had taught her how to use a knife in a fight. He was nearly ten years older than her, but he'd always treated her with respect. People said that Moy was Tio Isaac's most efficient killer, brutal and precise. He'd asked his father no questions. Gabriela was certain he had taught her well.

Moy was dead. Killed the same day as Tio Isaac.

When Gabriela returned to the container, Cristela was already asleep. Usually Gabriela would have curled up behind her sister, draping one arm over her and wedging their backpacks between herself and the wall. Tonight she spread out in front of Cristela, forming a wall between her and the entrance, holding on tightly to the shard of glass.

The voices woke her up.

"Quiet. Hold those flashlights."

The words were hissed by the Lion. Gabriela kept her eyes closed but could tell there was a new light in the shipping container. She had no idea what time it was. Maybe it was morning and they had come to wake her up. Time to keep moving. But she didn't feel rested. And Cristela was almost always up before her. She was like a rooster, instinctively awake at dawn.

There was rustling and stumbling. The sound of a body hitting the metal wall. The Lion swore under his breath as the Vulture laughed. The Lion shushed him.

"We don't want them both to wake up."

Unsteady footsteps approached the mattress. Gabriela cracked one eye just enough to see a shadow stumbling toward her. She smelled the alcohol before she felt the Lion gently nudge her shoulder.

"Hey, little girl. Beautiful dove. Wake up. I want to show you something."

Gabriela knew she couldn't avoid the Lion by pretending to sleep. She was young but not naïve. She knew why he was here. The girls in her class had said that the boys didn't even care if you were awake or asleep when you did it, as long as your legs were spread open. Gabriela tightened her grip around the glass shard. In her head, she heard Moy instructing her. *He is taller than you. So punch the knife up into his belly. Once it is in, go all the way to the ribs. That will get his attention.*

The Lion leaned in, inches from her face. His breath was worse than the dump, worse than the manure truck. Gabriela tried to steady her own breathing, hold in her tears. But she wasn't sure how to avoid what was going to happen. Even if she stabbed the Lion, there was the Vulture. And it wasn't just her to protect. She could feel Cristela behind her, blissfully asleep.

These were the wolves her mother was worried about.

"Wake up, my darling. Wake up."

She wanted it to be a different voice—her mother, Abuela, her father, even Tio Isaac. A different place. Her bed at home. But that was not what this was. Not where she was.

"Just get to it," the Vulture said. "She'll wake up soon enough."

The Lion snorted, a burst of hot air in her face. Gabriela couldn't help herself. She coughed. She felt a hand on her shirt, pulling it up.

Gabriela opened her eyes and abruptly sat up. The Lion, surprised, fell back away from her onto his ass. The Vulture laughed harder. Gabriela looked at the tall man, who held two flashlights over his head, pointing down at her, illuminating the scene. She held the shard of glass out in front her. Her hand trembled around it.

"Ooh, feisty. I thought you might be a tiger like that."

The Lion stood up. Only then did Gabriela realize he had already taken off his pants. His shirt was also unbuttoned, open from his collar to his waist. The tail ends of it fluttered around his penis, which was engorged and pointing toward the ceiling. Gabriela had seen penises before but not like this, only those of her cousins and the other young boys, who were always taking them out to pee on walls and trees. But those were floppy harmless things, like rag dolls.

"You're curious, aren't you? Take off your clothes and come outside with us. That way we won't wake your sister. Trust me. When it starts to feel good, you will make too much noise."

Gabriela felt tears on her cheeks. But she wouldn't make any noises for this man. Not now, not later. She shook the shard in his direction.

"No. Go away."

Her voice sounded too small, too weak. Exactly how she hadn't wanted it to. The Vulture laughed again, this time directly at her.

"Don't be like that," the Lion said.

He was watching the weapon, coming closer. Gabriela thought he was going to try to steal it from her. It bit into her palm as she clutched it tighter. He swung his arm toward her. Gabriela flinched, expecting to be slapped, but his hand fell away, palm open, before reaching her. The Lion looked at his own hand as if he didn't understand. But his intention had been clear.

Gabriela had an opening. The soft underside of his belly was exposed to her. The Lion was distracted. So she followed Moy's instructions, stabbing hard and upward into the soft flesh. The Lion yelped. Gabriela felt the shard give and assumed that was the feeling of it entering his body, cutting him deep. But there was no rush of warm liquid on her hand as she'd expected, no splash of blood on the floor.

The Lion's astonished expression hadn't changed. But now he turned it on her. Gabriela pulled her hand back toward herself. She still held the shard, but there was no longer a sharp point at the end. It had become pliable, bending in on itself. She had felt the Lion's belly against her hand; it was not impenetrable. The soft looseness of it seemed like it would be easily rent. Yet it had been the shard that gave. The razor tip had smooshed down to a blob as if it were made of putty, not glass. Still, in her hand, the rest of it was solid, the edges capable of slicing her palm. The Lion stood up again, hands patting his belly as if he had just had a big meal. He let out a relieved sigh at finding himself intact. That quickly faded to an angry leer as he considered Gabriela, his next feast. The Vulture moved closer, intensifying the light on her.

"I was going to be gentle. But now you'll get a real good fucking."

The Lion grabbed his own penis, pushing it down slightly so that its single eye gazed at her. It popped back up when he let it go. He rushed at her. Gabriela shrunk away, hoping to disappear into the mattress, deep into the ground below. But the Lion stopped before he reached her, his attention waylaid again.

His penis had gone limp. In this state, it hung weakly to the left, surrounded by a tuft of hair. The

Lion appeared upset. He batted at it lightly, trying to coax it back to life. But it wouldn't budge.

"Stop playing around," the Vulture said. "My arms are getting tired."

"I can't . . . it won't . . ."

"Fine," the Vulture said. "I will, then."

The Vulture stepped toward the mattress. Gabriela edged away, but he also stopped short. His clothes were still on, but he looked down at his crotch, scared. Whatever had happened to the Lion had also happened to him.

The Lion scurried away, collecting his clothing off the floor. The Vulture backed slowly away to the door, keeping one flashlight on Gabriela's face.

"What is she, a witch?"

"A witch. A bitch. It doesn't matter."

Their voices shook. They regarded her as if she were a rabid animal. That was fine with Gabriela, who tried to snarl but couldn't manage it through her trembling lips. She didn't feel lucky, but couldn't help but wonder if she was.

The men left. They closed the door behind them. Gabriela heard a clunk outside but was too relieved to consider the implications of it. Instead, without ever taking her eyes off the front door, she curled herself up behind her little sister, arms around Cristela, who sighed and shifted to fit into her shape. Gabriela would keep vigil tonight, knowing that sleep would be hard to find.

DAY

2

"GABI, GABI, WAKE up!"
Gabriela smelled eggs, scrambled together with cheese, garlic, and peppers, her abuela cooking downstairs in the kitchen, the aroma wafting up to her bedroom. It was perfect. She didn't want to open her eyes. She felt Cristela shaking her.

"Go away. Let me sleep."

"Gabi!"

The dream disappeared. The pleasant smell of her abuela's cooking was replaced by the stench of garbage. Gabriela opened her eyes not to the familiar decorations of her room back home but to the stark metal walls of the shipping container. And her sister's face looming over her. She was angry at first, mourning the loss of a simple perfect dream, but then she focused on Cristela, her face full of fear, tears brimming in her eyes. Now Gabriela was fully awake. She hadn't intended to sleep at all last night. She had meant to stay awake and keep watch over her sister. But she had dozed off, and the Lion must have returned. Bile rose in her throat at the thought that he had done something to Cristela.

"Are you okay?" Gabriela said, sitting up. "Are you hurt?"

"They locked us in," Cristela said. "I tried to go outside, but I can't open the door."

Relief flooded Gabriela. She pushed the worst of her thoughts from her mind.

"I told you not to go outside without me," Gabriela said.

Cristela's eyes narrowed, momentarily distracted from her distress by her annoyance with her sister. She spoke very slowly, a mother to a child. "We are locked in."

"I'm sure it's just a heavy door. You just need to push harder."

"I pushed very hard. It is locked."

Gabriela smiled at her sister, not believing at all that Cristela had pushed hard enough. She stood up and stretched. Her nonchalance served one purpose. Cristela's panic seemed to have given way to impatience with Gabriela.

It was no longer completely dark in the container. Sitting here in the elements, surrounded by trash, had taken its toll on the structural integrity of the box, which was coming apart at some of the seams between metal panels, letting in slivers of light from the outside world. Gabriela didn't know what time it was but figured that, given Cristela's tendencies, it must not be too long since dawn.

"I'll open the door," Gabriela said with a confidence that irked her sister more.

Gabriela made a show of it. She scowled at Cristela with an exaggerated snarl. Strutting to the door, she flexed and struck a pose every two or three steps, playing to the crowd like a luchador. Cristela laughed. At the door, Gabriela cracked her knuckles and put her weight into it. She pushed the door, fully expecting it to move. It didn't budge.

Enough with the games. Gabriela shoved her body into the door, straining against the metal. Cristela joined her. Together they gave everything they had to give. Their efforts were in vain.

A different urgency overcame Gabriela. Somehow the night before, the Lion had been unable to do what he wanted. He had been unable to hurt them. Maybe he had found another way. Was he that angry at his failure that he would leave them here to die, locked in a metal box in the middle of a junkyard?

Gabriela took a deep breath, reminding herself that they weren't going to suffocate. The straining seams were letting in air. She had two bottles of water and a handful of granola bars in her bag. Surely someone would find them before they starved or became dehydrated. Maybe there was another way out. Gabriela scanned the walls and the ceiling, looking for a loose panel or maybe a trapdoor. She found nothing.

"Gabi?" Cristela said, her voice small and fragile.

Now Cristela did start to sob softly, trying unsuccessfully to hide it. Gabriela hugged her tightly and tried not to cry herself.

"Don't worry," Gabriela said. "Someone will come open the door soon. I'm sure they closed it to protect us. You just woke up too early! If you slept to a normal hour, we wouldn't even know it was locked. They would have woken us up instead of you, stupid rooster!"

Cristela gave her sister a playful shove. She was smiling again. Gabriela wiped the tears from her cheeks.

"Let's have breakfast," Gabriela said.

They plopped down on the mattress. Gabriela rummaged through her backpack, emerging with one granola bar and a bottle of water. She broke the bar in half and held the two pieces in front of her, letting Cristela pick her share. After a few silent moments, punctuated by their crunching, Cristela spoke.

"What's it going to be like in America?"

"It's going to be wonderful," Gabriela said.

"How do you know?"

Gabriela didn't know. She had no idea what the United States was like. She wanted it to be wonderful. She wanted that to be true.

"You know what comes out of the water faucets in America?" Gabriela said.

"Water?"

Cristela's tone was jaded. She was on the cusp of losing her childhood. This journey would only speed that along. But in this moment, Gabriela needed her to be willing to play the silly games they'd relished when they were younger. She needed that for both of them.

"Orange soda!"

Cristela loved orange soda. Gabriela looked at her expectantly. For a moment, she thought her sister wouldn't join in, but then there was the huge smile again, the one that warmed and broke her heart.

"It comes out of the shower too!" Cristela said, giggling.

Gabriela laughed, thinking of her sister joyfully bathing in orange soda.

"And you know what every girl gets as a present at her quinceañera?"

Cristela's eyes widened. Gabriela paused for dramatic effect.

"A unicorn!"

They both laughed now, visions of the two of them in their poofed-out pastel dresses riding their brand-new unicorns.

"Where do they get the unicorns?"

"America is full of unicorn ranches!"

"And unicorn pet stores!"

They fell into each other's arms in hysterics, just as they used to at home in each other's beds. The game continued, each idea about America more ridiculous than the one before. But soon they were worn out from laughing. Silence overtook them. Cristela put her head down in Gabriela's lap. Gabriela stroked her sister's hair. Cristela's breathing slowed, leading Gabriela to think she might have fallen back asleep.

"What's it really going to be like?" Cristela said.

"Safe and free," Gabriela said.

The words were bitter on her tongue. They felt as much like lies as the unicorns and orange soda. But she felt Cristela relax, so they were the right words.

As the minutes passed, Gabriela thought of her abuela. She would tell her to pray. That was her answer to everything. Their mother had viewed the church with ambivalence, an attitude Gabriela had absorbed. She didn't believe her prayers were heard by anyone but the people sitting in the pew in front of her. Yet she and Gabriela had dutifully said their prayers every night under the watchful eye of her abuela. Gabriela realized she had neglected them since this trip had begun.

Once, Gabriela had said she didn't believe in God, and her abuela had responded that she didn't need to because God believed in her. Now, sitting here in this metal box that seemed to be closing in on her, Gabriela searched for a prayer, but found none. Asking God for help felt like a last resort, an admission that there was no hope, and she wasn't ready for that yet.

Somewhere outside, Gabriela heard a beeping and the low hum of an engine. A piece of heavy machinery backing up, announcing its intentions. She sat up straight, startling Cristela. Then her sister heard it too. The beeping stopped, but the engine got louder, closer.

They ran to the front of the container. They pounded on metal, echoes reverberating around them, hurting their hands and their ears. They shouted as loud as they could, calling for help. They heard the truck approach and pass by.

Gabriela leaned forward, pressing her forehead against the cool metal. She told herself there would be another truck. They would just have to be patient. She struggled to believe herself.

"Gabi, listen."

Gabriela looked to her sister. Cristela had her head cocked toward the door, face scrunched up in concentration. Gabriela closed her eyes and tried to hear what her sister heard. Nothing for a moment. Then, there it was. Someone in the distance calling their names.

They pounded on the walls with fresh vigor. They screamed at the top of their voices, the effort threatening to tear apart their throats.

A sound at the door. Gabriela and Cristela backed away, grabbing each other's hands. The squeaking of metal, the turning of a handle. Gabriela squinted against the morning light that suddenly filled the container. Only then did she realize how dark it had been inside.

"Gabriela, Cristela, are you okay?"

It was Oscar.

Gabriela wanted to run to him, but Cristela beat her to it, clinching him tightly around the waist. Oscar put a hand on her back but never took his eyes off Gabriela.

"They said they came to look for you and you were gone," Oscar said. "They said you'd run off."

"We didn't," Gabriela said.

"I didn't think I'd find you . . ."

Oscar trailed off. Gabriela knew the rest of his sentence. It was written on his face. He'd thought he would find dead bodies. Or not find them at all. This dump was an easy place to hide things.

"But you looked anyway."

"Of course. I'm sorry I left you."

"You couldn't know. How is your abuela?"

Oscar shook his head. He was an open book. He could have known. "She's fine. Last night . . . did they . . . hurt you?"

Gabriela took a deep breath. "They tried. They . . . couldn't."

Oscar nodded. Gabriela could tell he didn't want to ask the follow-up question. She didn't know how to answer it even if he did. Cristela finally let him go.

"I want to leave," Cristela said. "It still stinks here."

"Okay," Oscar said. "Let's go."

Gabriela ran back into the shipping container to grab their backpacks. Inside, she felt a crushing weight on her chest, a moment of sheer panic, and she glanced back to make sure the door wasn't closing her in again.

As they walked back along the winding paths of the dump, Oscar told them about the delicious meal his abuela had made him the night before. Gabriela assumed he would take them to his abuela's house and they could figure out what happened next. She was surprised when they arrived back at the clearing at the entrance of the junkyard to find the Lion and Vulture there waiting for them. There was a large truck with an open bed in back, the kind that usually hauled loads of vegetables, and all the other women and children were sitting in the dirt around it. They all stood up as soon as they saw Gabriela and Cristela. Their relief was palpable.

Gabriela turned to Oscar, who was staring at the Lion. It was clear he had not expected everyone to still be here.

"Thank god," the Lion bellowed. "We were all so worried! Don't scare us like that again!"

The Vulture motioned to the truck. The other women and children started to climb on board. The sides of the bed were tall enough that they weren't visible when they sat down. But it was nothing like the camouflage of the manure truck. The road ahead must be safer for everyone. Oscar warily approached the Lion. Gabriela and Cristela matched him step for step.

"I thought you were going to leave," Oscar said.

"How could I leave you and the girls?" the Lion said. "The others wouldn't even get on the truck until you got back."

A momentary flash of anger crossed the Lion's face as he watched the last woman board the truck. The Vulture glared at them coldly, then walked around to the cab. The engine came to life. The Lion looked to Gabriela.

"So, are we going?" the Lion said.

Oscar turned to Gabriela. "It's up to you."

Gabriela thought about the options. She knew she couldn't go back to her country; she doubted it had gotten any safer there in just a day. The world didn't change that much that fast. She and Cristela needed to go somewhere safe, even if the road there was dangerous. She thought about staying here, but she suspected the life in this foreign country wouldn't be as good for her and Cristela as it would be in the next one. They just needed to get there, and the back of this truck, so long as Oscar was in the front, seemed like her best choice.

"We will keep going."

"Great," the Lion said, though his tone was less than thrilled. "Get in the truck."

Gabriela grabbed Cristela by the hand and led her to the truck as Oscar went around to the cab. She helped her little sister climb in. She was about to pull herself up when she realized that the Lion had lingered behind her.

"Take care, little one," the Lion said. "Don't wander off again. We wouldn't want anything to happen to you."

Gabriela did not look back at him. She didn't want to see his smile.

D A Y

3

THE RAIN GREW heavier as they drove north, intensifying as they got nearer to their final border.
Oscar had told them they would cross into America the
next day. The rain seemed eager to stop them. It came
down in sheets on top of them, soaking their clothes,
their hair, their skin, as they shivered in the back of the
open truck and hoped they were getting close to their
final overnight stay. Water pooled around them. The
sky had steadily darkened throughout the day, so that
by the time they pulled into the weed-covered parking
lot outside the abandoned warehouse, it felt like the
dead of night, even though it was only late afternoon.

There were no beds, no mattresses. Just a cold,
hard floor in the middle of a cavernous room, surrounded by the empty, skeletal shelves that rose floor
to ceiling, the only reminder that this had once been a
place of commerce. The Lion and the Vulture herded
the women and children to the center of the open
space and motioned at the ground. They collapsed
there together in a heap.

The temperature dropped steadily throughout the night. They all huddled together for warmth. They sat or lay down, waiting for the next morning and the final leg of their journey, all of them mostly silent except for the youngest traveler, who had developed a disturbingly raspy cough on the truck, the sharp bursts of it echoing throughout the warehouse. There was a bathroom here, but it had crumbled from disuse, the toilets either overflowing or broken. The travelers chose to go outside, despite the rain, to conduct their business, clustering together in groups of four to five for safety and comfort. When night came, they pressed into each other's bodies and tried to sleep. The next day would be a long one.

The Lion was frustrated. He paced the perimeter of the warehouse like a caged animal. Once he told Oscar to go get food for everyone. Oscar refused to leave. The Lion stormed off to the truck himself, returning with a stack of soggy tortillas and two containers of mushy fillings, one an unidentified meat, the other likely vegetables. He threw the food on the ground near the group, leaving it to them to divvy up the night's meal. Oscar did not eat. He also never left their side. The Vulture lurked and watched everything.

At some point, Gabriela fell asleep. She dreamed of home. She heard her mother and abuela singing, each one her own song, under her breath, each unaware of the other's tune yet in perfect harmony. Cristela was in her bed, snoring, in the room they shared. Gabriela's father stood outside their window, laughing with Tio Isaac and Moy. They took turns absent-mindedly tossing sticks around the courtyard for the dogs to chase and collect. There was a boy there from school whom she had secretly liked, and a group of girls she had always wanted to be friends with. They had all gathered there to plan something for Gabriela, a party. A welcome home. Or a celebration that she had never left. Maybe her quinceañera. Conspiring about where to hide her unicorn.

"Wake up, little one," a voice whispered near Gabriela's ear.

She woke with a start, the Vulture's face filling her world.

Gabriela tried to dart away from him, but she couldn't move. Only her eyes could rotate in her skull, taking in the empty warehouse around them. She lay in the center of the room alone, save for the Vulture. She didn't know where anyone else had gone. She wanted to cry out for Cristela, but she had no voice. The Vulture held her tongue in his hand.

"You will never make it to America," the Vulture said.

And his nose elongated into a true beak. His arms, outstretched, grew feathers and spread like wings. He looked down on her and prepared to feed. Gabriela knew she was already dead.

She woke up with another jolt, this time fully emerging from her dreams. Cristela grunted and rolled over, annoyed even in her sleep to be jostled. Gabriela was surrounded by the other children, all in various depths of their own slumber. The youngest boy coughed. The women, the mothers, ringed them protectively. Outside the circle, Oscar dozed fitfully on an uncomfortable metal chair. Gabriela steadied herself, finding solace in not seeing the Lion or the Vulture nearby. They must have a better place to sleep.

Gabriela rolled over on her back and stared up at the warehouse ceiling, which seemed to be an infinite distance away. Blank and pitch-black, it might as well have been the inky, cloudless sky outside. Gabriela didn't want to go on the next day to America. She knew that the end of this journey was merely the beginning of the next one, which was equally unknowable, equally perilous. She wondered if Cristela also realized that troubles waited for them on the other side of tomorrow's river, same as on this side of the divide. She closed her eyes again, hoping for relief, but it never came. After a couple more hours, she was shaken again, this time by the collective movement of the women and children rising and returning to the truck.

It was still raining as they drove one final stretch, but not the monsoon of the day before, just a light mist that coated their skin with a soft sheen. The sun never came out, but the gray was less threatening than the black.

The highway became a small paved road that yielded to a dirt path that finally came to an abrupt end. There were two other men waiting for them with a car of their own. They stood out in the rain, seemingly unperturbed by getting wet. The truck engine died, and the Lion leapt from the cab. He approached the men while pointing at the sky and shaking his head. Then he threw his arms open and engulfed each man in a bear hug. Their expressions didn't change. The Lion seemed much happier to see them than they were him.

Oscar appeared at the back of the truck. He opened the bed and gestured to the travelers.

"From here we walk," he said.

For a moment, Gabriela thought they were about to be handed off to the new men, the strangers. Although she would be glad to be rid of the Lion and the Vulture, she preferred the familiarity of them to the specter of the unknown. She didn't like the idea of traveling with other men who wanted to hurt them but had not yet tried and failed.

Oscar was helping everyone out of the truck. When Gabriela took his hand and let him guide her to the muddy ground, she felt a surge of optimism that they were going to make it.

After two hours of walking toward the border, the optimism had washed away with the rain, which had only grown steadily stronger with each step. It was difficult to maintain her footing on the uneven, soaked earth. There was no path trod for them, but few obstacles either. The landscape was mostly bare, punctuated mainly by small bushes and shrubs. The occasional taller tree, striving toward the sky, looked like a misplaced exclamation mark. One of the other children asked if there were snakes. Oscar chuckled, saying that all the animals out here were smart enough to go deep underground in a rain like this. It was small comfort as they continued to grow increasingly waterlogged.

So they marched ahead, led by the Lion, trailed by the Vulture, with Oscar flitting back and forth, encouraging them forward. No one had the will to ask how long they had to go. No one believed they would be happy with the answer. So they stared at their feet, making sure the next step would be a sure one, the mothers doing so for their children as well. They walked with the knowledge that they were nearing their goal and the hope that they were right in seeking it.

After the third hour, there was sniffling mingling with the pattering of the rain, tears from the children whose feet hurt, who were tired and hungry, but the understanding that there was nothing to be done about it left them with only their sadness for company. Even the youngest boy, who had gotten piggyback rides from many of the adults, including for a short period Gabriela, had taken the initiative to stifle his cough, issuing it into his elbow. Each burst from his tiny lungs sounded like a distant apology.

As the rain increased, the human noises—the coughs and tears and footsteps and whispers—disappeared in the pounding of water on the already saturated land. The darkness returned, midafternoon transformed into nearly midnight. Lightning lit up the way with increasing frequency. The thunder shook them. They walked on, able to see those who trod with them but not much further into the desolate landscape.

"My stomach hurts," Cristela said.

Gabriela understood. Every part of her hurt, and each one in a unique way.

"We will reach the river soon," Gabriela said.

She didn't even convince herself.

"I can't wait," Cristela said. "I have to go."

Gabriela looked as far into the distance as she could, searching for a place with some privacy. There was a patch of low bushes nearby. That and the darkness would have to do. Others had diverted from the group during the hike to attend to their needs. But that had been when it was lighter out, when the rain had been more a nuisance than a threat. Gabriela considered the dangers. The land was flat enough; they were unlikely to come upon a cliff or embankment where they could be washed away. And she had chosen to believe Oscar when he'd said the animals were smart enough to shelter where they wouldn't be encountered. She grabbed Cristela's hand.

"Come on. Be quick."

Gabriela thought she heard another woman call after them as they hurried to the bushes. Oscar didn't see them; he had started scouting the way ahead. The shrubs provided less shelter than Gabriela had thought, but that didn't matter. It made her feel better that she could still see the marchers in the near distance.

"It hurts, Gabi," Cristela said.

"You'll feel better in a minute," Gabriela said.

Gabriela took her sister's hands and steadied her while she squatted next to the bush. She was relieved as she watched the pain fade from Cristela's face.

"Better?" Gabriela said.

"Yes, sorry," Cristela said. "Do you have paper?"

Gabriela had grabbed some paper towels from the warehouse bathroom. She let Cristela balance herself, then dug for them in the wet backpack. They were damp, but that might help the cause. She handed one to her sister. Cristela finished up and was straightening out her clothes when they heard a *click, click* over the sound of the rain.

Gabriela turned to the side, alarmed. The Vulture stood there. He had been watching them. He held a pistol, pointing it at Gabriela's head. The *click, click* had been him pulling the trigger twice. It must not be loaded. He must be playing games with them. The rest of the group was starting to disappear from view into the dark and rain and empty world around them.

"Just testing a theory," the Vulture said. "Something I heard on the radio."

Cristela melted into Gabriela's side. She held her sister close. The Vulture checked the gun's chambers for bullets and seemed satisfied with what he found.

"Move it," the Vulture said. "Remember what we said about getting lost. That's when accidents happen."

Gabriela didn't remember anyone saying that, but she wasn't going to wait for an explanation. She pulled Cristela away. They hurried toward the group, slipping and sliding. She didn't breathe until they were back in the line, at the back now, but finding comfort in the numbers.

Another half hour of walking convinced Gabriela that they couldn't go much further, particularly the children. Her own legs had become heavier with each step. There was a sharp pain between her shoulder blades and a duller ache in her temples. All of her skin had wrinkled in on itself, folds on folds. One of her knees felt weak, threatening to buckle under with each landing. She didn't know what would happen if she could no longer walk. Cristela would certainly help her, but did she have the strength? Maybe Oscar would help too.

It became a moot point when the Lion stopped them, waving them toward a small grove of trees. She could see more trees up ahead, blocking their view of what lay beyond. The storm had eased somewhat, and the world had brightened slightly. Another sound in the near distance, like the passing of cars on a busy highway, became audible above the rain and their own labored breaths. Gabriela knew it must be the river. Under the canopy of the trees, the rain struggled to find them. They fell into the mud happily, enjoying the shelter and the respite from walking.

The Lion nodded at the Vulture, who walked away toward the trees in the distance. He didn't seem to be in any hurry. Oscar came over and sat next to Gabriela.

"You okay?" he asked.

Gabriel just nodded. He seemed as tired as she was. She wondered how many times he did this, whether he was going right back down south to get another group of paying customers. But that wasn't what she really wanted to know at the moment.

"Why are you so nice to us?" Gabriela said.

Oscar cocked his head at her. She could see him thinking about who *us* was. Gabriela was reasonably sure she had been clear that she meant just her and Cristela.

"I have a sister," Oscar said to Gabriela. "You remind me of her."

Gabriela was happy that the wet and dark masked her blushing. It was not the answer she'd been expecting, or maybe not the one she'd thought she wanted, but now she knew it was the one she needed. She was about to respond when the Lion interrupted, shouting over the rain and the distant river.

"We have reached the end. There are three rafts on the other side of those trees. We will use them to get across the river. Once you are on the other side, you will be in the United States of America. Then you are no longer my problem. Once you cross the river, you are on you own."

The Lion paused and looked them over. There was an expectation in his eyes, as if he thought he should be given some appreciation for his service, some gratitude for his effort. He was disappointed.

"If you fall off the rafts, we aren't going to save you," the Lion said. "So make sure you hold on, and whatever you do, don't stand up."

He turned away from them, looking back to the trees in the distance. It was not as far to the riverbank as Gabriela had thought. The Vulture was already making his way back to them.

"Let's go," the Lion said.

He started to walk toward the Vulture. It took Gabriela a great deal of effort to separate herself from the earth. She could tell everyone was having the same problem.

"What happens on the other side of the river?" Cristela asked.

Gabriela didn't have the energy to lie. "Probably more walking. Hopefully we get picked up quickly and get a place to sleep tonight."

Cristela sighed. That was what she'd expected, but Gabriela knew her sister wanted to hear her say it.

"You won't be alone," Oscar said. "I'm staying on the other side with you."

"You're going to stay in America with us?" Cristela said, not trying to hide her excitement.

"Not forever," Oscar said. "I've seen it over there. It's better than some places, but not the promised land. It's like anywhere else. Full of its own problems. But I'll make sure that you get someplace safe."

Gabriela hoped she would have that perspective someday. In the last week, she had seen three countries, and they all seemed to have the same problems.

The mass of them slumped toward the Vulture, then past him to the river. They all appeared to be letting go of the tension, allowing themselves to relax as they neared the end of their journey, not thinking about how it only continued on the other side.

The Lion led them into the trees. It was only a few feet from there to the banks of the river. A narrow cut through the foliage led them down to a small swath of silty rocks at the water's edge. There were three rafts there, which seemed to be an agglomeration of wood slats tied to inflated rubber inner tubes. They looked seaworthy under the best of conditions, but Gabriela was worried that they wouldn't hold now.

Oscar had told her and Cristela that the river was as calm as a swimming pool. Like floating over on a sheet of glass. But that was not the river she saw now. This was an angry, roiling beast. The waters rushed by with a roar. They lapped at the banks hungrily and swirled recklessly in the middle.

Gabriela felt a hand on her shoulder. It was Oscar.

"Don't worry," he said. "I've crossed when it's like this before."

But he clutched her a little too hard, a little too long. She could feel his nerves through her shirt, which was already plastered to her torso. His reassurance fell flat.

The Vulture led the family of four to the furthest raft. The Lion guided the other five travelers to the middle one, leaving the closest and smallest vessel for Oscar, Gabriela, and Cristela. They watched the Vulture steady his boat as his passengers boarded. Once they were on, he deftly pushed them off the shore as he jumped aboard himself, oar in hand. One of the children screamed as the raft shot away, flying down the river. For a moment, it seemed to be spinning out of control. But the Vulture brought it right, and while it rapidly sped into the distance and out of sight, it also made slow but steady progress from one side to the other.

The Lion hurried his charges on board as well. He looked over his shoulder with a weak smile before he too shoved off into the raging waters. The river was fast, and as soon as the rafts launched, they receded far into the distance. Gabriela could only assume they would make it to the other side safely.

"When we're out there," Oscar said. "Stay low and stay calm."

Oscar moved the third raft into position. He looked to Gabriela, who strode confidently to it, stepping on board without hesitation. She turned back to help Cristela on. Oscar grabbed his oar, then took a deep breath and pushed them strongly onto the water.

The transition was sudden and jarring. Solid became liquid and all bearings below them disappeared. They were spinning and undulating up and down. Gabriela and Cristela clung to each other, flat on the raft's bottom. Oscar plunged his oar into the water. The tendons in his neck strained outward as he fought against the water, struggling to control the direction of the raft. He was losing the fight. He took his oar out of the water, then drove it back down, to little better effect.

Gabriela noticed that the entire raft was lilting to one side. She tried to scooch away from it, attempting to even out the weight. But that wasn't the problem. She could see that one of the inner tubes was shrinking, losing air fast. Oscar noticed it too. He rushed over to that side to assess the situation.

"That motherfucker," he said. "He popped it."

Gabriela could see the Vulture in her mind, watching her sister go to the bathroom, pointing the gun at them, pulling the trigger. Testing a theory. She knew that was who Oscar meant. She picked her head up slightly. The other rafts were nowhere to be seen. She had no idea if they were further along or behind them, already at the other side. She and Cristela and Oscar were titling and spinning out of control in the middle of the river.

Oscar put a knee on the side of the raft that wasn't sinking. He thrust his oar back into the water, fighting against the current, trying to bend it to his will. But Gabriela already knew he had lost. They were going under. Gabriela reached out for her sister, but it was too late.

In a heartbeat, the raft lost its structure beneath them. It disintegrated and disappeared. Gabriela went under, swallowing a lungful of water. As she careened along with the current, she pushed for the surface, which rose and fell around her.

"Cristela!" she shouted.

But she barely heard her own words. Everything was lost in the current, even sound. She treaded water, finding that pushing against the current brought her momentarily higher and able to see. Two bodies were floating in the water near her. She pushed herself in their direction. Then they came together and started moving toward her. She kicked harder, snorting out the water that kept getting in her nose. Soon, they were close enough for her to see that Oscar had a hold of Cristela and was keeping her head above water. Her sister's eyes were closed.

Gabriela and Oscar came together. They formed their own raft with their bodies, a surface on which Cristela could be supported. Gabriela couldn't tell if her sister was breathing. She didn't have time for that. They let the current carry them for a moment, catching their breath.

"No rocks . . . can float . . . kick toward shore . . ."

Oscar spit out words between taking in gulps of water and air. Gabriela strained her head above the rapids. She understood. There was nothing to hurt them in the water. Just the water itself. If the two of them worked together, slowly, steadily, they would move toward the other shore. But she was so tired already. If only her body wouldn't give out on her.

Gabriela let her head fall against her sister's hair. They were all floating only by the sheer willpower of her and Oscar. It would be so easy to go under.

But she had promised to take of her sister. She had sworn to get her to America. She felt Oscar's legs kick by her side. She waited until he was tensed and ready again. Then they kicked together. It would work. Together, they would get the three of them to shore.

Except that Oscar was wrong. There were no rocks under the surface in this part of the river, but the storm had created hazards nonetheless, ripping large branches from the trees along the banks and dropping them into the water.

The enormous branch, longer and thicker than any of them, came out of the darkness with startling speed. Gabriela had no time to react. Oscar surprised her by spinning them around. He must have seen it before her. She heard the crack as he took the full brunt of the impact. Then she was under the water, surrounded by the eerie silences below. Gabriela clung to Cristela, pulling her into her chest. But Oscar no longer held on to her.

Gabriela pushed upward again, fearing this might be the last time she could summon that strength. The giant log was now in front of her, within arm's reach. She lunged for it, hooking her arm over its smooth trunk. She kicked her legs under the surface, enough to keep both her and Cristela's heads above water.

"Oscar!"

Shouting was futile. The word merely echoed in her own head. Yet she tried again.

"Oscar!"

Gabriela felt Cristela shift in her arm. She still didn't open her eyes, but she was alive. Gabriela added her tears to the world, which was already drowning in its own.

Off in the distance, moving much faster down the river, she saw a shadow on top of the water. It could have been another log. Or a body. It didn't move. There was no way she could get to it. It sped away from them.

Gabriela was spent. She could do nothing more than hold on. To this log. To her sister. She repeated a mantra in her head. Maybe out loud.

I will never let you go.

EXCURSUS F: THE DEAR LEADER

FOR THE FIRST two days, the Dear Leader stayed inside. He did not watch any news programs. He did not allow anyone to speak to him. He wanted to be alone and watch DVDs from his extensive private film collection. For two days, the Dear Leader pretended the rest of the world did not exist.

THE EMPTY SHELL

DAY

1

THE EMPTY SHELL woke up to the dingy light of the rising sun. It filtered through the small window of his small cell. He had been in this prison for three days. At least he thought it was three days, given that he had woken up here, lying on the cold dirt floor, three times. He looked up at the window, which was really just an open slit at the top of the wall near the ceiling. It could be sunlight he was seeing. Or it could be a spotlight shone on the wall from outside by his captors. It could be early morning or it could be the dead of night. In the Empty Shell's country, it was hard to tell the difference.

The Empty Shell raised himself off the floor slowly, by degrees. First, he pushed upward against gravity onto one elbow. He took a moment to catch his breath, then pressed on with one hand against the dusty floor until he was in a seated position. He looked at the palm of his hand, coated anew with the grime of this place, as was the rest of his body, his face, his lungs.

The Empty Shell had grown used to the stench of human fluids. There were no toilets in cells. Prisoners urinated and evacuated bowels in a corner of their choosing. No one came to clean it up. It soaked into the floor, leaving a stain but gradually disappearing. Even after only three days, everything that came out of the Empty Shell's body was already liquid—piss, shit, sweat, tears. There were no showers in this place, not for the prisoners, no ability to wash anything away.

The Empty Shell picked up the tin plate that had held his dinner the night before, a thin gruel that slopped over the edge and soaked into the floor if you didn't hold the plate exactly level with the earth. Any slope meant the loss of food, the minimal nourishment that the Empty Shell, who was not yet ready to die, knew he needed. The other option was to leave the plate on the ground, kneel before it, and lick the gruel off like a dog. But, as in any situation, there were always tricks to learn. Overnight, the gruel had crusted onto the plate, a hard coating. The Empty Shell picked up the tin disk and brought it to his mouth, licking clean any stray vitamins and minerals that might exist in the residue. He was thirsty. There was a cup of water just outside the rusty iron bars that formed the fourth wall of his cell, the other three made of solid concrete, stained by random darker splotches of what the Empty Shell assumed was blood.

The Empty Shell finished the last of his gritty meal off the plate, carefully threading it through the bars to place in the outside hall next to the cup of water. He was thirsty. There was plenty of water in the cup to fulfill him. But the vessel was an awkward shape, designed to not fit through the narrow bars. So while a prisoner could reach through the bars and grab it, it was impossible to pull it back through and drink. The Empty Shell stuck each hand through a different opening, each one momentarily free from the cell. With one hand he picked up the cup, the other forming a second inadequate cup. He poured a splash of water from one to the other, then quickly pulled his hand back to his face. Half the water was lost instantly to the porous floor. The Empty Shell lapped the rest up greedily from his palm. He repeated this again and again until the cup provided by his captors was empty. Each time he pulled his hand back, it scraped against the bars, tiny needles of the rust cutting his skin and mixing with his blood.

Done with his meal, the Empty Shell scooted across the floor to the back wall. He leaned against it and waited. That was what this section of the prison was for, waiting. They had brought him to his cell past a dozen other men in identical cells. Each one waiting. The men made no noise. They lamented and cursed in silence. Each of them still had a single refuge in their own mind, though they knew that would soon be lost too. The Empty Shell knew his own crimes, but not theirs. Not that it mattered. All crimes in their country were crimes against the Dear Leader, and therefore punishable equally. The Empty Shell knew that this was the best that his time in this prison would be, as did his compatriots in the neighboring cells. They all knew the stories, the possibilities. Cells so constricted that one could only stand or sit cross-legged without relief. Spaces where you were slid in on your back with the ceiling millimeters from your nose. Of course, while here, the Empty Shell had as yet been untouched, but he knew there were no limits to the Dear Leader's imagination when it came to degradation of the human body.

The Empty Shell had been committing his crimes against the Nation for twenty years. He marveled at his luck at having been caught only in the last week. Actually, he hadn't been caught. He knew he had surrendered. The Empty Shell was tired. His body was worn down from years of working in the artillery factory on the outskirts of the capitol. He was ready to be done. He'd considered suicide. It would have been easier, but ultimately it was not the way he had lived and not the way he wanted to die.

So he had retrieved his pen and paper from where they were hidden in his apartment, which wasn't much bigger than this cell. Although there was no air conditioning or discernible heat in his building, there were metal grates in his room, suggesting ductwork. Behind one of them was his hiding place for the tools of his trade. After his shift five days ago, before going down to the cafeteria for dinner, he had written his last work, signing it *The Empty Shell* as always.

Your fiction is our reality. Your reality is our dream.

The next morning, instead of going to work, the Empty Shell had walked into the capitol. For two decades he had been writing his missives on scraps of paper that he carried folded or rolled with him until he found a place to deposit them. He didn't publish his work. He didn't even understand how that would be possible in this country. But he did release it. Crumpled up as trash on the ground. Nestled into the crack between bricks of a crumbling building. Dropped under a table in a park. Left inside a plunger in a dormitory restroom. For two decades, he had tried to never repeat locations where he left his writing. He trusted that it would be found, and that trust had been rewarded.

It had been years since the Empty Shell had begun rolling his papers tightly and sliding them into empty shell casings of random calibers that he had stolen from his work. One of his jobs, depending on the day, was to sift through the laundry bins of spent casings that were collected from around the country. Every single one was to be reused. Sanctions had made recycling a necessity in his country. It was considered unpatriotic to waste anything, and of course, being unpatriotic was a crime against the Dear Leader. So spent shells were gathered from wherever they were found, shooting ranges or the homes of dissidents, military bases or dead bodies, and sent to the factories for assessment. The Empty Shell spent entire days determining if a casing could be reloaded or needed to be melted down and recast. And each one he held in his hand led him to consider where it had been, who it might have killed or maimed or just frightened. One day, considering the empty impotence, he'd decided to fill it with his words. Without thinking, he'd slipped a single shell in his pocket. Later, his first poem coddled inside it, the Empty Shell had dropped the casing outside a nearby university building, knowing full well that anyone who picked it up, anyone who read it, was in as much danger as the writer.

His final work had been handed directly to a Swedish diplomat outside his embassy. The Empty Shell was not expecting to give it to a person. His plan had been to place it just inside the gates. He assumed that whatever guard was on duty would pick it up. Maybe they would exchange a sad glance, the foreigner knowing as well as he that the embassy was under constant surveillance and that the Empty Shell would be picked up by his country's enforcers within blocks of walking away. But instead, as the Empty Shell approached the gates from one direction, a tall man with almost white-blond hair and translucent skin, so insubstantial that he seemed to be the morning mist personified and ready to disassemble in the sunlight, walked toward him. They met in front of the embassy. The diplomat looked momentarily spooked, as if the Empty Shell and not he himself more closely resembled a ghost. The Empty Shell understood. This man was wondering if he was on the cusp of an international incident, whether this local before him was about to request help, to ask for asylum. The diplomat would have to turn him down and live with that guilt for the remainder of his tour. So he was relieved when the Empty Shell smiled and shook his head, holding out the small scrap of paper. The diplomat, not thinking, accepted the gift. Mission complete, the Empty Shell walked away. Three long blocks later, he was picked up by the watchers and taken away in a black van.

The Empty Shell had a name. It was seldom used, and sometimes even he forgot it. In this prison, he knew it would be completely gone soon. The Empty Shell had been born during a famine. He had parents and siblings he had not seen in years. He was part of a family that did not matter. Every citizen of the country was part of the same family and had a single Father.

The Empty Shell had a birthday. He did not remember the month or day. It was never celebrated. Only the Dear Leader's birthday was important.

The party members in charge of the Empty Shell's dormitory had tried to convince him to marry. He had refused. It turned out to be one thing they were unwilling to force upon him; most likely they didn't want to doom some poor woman to the same fate they sensed was coming for him. The Empty Shell didn't understand how his fellow citizens could fall in love and bring children into this world, but so many of them did. A facet of human nature, he supposed, that thankfully did not afflict him.

"The elusive Empty Shell. A pleasure to finally meet you."

The Empty Shell opened his eyes. He had not realized he had closed them. Darkness and light, like so many opposites, sometimes were hard to differentiate in his country. There were three people standing outside the bars of his cell. One of them carried two metal chairs, one hanging from each arm. There was no furniture in the cell; they had to bring their own. The second man, the one the Empty Shell assumed had spoken, was wearing a military uniform. Medals bedazzled the front of his jacket. The third man, who was dressed in the same prison guard garb as the first, held a long leather strap in each hand, the ends of which dragged on the floor.

The Empty Shell let his eyes wander from the leather straps to the medals to the chairs. He had not been beaten yet but knew that it was only a matter of time. The first guard put down a chair and retrieved a key from his belt. He opened the cell door, then picked up the second chair and entered. He placed the chairs precisely two feet apart, facing each other, effectively creating an interrogation room. Then he turned on his heel and marched away, out of the cell and down the hall, proving his military bona fides to the man in the uniform.

"You can call me Colonel," the man in the uniform said. "I've been looking forward to this. We are beginning a long journey together."

He came into the cell and sat in one of the chairs with his back to the door. He motioned to the other chair. The man with the leather straps followed and stood behind him. When the Empty Shell did not move immediately, it seemed as if the guard was going to come help him. But the Empty Shell pushed himself back against the wall and came to his feet of his own accord. Slowly—there was no motion he did not undertake slowly—he arrived at the open chair and sat down.

"Excellent," the Colonel said. "As usual, the writing is stronger than the writer."

"Yes," the Empty Shell said. "That is usually the case."

The Colonel was surprised by the response. But he looked amused, not angry. It was the expression of a man who knew he had the upper hand and it could not be taken away from him.

"Did you know that there is a book of your writing?"

The Empty Shell did not hide his surprise. The government had printed his work? That didn't seem likely, unless they had perverted his words. Had he been turned into propaganda and not even realized it? That would be the worst fate he could imagine. The Colonel smiled at his discomfort.

"Some American university. They collected everything you've written and published it. It's a short book."

The Empty Shell breathed out. He tried to stifle his own smile. The look on the Colonel's face showed him that he'd failed.

"You have always been able to distribute your work effectively. There are people in ministries that have studied the permeation of the Empty Shell. They have created maps of where your poems have been found, plotted the migration of your words. For some, it has been their life's work. They will be disappointed that your writing has disappeared.

"How did you do it? Some of the stories sound more like miracles that facts. One man said he was cutting open a fish to prepare for dinner and he found the words of the Empty Shell in its stomach. Is that possible? Have you been nourishing the fish in the sea as well as the people on the land?"

The Colonel's smile never wavered. Even the Empty Shell doubted the veracity of that story, although he had on occasion popped a rolled-up scroll into a plastic bottle and let it float down the river.

"Another woman insisted that a bird had brought her an Empty Shell poem. A bird! You have such control over the world's fauna! I expect any moment that an elephant will escape from the zoo and crash through that wall to save you!"

The Colonel laughed. The guard behind him was stone-faced. He had a job. It was not to laugh at the Colonel's jokes.

The bird story was true. The Empty Shell had found a pigeon with a broken wing behind the dormitory. He had collected bugs for it and given it water. Before it flew away, he had tied a piece of paper to its leg. The woman had probably killed the pigeon to eat it. Meat could be hard to come by in their country.

"The illustrious Empty Shell! The esteemed Empty Shell!"

The pleasantries were coming to an end. The Empty Shell knew this, as did the man with the leather straps, who flexed his muscles and shook out the straps.

"Those people in the ministries have been reading tea leaves. But they don't have to anymore, do they? Now we have you. You can tell us exactly how your words entered the world."

"It is no more than reading tea leaves for me as well," the Empty Shell said. "The words appeared in my mind. I wrote them down."

"No one helped you. Your family maybe?"

"I have no family."

"You do have family."

"They are alive? I have not seen them since I was a child."

"How about friends, then? Surely some of them would find it exciting to help the world-renowned Empty Shell."

"I have no friends."

"Acquaintances, maybe. Lovers?"

"I am alone."

The Colonel nodded. "That is most certainly true."

The guard with the leather straps took a step forward. He now stood next to the Colonel. The Empty Shell had seen no discernible communication between the two of them. How did he know it was almost time? They said that the Dear Leader could read minds, could make you do things just by looking at you, but no one claimed the same of colonels in the army.

"You know, even one or two names could make your time here easier," the Colonel said. "Much easier."

The Empty Shell did not hesitate. "I am alone."

This time he saw the Colonel nod. The man with the straps stepped forward and pulled back his shoulder. The Empty Shell could see the muscles in his chest tense as he swung the leather straps in his direction like whips. They would land hard. The Empty Shell braced himself, expecting to be knocked out of his chair. Instead, the straps danced around his head and returned to the guard. The Empty Shell was untouched still.

"Why are you fooling around?" the Colonel said.

The guard looked down at the hands that had betrayed him. He took a deep breath, filled with resolve, and tried again.

The guard's arms oscillated up and down, like a traditional drummer's at a New Year's celebration. The leather straps floated in the air between them, fluttering delicately, as the guard became increasingly frenetic in his movement, trying to get them to obey. But instead the straps flitted about freely, studiously avoiding their target. It reminded the Empty Shell of a demonstration in the main square of the capitol many years before where the Dear Leader was celebrating the country's Olympic athletes before they left to compete in a foreign land. The Empty Shell had been fixated by the rhythmic gymnasts, tiny girls who danced with ribbons that seemed to have their own lives. These leather straps and their frustrated guard were the drab counterparts of those colorful creatures.

Finally, tired, the guard let his arms fall to his sides. He looked to the scowling Colonel, who gave him no comfort.

"Give me that!" the Colonel barked.

He grabbed one of the straps from the guard. But it was wrapped around the guard's hand tightly, the better to do his damage. The Colonel continued to yank on it as the guard struggled to free his hand. When he succeeded, the Colonel folded the strap in half, then in half again. He looked it over, then slapped it into his own hand. It made a loud smack. Satisfied, he approached the Empty Shell, considering the whole of his body. With a sadistic leer, he chose his target.

The leather strap cleaved the air, heading for the Empty Shell's crotch. Again, he braced himself. But the strap came to rest gently in his lap. He was surprised when the Colonel left it there.

The Colonel backed away from the Empty Shell. The guard followed him out of the cell. They locked the door behind themselves. Before they walked away, the Empty Shell heard the Colonel say, "We will find a way."

The Empty Shell had acquired a leather strap and two chairs. He knew they didn't belong to him. He stood up and carefully reached through the bars, placing the leather strap outside his cell. If possible, he would try to keep the chairs.

2

The Empty Shell's father was a hollow man. As a child, he had never heard him speak, not inside the house or out. His father went to work every day. The Empty Shell did not know where he went or what he did. His father did not talk about it or anything else, and his mother never mentioned his father's life outside the family. The Empty Shell's mother filled the silence admirably. She talked constantly. For reasons the Empty Shell could never understand, his mother was a true believer in the Dear Leader. Much of her breath was dedicated to praise of that man, who was the father of the current Dear Leader.

Even during the famine, which occupied much of the Empty Shell's younger years, his mother was unwavering in her devotion. He loved his mother. And she did everything in her ability to keep them alive during lean years, scavenging for edible plants, often roots and bark, to add to their hot water, calling it soup. She captured animals too weak or young to escape her own frail frame so they could have the occasional serving of meat. Whenever she returned home with something, she genuflected before the portrait of the Dear Leader by the front door and thanked him for providing it. Often she refused to eat so that her children had more.

The Empty Shell's father brought home the weekly rations provided by the State—rotten vegetables and stale grains better suited for livestock, occasionally packaged goods provided by nearby countries that shared the State's ideology but not its poverty, brightly colored boxes covered with foreign writing that no one in the house could understand. The Empty Shell's mother blamed the imperialists who lived far across the sea, those who had once waged war on their country, for any shortcomings. When the rations came, she thanked the Dear Leader's portrait for his generosity. His mother refused to hear a single negative word about the Dear Leader in her house, and the Empty Shell was convinced that was why his father never spoke.

The Empty Shell thought about his parents as he sat in his cell on one of his new metal chairs. He thought about his siblings as well. He suspected he knew where they were and what their lives were like, but he wondered all the same.

It had been almost a day since the guard had failed to beat him with the leather straps. The prison had been quiet since then. The Empty Shell realized that even in the short time he had been there, the daily sounds of the prison's rhythms had become familiar to him. Screams and pleas, near and far. Gunshots of all calibers. The familiar cadence of military officers berating ordinary citizens. The stomping of boots and dragging of bare feet across the dirt floors. Cracking, breaking, moaning. But all of that had disappeared in the past twenty-four hours, all of the echoes of violence.

The silence did not please the Empty Shell. It was more ominous than the noises themselves.

Other routines had also been interrupted. No one had brought him food or what they considered passed for such. The Empty Shell's stomach complained, his intestines contracting uselessly and painfully. But these were sensations familiar to him, from his childhood and from his recent past. Hunger was an old and constant companion. Only once in the past day had a guard stopped outside his cell. This guard had said nothing. He'd left a cup of water and took the leather strap away. On other days, the Empty Shell had come to expect visitors upwards of a dozen times a day, sometimes to bring him something but usually just to leer and taunt him, recite his work mockingly, spit and piss through the bars in his general direction.

But today, no visitors. Only silence.

The Empty Shell had spent time the night before trying to turn his two chairs into a bed, but it had proved impossible. There was always a part of him hanging off in a manner that made the arrangement more uncomfortable than sleeping on the floor. Now, however, he scooted the second chair in front of the first and put his feet up, an unexpected luxury while he stared and thought. He was comfortable enough that it took him a moment to realize there was a guard opening the door to his cell.

"Come with me," the guard said, gesturing to the hall.

The Empty Shell still wasn't sure what had happened the day before, but he didn't think it significant enough to allow him to ignore orders from guards. He followed the guard, who didn't lock the cell behind them, out into the corridor.

All of the cells were being emptied. Each prisoner had a guard. They walked in two solemn lines, like couples at a deathly ball. The prisoners who were too weak to walk a straight line were steadied by their escorts.

They were led to the opposite end of the building from where the Empty Shell had been originally brought in. He had never left this wing. Once he'd arrived, he had not left his cell. The Empty Shell was surprised that it opened onto a large courtyard, as spare as the space inside, surrounded by four concrete walls and undergirded by a dirt floor. Along one wall was a set of low bleachers, risers five tiers deep. There were already other prisoners sitting on those metal benches, watching them walk in. The Empty Shell could discern no difference between the bedraggled prisoners in the bleachers and the forlorn marchers he entered with. He supposed the difference was that they were the audience and his cohort was the show. Everything that happened in the Empty Shell's country required an audience.

It was never good to be the show.

The Empty Shell's guard patted him on the back and pointed him toward the center of the courtyard. The other guards did the same with their prisoners. The Empty Shell expected a harsh shove, a more definitive instruction, but it didn't come. The other prisoners also seemed confused by what seemed like a polite request. There was nothing else to do, nowhere else to go, so the prisoners complied, huddling together in the center of the open space while the guards circled around them. They stood there for a while, not sure what they were waiting for. The prisoners in the bleachers watched in silence.

Then the Empty Shell heard the barking. He had always been frightened of dogs. They were rarely seen in his country outside the military. Still, it had always struck him as odd that it was dogs that brought a dread to the pit of his stomach despite his having seen far worse depravities committed by his fellow man.

From a different building, the dogs emerged into the courtyard. Their handlers struggled to contain them; the thin leashes seemed ready to snap under the strain. But the dogs were led, snarling and snapping, into formation around the circle. The guards already standing there tried not to betray their nervousness around their new companions but largely failed, shuffling their feet. The handlers were unperturbed by their animals' eagerness to get at the prisoners. The Empty Shell, attempting to stand tall and stoic in the face of his greatest fear, wondered how the dogs knew who the prisoners were. Their unwashed scents must be strong and enticing. With their pointed ears and long snouts, these German shepherds had already homed in on their targets. Then the handlers all shouted a command, and the dogs all sat at silent attention.

"Some of you have experienced unusual occurrences over the past few hours," a voice boomed over them.

The Empty Shell turned to see the Colonel's head and torso above the circle of guards. He was on the opposite side of the courtyard from the bleachers and was addressing the prisoners who sat there through a bullhorn. He had to be standing on a box or a stepladder; he wasn't that tall. The Colonel ignored the prisoners surrounded by the dogs. The Empty Shell knew then that they were already dead.

If his mother were here, she would be praising the Dear Leader through her tears. His father would say nothing. The Empty Shell suddenly realized that he would never write anything again. The two lines he had handed the Swedish diplomat had been his final work.

"You have whispered to each other about impotency," the Colonel continued. "You have committed blasphemy against the Dear Leader, doubting his ability to serve justice through our hands. You have questioned the Nation. You have doubted our strength."

He held out the megaphone and waved it over the crowd. It felt more like a benediction than an implication of everyone's guilt.

"There will be no more whispers. No more blasphemy. No more questions. No more doubt."

The Colonel nodded at one of the dog handlers, who gave a signal to the others. In unison, they reached down and undid the leashes from the dogs. After standing back up, in one voice, they all shouted the same command. The other guards tensed, one foot forward, ready to force any prisoner who tried to flee back toward the dogs.

The dogs burst forward, teeth bared, ready to rip into the prisoners, who cowered into each other, becoming a single mass of humanity ready to be dismantled, chunk by chunk. The Empty Shell conjured up one last blasphemous thought. He was ready for the first tooth or claw to bury itself deep in his flesh. One of the animals locked in on the Empty Shell, who leaned back and held his arms in front of himself defensively. He closed his eyes. The blow came. But it was softer than expected, the pads of the dog's feet landing on his chest rather than sharp teeth at his throat. The force was still enough to knock him backward, sending him sprawling to the dirt floor in a cloud of dust. He felt something wet on his cheek.

The Empty Shell opened his eyes. The dog licked his face again, then playfully tapped its paw on the Empty Shell's chest. The Empty Shell sat up and backed away, expecting another trick, that the handlers would shout a second command that would lead to the real attack. The dog looked at him with its tongue hanging from its mouth, expecting something. When it didn't come, the dog approached again, head down, nuzzling its nose under the Empty Shell's hand. The dog's fur was slightly coarse and bristly to the touch but smoother than the Empty Shell had expected. The dog lifted its head, guiding the Empty Shell's hand to its ears, which felt like velvet on his fingertips.

The dog wanted to be petted, maybe scratched. The Empty Shell didn't know; he had avoided dogs his entire life. Their wants were alien to him. Still, he rubbed the dog's head around the ears, using a circular motion similar to how his mother had caressed his back as a child as he cried over the aching shallow pit of his stomach. The dog seemed satisfied. It fell heavily into him, looking momentarily annoyed when the Empty Shell paused. When he continued, the dog rolled onto its side and lifted its foreleg, exposing its belly. This animal was as transparent as glass. The Empty Shell instinctually understood its desires, scratching the exposed belly at the same time as he ruffled the fur on its head.

The Empty Shell looked around him. The animals were all seeking the same from the other prisoners. Some of the dogs were content to loll in the dirt and receive their love, while others, probably the younger ones, bounded back and forth, hoping to wrestle or play. No teeth were bared, though there was the occasional nip or hopeful bark. The

prisoners had become children enraptured with a lit-
ter of puppies.

But there was still an audience. The guards that
encircled them shifted uncomfortably. The dog handlers in particular didn't know what to do, lacking a
command to control this situation. The Empty Shell
couldn't see the prisoners in the bleachers, but he knew
they were feeling an unfamiliar hope, as was he. What
was happening was not possible. And yet he could feel
the gentle breathing of this animal against his hand,
measured and calm, so unlike the snarling beast that
had been ready to devour him moments before.

The circle of guards opened up, allowing the Colonel to have a better view of the events unfolding in
the center. The megaphone hung limply by his side.
He was indeed standing on an upside-down wooden
crate that was meant to carry fruit, his skin sallow and
pockmarked by years of malnutrition, as was all of
theirs. His face was a blank mask, betraying nothing.

The Empty Shell considered the past two days. The
attack dogs were no less a tool of violence than the leather
straps wielded by human hands. Both were methods used
to hurt, to main, to kill. They were merely implements of
human intent. Left alone by humanity, the leather straps
would hang limply over the back of a chair, the dogs
would live peacefully in search of a game or a compas-
sionate touch. Only a person could turn them into a
weapon. And over the past two days, both had failed.

The Empty Shell extricated himself from his canine
companion, much to the dog's disappointment. He
wanted to try something. If he was wrong, his time in
this prison could become far worse, though he knew
that the progression in that direction was inevitable

anyway. Among the guards, he recognized the man who had tried and failed to beat him with the leather straps the day before. He stood and walked to the guard. He made a fist and formed the thoughts in his head.

I am going to hit you. I am going to hurt you.

The Empty Shell cocked his arm back and thrust it forward, intending to hit the man in the jaw. Instead, his open palm came to a rest on the guard's shoulder. The touch itself was enough of an infraction to end the Empty Shell's days. But the guard only looked at him, surprised, and the Empty Shell knew that he had now experienced what this man had the day before. The dizzying confusion of being unable to harm his fellow man.

The Colonel had seen enough. With a wordless gesture, he brought all the guards to quick attention. They clopped their feet together and stood taller. Another gesture and they marched out of the courtyard, ignoring the prisoners. The handlers clapped their hands twice. Their dogs reluctantly obeyed, returning to their masters and their leashes to be led into one of the buildings.

The Colonel trailed his men. The prisoners considered each other, none of them sure what to do. They were being abandoned, experiencing a relative freedom that had become foreign to them. The Empty Shell knew it was illusory. They were still locked in this prison. Their jailers were merely considering their next steps. His thoughts were confirmed by the Colonel, who glared at him before leaving the yard. In that moment, the Empty Shell remembered the Colonel's words from the day before.

We will find a way.

3

THE MORNING AFTER the dogs, the Empty Shell awoke to find the door to his cell still open. After the guards had departed the day before, a voice on unseen speakers had boomed over the courtyard, demanding that they return to their cells. Like Pavlov's dogs, most of the prisoners obeyed, even when no guards appeared to enforce the order. No one had come to lock them in.

This new morning, there were still no guards in the corridor outside. The Empty Shell approached the opening to his cell with care, stopping at the threshold, concerned that a trap had been set in the dead of night. He scrutinized the ground, squatting for a better view, checking for a trip wire that might set off a bomb. He pressed his face into the floor to check the contours of the dirt, any rises or small ridges that might suggest a buried mine. An open door in his country usually meant someone wanted you to walk through it. Rarely with good intentions. The Empty Shell, as any of his fellow citizens would be, was wary of opportunities.

But he found nothing of concern, nothing to trigger an alarm. Still, he doubted. The Empty Shell picked up one of the chairs and tossed it through the gateway. It clattered into the corridor, coming to a rest on its side, impotent and safe. The Empty Shell followed it out of the cell, pausing after the first step, flinching involuntarily as he braced for the blow that never came.

All of the cells on this hallway were open. Most were empty. There were still men in a few, those who had just woken up, like him, and those who were paralyzed by the uncertainty of the situation. Most of them fell in behind him as he walked down the hall. The Empty Shell remembered arriving at the prison. It had not been that long ago, nor had his time here yet been traumatic enough to make him lose time or memory. The courtyard was through a door to the left, the prison's front entrance to the right, past two guard stations and some administrative offices. All of these posts were unmanned now. The checkpoints, each with a set of bars that had been swung open, posed no barrier to their leaving the prison. This place had been well and truly abandoned. Left to the inmates to determine their own fate.

Other men appeared from other areas of the prison. The Empty Shell realized that everyone had been freed. Others were ahead of him. He could see them exiting the front door, having limped and lurched through other unguarded checkpoints. As he got closer to freedom, the Empty Shell could see men lingering outside, squinting against the bright sun of the day.

The Empty Shell too narrowed his eyes as he left the building. The entrance was on the edge of a paved road that stretched north and south for as far as he could see. There were no other buildings, other than the complex of the prison, anywhere in sight. In front of him, the landscape rose into hills that became mountains in the distance. Behind him, he could only face the brick walls of the prison.

Men were already walking away briskly in all directions. Most headed one way or the other on the road, but some plowed straight ahead toward the spare wilderness of the distant plateaus. The Empty Shell did not move. These men, he assumed, had destinations in mind. Some must have family to return to—wives and children, brothers and sisters, parents who loved them. They walked as if they knew where they were going. Or they still had the will to escape, something the Empty Shell tried and failed to conjure up in himself. Maybe they believed they could walk to the borders to be found in three directions, the fourth leading only to the sea, and they would find a refuge on the other side of them.

These men who left likely saw more hope outside than inside, but the Empty Shell knew that his entire country was a prison, with or without the walls behind him. He wondered where he might go. Back to his apartment on the edge of the city, his job at the ammunition factory? Out into the countryside to return to his childhood home, to see his parents and his siblings, to discover if any of them were alive? Neither option held any more appeal than wandering aimlessly away into nothing.

"It is a trap."

The man who spoke came up next to the Empty Shell. He was both shorter and rounder, amazingly plump given the dietary restrictions he had no doubt suffered through his life. He looked up at the Empty Shell with a sad smile.

"Every step away adds to their crimes. Escape is treason."

The Empty Shell heard the regret in the Round Man's voice. These were not the words of a true believer or a party official but of a man who knew the unfortunate truth. It was also the voice inside his own head.

"Don't you have somewhere to go?" the Empty Shell said.

"Where would I go?" the Round Man answered.

The Empty Shell could have been talking to himself. Together, they turned back to the prison and went inside. Men pressed past them, regarding them with suspicion as they walked the wrong way through the checkpoints. Every man they passed shrank away, expecting to be returned to their cells, despite the fact that they wore the same inmate jumpsuits and caged expressions.

The Empty Shell followed the Round Man into the courtyard. There they found six more men waiting, possibly too scared or weak to leave. Or like him, with nowhere to go.

There was a tall man who held himself upright in a noble posture. A former party official perhaps, someone who had known power but had lost it when he crossed the wrong person, likely unwittingly. Huddling together conspiratorially were identical twins. Upon closer inspection, the Empty Shell could see that they had the exact same scar bisecting their right cheeks and were each missing the middle finger on their left hand. Someone had decided to be meticulous in ensuring that their natural lack of differentiation would be preserved. Two other men milled about, each so nondescript as to be nearly indistinguishable from the other. The last man, older than all of them, sat on the bleachers. Bald with a wispy beard, his body was permanently bent into a right angle. When he finally broke the silence, the Old Man spoke directly to the ground at his feet.

"There are others," the Old Man said. "Others who could not leave. They should not be abandoned to die in the dark."

The Old Man was right, as old men sometimes were. They split up into teams to explore the grounds and buildings. The Twins wandered off together, as did the Undistinguished. The Empty Shell and the Round Man wordlessly agreed to work together. The Empty Shell thought that the Party Official might opt out, choosing instead to stay in the courtyard and take notes on the others. But he too squared his jaw and stalked off, seemingly more determined than any of them.

There were many more cells in the building that they first entered. On the ground floor were wall-to-wall cubicles for the accused. These cells were smaller and dirtier and thankfully all empty. There had been many more prisoners here than the Empty Shell realized. There were stairs at the end of the row, and the two men went down. They found another line of cells, similar to those above, but the feel was more decrepit. The stains on the walls and the floor, occasionally the ceiling, were bigger and still wet. The little light that emanated from the bare bulbs was gray and full of camphor. Items had been abandoned, left on the floor as reminders: restraints, spikes, shreds of clothing. But unexpectedly, the Empty Shell and the Round Man found no occupants left. Every man here, regardless of the damage done to them, had managed to walk away into the light.

At the end of the row was yet another stairway, going down one more floor. The stench of death and decay greeted them at the top. The men considered each other's resolve, their commitment to the Old Man's words, his plea for humanity. They thought about what was left of their own and, after a long pause, went down.

There were no cells in this basement. It was a large room dug out from the bowels of the earth. The floor gave under their feet, spongy as peat moss, releasing fragrant gasses with each step. The air clung to their clothing, clawing at it with moist little talons. There were tables and chairs and manacles and a table saw and in one corner a white box against the wall that could have been either a coffin or a refrigerator. And there were also four bodies, lying on the floor.

The Empty Shell now understood that there was a difference between knowing how far from morality his country had strayed and seeing it firsthand. Every word he had ever written suddenly seemed inadequate.

The Round Man approached one of the bodies first. He rolled it over from its side onto its back, taking care not to bend the thin arm underneath it. He leaned over it and touched the papery skin on its neck. He pulled back as if he had been shocked.

"He's alive."

Together the two men went from body to body, assessing the state of their vitality. All four of them were alive, though barely, and for who knew how long. But the Old Man was right. They should not die in the dark. Not down here. The Empty Shell allowed himself to think that maybe they shouldn't die at all.

"Which one first?" the Round Man said.

The Empty Shell was considering the question, trying not to gag on the stale air that continued to permeate his lungs, when a faint thumping came from the box in the corner, accompanied by a tiny, living sound, like that of a baby animal crying inside a burlap sack. The Empty Shell ran to the box, confirming his initial impression that it was both a refrigerator and a coffin. He pulled open the door. Inside, he found a man folded up on himself. A new stench pummeled the Empty Shell as he reached in to exhume the man.

The man let out an exhalation as the Empty Shell took him in his arms, a sigh more than a moan. The Empty Shell breathed for them both and, with the Round Man's assistance, ascended back to the courtyard.

There they found that the others had also returned, each with their own addendum. The Twins held up a man with no nose, the Undistinguished a man with no ears. The Party Official cradled a man in his arms with no legs. The Empty Shell and the Round Man had recovered the only whole man, the only one who had not lost a piece of himself in this prison—but even as the Empty Shell thought that, he knew it was a lie. They all looked to the Old Man for guidance.

"Lay them down," the Old Man said. "And get the rest."

As they all left the courtyard again, their orders clear, the Old Man rose to his feet, an accomplishment of great effort. One last glance over his shoulder let the Empty Shell see the Old Man approach the first body, whispering down at it. Words of encouragement, the Empty Shell hoped. Or possibly this Old Man was the last person in his country who remembered a prayer.

When they were finished with their task of gathering the damaged and degraded, the beaten and the broken, there were twenty-seven men lying on the dirt of the courtyard. The seven able bodies standing among them looked to the Old Man for what to do next. But the Old Man had returned to the bleachers. He sat and stared at his feet. He had given them the last of his wisdom.

"There's a kitchen," the Party Official said, his voice exactly the rich baritone the Empty Shell would have expected. "For the guards. And showers."

He said it like a man who had been here before under very different circumstances.

They followed the Party Official to the kitchen. There were bags of the thin grains to make the porridge for the prisoners. But there were also containers of heartier oats and wheat flour. Vats of rice. Cans with Chinese characters filled with cut vegetables and cubed fruits in syrup. There was even some meat, not fresh, but strips of dried pork and salted fish that made the Empty Shell's mouth water.

The seven of them made some rice and ate a meal together, opening a can of green beans and another of water chestnuts. They split a single ropy length of jerky. They sat at the table usually occupied by the guards and watched the empty road in front of the prison through a dirty window.

The Empty Shell carried a bowl of rice and vegetables to the Old Man, who thanked him with a small bow a few degrees beyond his permanent ninety. Several of the men on the floor of the courtyard stirred at the aroma of food. The Empty Shell carried his guilt with him back to the kitchen but found it assuaged by the activity he found there. The seven of them spent the rest of the afternoon preparing food of various strengths and consistencies. By dinner, they were ready to try to feed the starved and starving.

They gathered the ones who could stand and walked them into the kitchen, nearly a dozen in all. The men crowded around the guards' table, where they were served. The former prisoners regarded the chopsticks and spoons with suspicion but took them up in their hands when the food arrived. They ate to the best of their abilities, reminding their stomachs and palates of the sensation of real food. For a couple of them, it was too much too fast. They were helped into the bathroom to throw up into a toilet that took the human waste away instead of leaving it with them as a companion.

For those too weak to leave the courtyard, the seven brought the food to them, walking among the bodies with ladles and pots, spooning small amounts into their mouths. Some swallowed without problem. Others choked on it and needed to be raised up to clear the path. But the Empty Shell felt the appreciation in every blink and twitch of the lips as he wiped the excess from their chins and moved on to the next one.

On the second day, the seven decided to cleanse themselves and all who could move or be moved. First, they tested the showers themselves, reveling in the water that fell from above and tickled their skin. Though it was only lukewarm, it refreshed them as nothing else had. They didn't bother to get dressed. There was no need for modesty here. The seven wore slippers they had found in the guards' locker room as they padded back and forth to the courtyard. They monitored the men who were strong enough to stand

and use their own hands to manipulate the soap, which smelled like lavender. For the rest, one or maybe two of the men would enter the shower with them, holding them up and turning them around, using their own hands as if they belonged to the one needing the shower, helping to wash away the dirt and blood and shit and pain that had coated the prisoners for the duration of their time in this place. The ones who did not take additional showers ferried the ragged clothing into the small laundry room, where it too was cleaned to the extent possible. Former prisoners whose clothes could not be adequately recovered, either because they were being held together by filth or had disintegrated altogether, were outfitted with guard uniforms that had been left behind. By the end of the second day, everyone was one step closer to remembering who they were before.

Except for three prisoners who had died over the course of the rejuvenation. The ones who had never managed to eat a single spoonful. The ones who could never walk or even open their eyes. The ones whose breaths had been barely detectable, their heartbeats not even a tap inside their chests. They had been found too late. They were never going to be saved.

"There is a crematorium outside," the Party Official said.

Another procession for the seven, this time beyond the walls of the prison to a small building next door. It was surprisingly easy to fire up the furnace. The Empty Shell shied away from the heat. The three bodies were held upright between them, as if they were merely companions too drunk from a night out to hold their own ground. The Old Man had come with them. None of the rest of them knew what to do. The Old Man spoke to the floor, waving his gnarled hand in the direction of the three corpses.

"I have washed you. I have fed you. I have clothed you. I have taken you home."

All lies that the Empty Shell wished were true. The Old Man had said all he was going to say. He waved them toward the furnace and its human-body-sized opening. One by one, the bodies were lifted and shoved inside to burn away into the night.

On the third day, the Nation returned to claim them.

One of the Twins came into the courtyard, where they had all been lounging on the bleachers, enjoying the sun. He was out of breath and red-faced.

"There's a bus outside," he said.

The Twins and the Party Official had been preparing lunch in the kitchen. The rest joined them at the window. There was a bus in front of the prison. The driver was loitering by the front bumper, smoking a cigarette. There was no sign of anyone else.

The seven returned to the courtyard to report back. There was a new figure standing in the middle of the recovering mass of humanity. He turned and smiled when he saw the Empty Shell.

"I did not expect so many of you to still be here," the Colonel said. "But I thought you might stay."

The atmosphere in the courtyard changed. The Empty Shell had grown used to the difference over the last two days, as if somehow, in this small plot of land, they had been transported away to somewhere better. But the Colonel had returned and brought his country back with him. The feeling was palpable among the Empty

Shell's companions, who all moved away from him out of habit, given the Colonel's interest in him. It was the fear that had returned. The Empty Shell looked sadly at Round Man, remembering his first words. *It is a trap.*

The Colonel opened his arms and addressed the courtyard rather than the prisoners.

"You have all been pardoned," the Colonel said. "Dear Leader has been impressed by the will of the people in this time of challenge. Those who are able will be taken by bus to a facility to be immediately processed. Those who cannot will be processed here at a later time. But the most expeditious route to your freedom is to come with me."

The Empty Shell noticed that the Colonel had to force out the word *freedom*. It had stuck in his throat. He wasn't the only one who heard the stutter. Yet the Empty Shell knew that they weren't really being given a choice. Whatever would happen on that bus or at its destination would also happen here in this prison. The only question for each individual was whether he wanted a change of venue.

"We can still walk away," one of the Twins whispered to the other.

The Empty Shell hadn't considered that possibility. Even now, hearing it out loud, he didn't believe he could leave of his own accord. The Colonel might have heard them. It was impossible to know.

"No one has to go with me," the Colonel said. "You are free to make your own choices. However, you must make them now. The bus will be leaving immediately."

The Colonel walked out of the courtyard, weaving his way through the prisoners, none of them knowing if they were still captives or not. A few of them struggled to their feet and followed the Colonel. The Party Official went, the two Undistinguished directly behind him. The Empty Shell was surprised to see the Old Man also moving in that direction.

"It is time for me to leave this place," the Old Man said as he passed by them.

One of the Twins took a step, and the other stopped him.

The Empty Shell looked to the Round Man, who shook his head.

"I'm not going with him," the Round Man said.

"I am," the Empty Shell said. "It's a trap, but I have to see it."

He shook the Round Man's hand. There were tears in the man's eyes, though they had known each other only two days. They didn't know each other's names; none of them did. It hadn't come up. In a place like this, it was assumed that all names had been forgotten.

"Good luck to you," the Round Man said.

The Empty Shell nodded. "And to you." Then, to him and the Twins, he said, "Take care of them for as long as you can."

There were more than a dozen of them already on the bus. The Empty Shell got on last, just before the driver closed the door. The Colonel sat in the front seat.

"I knew you would come," the Colonel said.

The Empty Shell took a seat toward the back of the bus, which made an awkward jerky U-turn to get moving in the right direction. They were driving south, toward the capitol. If the world had changed in the past few days, the Empty Shell couldn't discern it from the scenery as it passed his window. The world was still stark and bleak and colorless, the people still gaunt and frightened and unable to make eye contact.

An hour into the drive, the Empty Shell became convinced that the "processing facility" would merely be another prison. That this was all an elaborate mind game being played by the Dear Leader and his cronies.

He was less sure of that conviction when the bus arrived at the outskirts of the city. They did not slow or stop all the way to the capitol center.

They were approaching the main square. The bus was stopped at a military checkpoint. There were soldiers everywhere. The Empty Shell craned his neck to see ahead into the square. He could see flutters of the national flag. The familiar voice of the Dear Leader droned on through the loudspeakers, occasionally punctuated by the sounds of the masses, cued to agree or applaud or lament at the appropriate moments. The Empty Shell had attended enough rallies in his lifetime to feel the rhythms of them deep in his organs. His heart, his lungs, his intestines, his spleen all started to palpitate in anticipation of what they were going to be asked to do.

They were not being taken to a processing center or a prison. The only reason a busload of traitors would be driven into the main square for a rally was for an execution. But the Empty Shell wasn't sure that was still possible, though the experience of the last few days could easily have been a setup, elaborate mind control designed for this payoff. He realized that the Colonel was standing up in front of the bus, staring back at him.

We will find a way.

The military checkpoint blocking the street parted for the bus. They drove on. Everything in front of them moved aside. The Dear Leader's voice grew louder around them. The Empty Shell heard only snippets of the speech, but he could tell it was winding down. The end was nearing.

The bus drove to the center of the main square. The monolithic buildings loomed over them: The Hall of Heroes. The Parliament. The shrines to the Dear Leader's father and grandfather. Statues of marble and stone looked down on them from all directions. The soldiers closed ranks back around them. In every direction, citizens filled the bleachers, a far larger audience than they'd had in the courtyard.

The prisoners on the bus—and they all knew now that that was what they still were—did not bemoan their fates. This was what was expected. Anything else would have been a surprise. They deflated into their seats, and when the Colonel said to stand and exit the bus, they did. The Empty Shell disembarked last. As soon as he was clear of the door, the bus drove away. The soldiers on the other side of the square let it through. The Empty Shell looked around for the Colonel, but he had also disappeared.

There were fourteen of them there, standing in the dead center of the main square. Out of habit, they had all tucked their hands behind their backs and turned to face the Dear Leader as he talked. But they also glanced around without moving their heads, taking in the scene, marveling that they were the center of it all.

The Empty Shell, in that moment, decided that it truly was time to give up.

They listened to the Dear Leader's final words.

"To those at home and abroad that doubt our strength. To those, enemy and friend alike, who doubt our will. To those who no longer respect our preeminence and divinity. To those who think the world has changed. To those who don't understand the truth behind our power. To those people, and to everyone else, I give you this."

The Empty Shell stepped backward at the sound of two hundred boots hitting the concrete plaza at once. The soldiers formed a tight circle around the prisoners, maybe thirty or forty of them linking arms and closing in. Another circle seemed to be forming outside that one and a third beyond it. The Empty Shell had no idea what was going on. None of the soldiers were carrying weapons or had them drawn if they were.

The first circle closed in tightly enough that the fourteen of them had nowhere to move, so they jostled each other. Then the Empty Shell noticed something odd about the soldiers in the circle. They each had small wooden platforms on their shoulders, like epaulets. It distracted him. He could think of no purpose for them.

Then the soldiers from the second circle started to climb up the backs of those in the first circle. The fourteen prisoners went silent at the spectacle as the walls around them were quickly two soldiers high, the second layer with their boots planted firmly on the platforms of the first. The Empty Shell was reminded of a class trip in elementary school when they had been brought into the capitol to see a special performance by a Chinese acrobatic troupe. His memory was reinforced even further when the third circle of soldiers began to scale to the top of the first and second.

There was no way that they could maintain that balance, the Empty Shell thought. They were not trained acrobats. They were soldiers, conditioned to do what they were told, no matter how unusual or ill-advised it seemed.

And as the third level started to peer down on them, the Empty Shell realized that they were not supposed to balance. Not for long. They were supposed to fall onto the prisoners. As the first soldier lost his bearings at the top of this shaky pyramid and dropped toward them, the Empty Shell knew that this was the way they had found. No individual soldier could kill them. But if enough accidentally fell on top of them, the prisoners at the bottom would be crushed just the same.

The light from above was blocked out as more bodies fell toward them. The Empty Shell held his arms above him in a hopeless attempt to shield himself. The first soldier did pass by harmlessly, missing the prisoners and crunching onto the ground. But more were plummeting toward them, body after body. Some of the prisoners dropped to the ground, pulling their legs in tightly, coiling into a fetal position for protection. Others rushed the first circle before futilely realizing they couldn't push past. And the bodies kept falling. And others climbed up the outside in their place, lemmings to the edge of a cliff. Above them, most towers were three high, briefly then again, though a couple reached loftier heights four tall.

Bodies on the ground and from above made it impossible for the Empty Shell to keep his feet under him. He fell like the rest. They piled on top of him. He searched for cushions of air, places where there were no bodies, no soft flesh or scratchy fabrics blocking his airways. The light disappeared completely at the bottom of this human silo that was rapidly filling up on top of him.

This was the end. He felt no pain, though he knew he was being crushed. He felt no fear, though he knew that soon there would be no air to breathe. The Empty Shell was calm, at peace and ready.

The stack of limbs and torsos grew above him. The Empty Shell was sinking into the earth, through the concrete of the square, into the ground below. He felt himself losing consciousness, losing himself, disappearing.

Then the world shifted again. Like an earthquake, bodies jerked and twitched around him. Not the agony of the dying. Not the spasms of the lost. This was something else. Bodies were being moved. Against their will in some cases, to their delight in others. They rolled away from each other, each on its own unseen conveyor belt, making its own space apart from the others. And the light above him returned. The towers of men were no more. The circle of soldiers around him burned off like mist.

The Empty Shell found himself lying on his back looking up at the perfect blue sky. There was not a single cloud. The sun had dipped behind the monument to the first Dear Leader, illuminating the square but blinding no one. The silence around him was utter and complete. He was wedged between bodies, a soldier to his left and prisoner to his right, his head touching a boot and his own foot on the arm of another man. Yet he was on top of no one and no one covered him. They had each found their own space, had been moved into their own places, forming a tapestry of humanity before the assembled crowd, a quilt of living bodies.

The Empty Shell was unharmed. Nothing broken, nothing cut. A miracle never to be explained. He breathed in deep, easily, the air sweet in his lungs. He tasted the vaguely sooty pollution of the capitol on his tongue and relished it.

No one moved. In that moment, the Empty Shell knew what he had to do. He had to stand up. An action more important than any of his words. Either a final act or a first one.

So he pulled his legs toward him, arching his back and sitting up. The crowd tried not to react, but there might have been a stifled gasp here or there. The Empty Shell rose to his feet. He turned toward the stage where the Dear Leader had been speaking. He looked to the podium where he had been standing.

That space was empty now. The Dear Leader had gone. And for a long moment, the Empty Shell stood alone.

EXCURSUS G:
KAHALE

A ISAKE HELD THE fish out in front of him, pointed in Kahale's direction. He did his best Aretha Franklin impression as the gasping fish lip-synced along with him.

Kahale sighed deeply. Aisake was a jukebox filled with a bottomless collection of Motown records. Every morning for three years, ever since Kahale had agreed to take Aisake on as an apprentice on his boat, he had been serenaded by the first catch of the day. When the net first came up and the initial load slopped out onto the floor of the boat, turning it into a roiling mass of all manner of creatures flopping and scuttling and gasping for air, Aisake picked a companion for his duet. Unfortunately, Aisake's voice was barely even suited for karaoke, let alone soulful renditions of the greatest hits of American music.

Aisake laughed at his own final horrific note. Turning the fish to face himself, he smiled.

"You sing like Jesus resurrected," Aisake said.

"There was nothing heavenly about that," Kahale said, not hiding his annoyance.

Aisake laughed again and got down to work. He tossed his singing partner into the resort cooler, then dove into the writhing pile at his feet. Within minutes he had finished most of the sorting for the first load. Fish for the resort. Fish for the local market. Those to keep for his family and Kahale's. Those that were good for nothing but being tossed back into the sea.

Kahale considered this man, who had long since graduated from apprentice to employee. Aisake was annoying. He was an idiot, though a harmless and jovial one. Shirtless and unconcerned, Aisake had a robust middle that jiggled around the waistband of his shorts as he stooped and shuffled through the pile of potential seafood. Nothing seemed to faze this man. He was always happy. And all of that would be fine for Kahale in a friend, a drinking buddy, a coworker. But Aisake was in love with his sister. He wanted Kahale's blessing to marry her. The equation changed significantly in considering Aisake as a possible family member.

But the morning was perfect and the ocean was calm, which eased Kahale's mind. Out here, staring into the insubstantial blue of the sky and the undulating water roiling below them, both of which stretched out into the infinite distance only to meet at a thin white line, everything seemed less troubling to Kahale. Even Aisake's unwavering love for his sister. Even the fact that his sister loved this buffoon with equal if not greater fervor.

His sister thanked him every day for giving Aisake a reason to stay on their tiny island, a way to make a living that didn't require him to move to Majuro to work on the big commercial boats run by the Chinese and Japanese, catching tuna and swordfish to be shipped off to foreign countries. Accidents were not uncommon on those boats. Even those who didn't get hurt developed long-term problems from the back-breaking work, driven by unforgiving supervisors.

Kahale's sister was ten years younger than him, as was Aisake. He loved her like she was his own daughter. Of course, his own daughter loved her aunt more than her father, and made no secret of it whenever she got mad at him in a six-year-old pique. His daughter wasn't the only one mad at him. His wife also thought he was being an ass for withholding his blessing, and made no secret of her feelings.

Aisake had turned his attention to belting out *R-E-S-P-E-C-T* with his back facing Kahale and his abundant ass shaking in his direction. It only hardened Kahale's convictions. Once all the fish were cleared and Aisake had taken up the push broom to slosh the excess water over the open back edge of the boat, Kahale joined his sole employee to reset the winches in preparation for dropping the net back into the water for a second pass. They made decent money selling to the locals and the resort, where rich Americans and Europeans came to fish for marlin and feel good about the fact that their own meals were all being sourced from native Marshallese fishermen and farmers.

"Something's stuck up there," Aisake said.

Aisake was looking up at one the main struts that supported the winch and net. Kahale followed his eyes to a wire that had gotten tangled in the cable. Before he could say anything, Aisake was scaling up to free it. He was a big man but remarkably agile. Kahale almost called out for him to be careful with his fingers; the last thing he needed was to bring Aisake back without all his digits. His sister and his wife and his daughter would never let him hear the end of that. His daughter also loved Aisake more than she loved her father. Kahale couldn't help but grin as he thought of her little scowling face.

By the time he turned back to Aisake, the cable had been cleared, but his employee wasn't coming down, instead hanging on to the post ten feet up, looking out over the ocean.

There was a large ship in the distance, a dark smudge on the horizon. Kahale shielded his eyes with his hand, trying to get a better view without the glare of the sun. The ship was moving, long and sleek, like a dagger bisecting the sea and sky. Nothing like the plodding commercial fishing boats that lumbered around the islands. The ship was getting bigger. It seemed to be moving their way. It took only a few more moments before Kahale realized it was an American warship.

These islands used to belong to the Americans, and they still kept a military base on one of the atolls, where they tested missiles and other weapons. The islands had been a guinea pig for the Americans for decades. The elders on the island still told stories of their childhood, of when the Americans had set off their world killer, the bomb that turned night into day and set the sky on fire. They told of birds dropping out of the sky and fish washing up on the beach with a dozen fins and no eyes. They told of the new diseases, the dying men and women whose bodies bloated and blistered and grew lumps the size of coconuts. Unlike the other ancient stories they told, of willful gods and wily tricksters, myths meant as cautionary tales, these stories were all true.

Kahale had seen the warships on the horizon on occasion. But his island and the military base were on opposite ends of the island chain. There was little occasion for the Americans to visit here except to do some deep-sea fishing on leave. There was no reason for one of their warships to be approaching his home.

"Aisake! Come down! We're going in!"

Aisake looked down on him like he was crazy. They had pulled in only one catch. An average morning was four or five, if not more.

But Aisake scurried down as Kahale rushed to the front of the boat. With a quick check to make sure that everything was secure, he fired up the engine and made a U-turn. This boat was not built for speed, but it could move when it had to.

"What's gotten into you?" Aisake said, joining him at the helm.

"Just a bad feeling," Kahale said.

He didn't have any better explanation. He was just suddenly overwhelmed by the need to be home with his wife and daughter. He looked over his shoulder. The American warship was definitely coming their way. It made no sense, but there it was. Kahale always trusted his instincts. They hadn't failed him yet.

But why would the Americans be coming out here? There had been a minor sensation in Parliament the previous week. Even in their tiny island country, Kahale's even tinier island was generally ignored— only a few hundred people living at the end of the world. Just as he liked it. Their chief had a seat in Parliament like all the chiefs, but he rarely spoke and was even more rarely listened to. Until last week, when he'd decided to declare his island an independent nation. It was ridiculous, of course, and treated by everyone as a joke. Their chief was a bit of a communist, but also more than a bit senile. His antics were harmless and he was generally tolerated. But the Americans didn't like communists. Surely they didn't care about this one. Yet here was the warship coming their way.

Kahale pushed the ship harder. Aisake stood on his chair and held his arms out to his sides, letting the air pummel him fully. His tongue poked out of the corner of his mouth as if he were a dog hanging out a car window. Their home grew in front of him. Soon Kahale could see the docks.

The boat eased into Kahale's berth. The dock boy rushed over and tied it to the moorings. Kahale killed the motor. Only when the boat went silent did he realized that his heart was racing as fast as the engine. He wondered if he was having a panic attack. Maybe this had nothing to do with the American warship. Maybe he was just losing his mind. The way Aisake was looking at him now did nothing to dissuade him from entertaining that possibility.

They weren't the only ones who had noticed the visitor on the horizon. The docks as well as the beaches down the shoreline were lined with people gazing out at the approaching ship, pointing and chattering. But the mood was celebratory. No one else seemed to be sharing Kahale's sense of impending doom. He felt like he was running out of time.

Kahale leapt out of the boat. He ran toward his pickup truck in the lot.

"Hey!" Aisake yelled after him. "What about the fish?"

The fish could wait. He needed to get home. Now.

The truck was unlocked. Kahale jumped into the driver's seat. Only then did he realize that he had left his keys on the boat. He heard a jingling through the passenger-side window.

"You probably need these," Aisake said, climbing in. "You're looking kind of scary."

Kahale glanced in the rearview mirror. He was sweating, his face darker than usual, flushed with blood. He didn't know the man staring back at him. If it was a panic attack, a mental break, that just made him want to be at home even more. That was the easiest place to come to grips with what was happening to him. He grabbed the keys and jammed them into the ignition.

As they barreled over the dirt roads, Aisake seemed even happier than usual, if that was possible. He even stuck his head out the window and howled. They tore out of the main village. The trees rose around them, shrouding them from the world outside. The pickup skidded off the main road onto the smaller driveway that led to his family's property, past the rows of coconut and breadfruit trees they harvested for some additional income. He came to an abrupt stop in the clearing, within sight of the various buildings on the property, solid but modest, kicking up a cloud of dust around them. Aisake stared at his boss and aspirational brother-in-law with concern.

"Don't go scaring anyone with those crazy eyes," Aisake said, only half joking.

A quiet descended around them. That was when they heard the whistling. Not a pleasant tune but more of a screeching high in the sky, getting louder. Underneath the constant squeal of that noise, they could make out a series of booms in the far distance, out in the ocean where the warship floated.

Kahale scanned the area until he found his wife and daughter nearby, feeding the chickens. They were looking at him, confused. He shouldn't be home at this hour. Kahale ran to them. He took his wife and daughter in his arms just as the first missile screamed over their heads, falling toward the far end of the island. Aisake also watched it fly past, eyes wide with wonder and fear. He called out Kahale's sister's name and ran toward the low-slung house where she still lived with her parents.

Two more missiles screamed overhead. Kahale and his wife and their daughter fell to their knees, anticipating the blasts that would rock the island and make the trees fall, engulf them in fire and death. They clung to each other as more missiles filled the sky, one after another after another, and whispered words of love to each other.

One of the missiles grew larger than the other, its nose pointing down at them. It had targeted them. It wanted them. Kahale pulled his family closer and started to mourn the loss of everyone he loved.

The missile made impact with his parents' house, sending the splinters from the roof scattering in all directions around it. Kahale closed his eyes, expecting to die.

But he lived. There was no explosion, not here and not in the distance. Not a single earth-shattering blast to be heard anywhere on the island. Kahale and his wife looked into each other's eyes, reassuring each other that they were still here, still whole. They whispered strength into their daughter's ears. They peered up at the sky. The perfect blue had been marred by a latticework of vapor trails, which were rapidly dissolving into an artificial layer of clouds. But no more missiles cleaved the air above them. Kahale's parents' house was still standing, though the tail of the missile protruded out of the hole in the roof it had made, like a new chimney.

Kahale ran to the house, trailed by his wife and daughter. He stopped them at the door and went in alone, afraid that the structure had to be unstable, that it could fall at any provocation.

Aisake and Kahale's sister were huddled on the floor in the middle of the open common room. Aisake had folded his body around her, enveloping her and protecting her with his ample size. She looked warm and comforted within him. They fit together perfectly.

The missile hung in midair above them, the angry red tip of it, where the explosives were likely housed, pointed at Aisake's back, nearly touching the midpoint between his shoulder blades. It would have to go through him to get to Kahale's sister. But it couldn't penetrate Aisake, the bulk of him an immovable shield.

Kahale thought this couldn't be real. Maybe they were dead, frozen in a way station before moving to the next world.

But then his sister and his future brother-in-law looked at him. Their eyes were alive. Cautiously, he beckoned to them. They ran to him, out from under the missile, which fell the remaining feet as soon as they vacated the space, driving itself two feet deeper into the floor of the house. But still it did not explode.

Kahale embraced both of them, and they hugged him. They cried together.

"You have my blessing," Kahale said.

MEMORIAL

DAB

USUALLY ON WEEKENDS, Dab and his mother filled their time with excursions. Dab had no idea where she found these things, but on Friday she always had a list of activities for the two of them. Concerts, festivals, hikes, museums. There was always something going on in the area, and Dab's mother had a strong allergy to staying in the house, no matter what the weather. It had been going on for as long as Dab could remember. It was always just him and his mother, even though the outings had started when his brother and sister still lived in the house. Only recently had Dab put together that it was a way for his mother to escape the near constant fights she had with her teenage children. Time with her compliant child to avoid her surly ones.

This weekend was different. Dab's mother didn't want to go anywhere. She never strayed far from the TV, which was locked on the news. When school had ended, Dab had run home, using the same escape route as a couple of days before, through the backyards, even though no one was chasing him. They didn't need to. He could feel them, mere steps behind, dabbing away. Dab had not stopped running until he was locked inside the house, facedown in his pillow, crying. He tried to comfort himself by imagining the bizarre events his mother might have planned for the next two days. She lived her life in a constant state of disarray and always required the distraction as much as he did right now.

But she had arrived home from work and turned on the television before even saying hello, before coming to find him in his room. She didn't seem to notice he was upset. She didn't cook dinner. They ordered a pizza and ate it on the couch. The next day, Dab had cereal for breakfast, made them both mac and cheese for lunch, and convinced his mother they needed to eat dinner, at which point she ordered Chinese. On Sunday, they both ate leftovers whenever they were hungry.

Dab worried that his mother was having a breakdown. He had memories of such events happening when he was younger. His brother used to say that Mom was going dark before he himself decamped to wait it out at a friend's house. College had offered Dab's brother the ultimate escape plan; he'd fled to the opposite coast and never come home. On the other hand, Jane had never abandoned Dab when their mother disappeared into herself—she had picked up the slack, getting him to activities and playdates, Even after Jane left for college, she had stayed around, choosing a school only an hour or so away.

Jane would always try to explain what had set their mother off. It was always something external, something in the news, a school shooting or an election, a natural disaster or a war. He wanted to talk to Jane now. She always seemed to know why this was happening and also that it would pass. Dab wanted Jane to come home. But she had gone on the camping trip and wasn't answering any texts. Dab hoped she had no cell service. At this moment, the thought of his sister ignoring him was too devastating to consider. He could call his brother, but he decided this was not a crisis of such proportions yet.

The news that played on an endless loop throughout the house all weekend seemed to be good. But it was clear that it was also the source of his mother's agitation. She sat curled up with her legs tucked under her, an air of disbelief etched on her face. The newscasters, despite being made up and perfectly coiffed, mirrored his mother in their voices. Some displayed a sense of wonder at the events happening around them. But most of their voices were tinged with fear and laced with confusion as they tried to figure out what was going on without resorting to folding themselves into a perpetual hug like Dab's mother had.

She didn't spend the entire weekend on the couch. She went to the bathroom. She got food and water from the kitchen. At some point she closed the blinds to avoid the light of the day outside. At times, Dab heard her on the phone with friends, discussing what they didn't understand about the state of the world.

Dab spent most of the weekend in his room on the computer, alone. He didn't watch the news when he wasn't with his mother. He'd had enough of it. Though some of it was fascinating, such as the clip one network played repeatedly, each time trying to give it new context.

In the footage, a group of women in an African country that had suffered for years under a dictator formed a circle and linked arms around a young man with a gun. The man grew increasingly agitated, shouting, pointing the gun in their faces, spitting at the ground. But the women didn't move. They merely swayed around him and started to sing. The man, who might still have been a teenager, wanted to push his way out of the circle. But every time he approached a woman or tried to break the link between their arms, he seemed to lose control of his muscles or maybe his will to fight. After a couple of minutes of seething, the young man put down his gun. Only then did the women open their arms and let him pass. As he ran away, they continued singing.

The footage made Dab feel safe. He wanted to be in that circle with those women. But that clip, like all the commentary and video, made his mother fidget. At one point, late on Saturday night, Dab asked her why it was bothering her so much. She just turned to him as if she didn't recognize her own son.

"Do you believe it?" she said, making it clear that she did not.

And Dab understood that. It was hard to believe. There were interviews with police officers swearing that there had been no violent crimes in days. There were reporters, still wearing helmets and flak jackets, wandering around war zones, surrounded by collapsed buildings, claiming that no bombs fell anymore, no gunfire kept the children of this devastated country awake at night. There was the security cam footage of the attempted suicide bombing in a shopping mall in Paris. The would-be bomber disappeared in a bright blast that became a supernova imploding on himself.

When the bright light cleared, all the stunned people who would have been his victims formed a wary circle around his charred, mangled body. The story was the same everywhere in the world, yet every story was different. The implications overwhelmed Dab's mother.

Dab desperately wanted to watch the news with Jane. She would see it as a miracle, laughing and smiling at the wonder of it all, and Dab would be able to feel the same. Instead, his mother's agitation infected him.

"If this can happen," she said once, to no one in particular, as Dab lingered in the doorway. "Then what comes next?"

Throughout the weekend, Dab mainly stayed in his room with the internet for company. The videos were proliferating, falling into two major categories. There were those taken by people testing the boundaries of their limitations. People shooting at other people with guns, crossbows, slingshots, flares, anything they could find, all failing to hit their mark, to the delight of both the target and the attacker. People trying to get into fights—kicking, punching, biting, headbutting—to no avail. All manner of attempts to do physical damage, all dutifully archived, had proven unsuccessful.

But the videos that racked up even more views focused on the idiots who hadn't quite figured out the rules of the new order, those who didn't understand the distinction between an inability to hurt others and the inability to get hurt. The morons who jumped off the roof like superheroes or rode their dirt bikes into brick walls or jumped headfirst through plate-glass windows expecting to be invincible. Other idiots stabbed their own hands or lit themselves on fire or shot themselves in the foot, expecting similar results. Some of the news stories his mother was watching were about these kids filling the emergency rooms or arriving at hospitals dead on arrival.

But most of the time, the videos barely distracted Dab from his real problem: he couldn't get Connor off his mind. Sometimes he just found himself thinking about his classmate. Other times, he realized he could still feel Connor's body pressing against him in the backyard. Confused and nervous, Dab headed down another rabbit hole that started with a simple three-word Google search: *Am I gay?*

He had to engage the safe search function to filter out the porn, which he saw a little of only to find himself so disturbed and disoriented by not knowing whether this was really what sex was like that he had to clear his mind with funny animal videos before continuing. Once his search was sanitized, Dab found himself starting with quizzes, of which there were a surprising number. Most were of the multiple-choice variety: *do you like this or that?* This being the internet, many of them trafficked in the most blatant of stereotypes. Rock music or show tunes? Barbecue or brunch? San Francisco or Dallas? But others were harder to game out. Cats or dogs? Red or blue? McDonald's or Burger King? Dab trudged through them all, answering hundreds of questions on dozens of quizzes. He tried to answer every one of them honestly, hoping for some guidance and clarity. He got none. Some said he was gay, some said he wasn't. A few determined he was somewhere in between.

So, after that dead-end exercise, Dab turned to the videos. He entered a one-way conversation with the world, watching person after person, gay, straight and in between, telling their stories. Coming out to family and friends. Learning that their siblings were gay. Being bullied and scared. Fighting back with varying degrees of success. There were kids who had been rejected by their parents and kids who had been embraced by their grandparents. Boys who'd waited until college to come out and girls who had known since middle school. So many videos of people who had found love and learned to love themselves. So many videos of people who felt trapped and judged by their families and communities, who were desperate and ready to do something drastic to end their pain. It was dizzying and frightening. Dab tried to process it, but there was too much information and the compendium of it only proved to him that his own life could spin out in any of those directions.

Dab wanted to talk to his mother. He wanted to ask her questions. But every time he emerged from his room, she was immersed in the unending news cycle, so he would just sit with her in silence before retreating again.

By Sunday, the talking heads had shifted to commentary, trying to make sense of the events around them. Some saw the dawning of a new age of enlightenment for humanity, a chance to be better than before. Others saw an impending apocalypse, a complete collapse of societal norms, unable to envision a world where order was maintained in any way other than the ultimate threat of violence.

As he fell asleep Sunday, more confused and concerned than he had been on Friday, Dab wondered if his mother would go to work in the morning. He didn't know if he had to go to school. In the morning, he smelled the coffee coming from the kitchen, heard his mother clattering around making breakfast, and he had his answer.

"Hurry up," his mother said. "You don't want to be late."

It was as if the weekend had never happened, as if Dab had slipped into an alternate universe for two days only to wake up this morning back at home. His mother had gone dark, then returned to the light. Dread rose inside Dab as he realized that he had to go back to school.

Dab and his mother left the house together. She got in her car, headed for work. He began the long walk to school, which he lengthened to the greatest extent possible through his shuffling steps.

His phone dinged, reminding him he had to silence it for school. He had left it on all weekend, hoping to be alerted immediately when Jane popped up.

A text from Jane:

I'm later than I thought. I'm coming to get you.

Dab stopped and read it again. He didn't know what it meant, but it thrilled him. Had he made a plan with Jane that he'd forgotten? That didn't make sense. There was no chance his mother would let him do something with Jane instead of going to school. He stood in the middle of the sidewalk, paralyzed. Where was she coming to get him? He texted back.

Coming to get me? I'm headed to school.

It sent. He waited. His phone was silent. Dab didn't move, even as the world streamed around him. Kids he recognized from school. Parents walking the smaller children to the elementary school next door. After a few minutes, Dab continued toward school, even slower than before.

The late bell rang as Dab turned the corner. He could see the principal turn on his heel and head into the building. Everyone would be seated in his first class when he walked in. He imagined everyone giving him a simultaneous dab, including the teacher. With a sigh, Dab trod up the walk toward the front door.

"Dabney!"

His name was accompanied by some familiar honking. He turned to see his sister's beat-up, belching old car roll to a halt at the curb. Dab had never been so happy to see that piece of crap. Jane was leaning over the passenger's seat, beckoning for him to come. Dab ran over.

"I tried to get home before you left. Sorry. Get in."

Dab looked through the open window. The front seat was covered with food wrappers, notebooks, clothing, some plastic silverware. Jane noticed the mess and started tossing it all into the back seat. Still, Dab didn't get in.

"I have to go to school," Dab said.

"Not today. I need you."

Dab smiled. She needed him. He almost forgot he was angry at her for abandoning him all weekend. He opened the back door and tossed his backpack on top of the mess, then climbed into the front seat. Only then did he see his sister clearly. She was wearing a fancy dress, possibly the one she had worn at her high school graduation. And she had makeup on, which was a rarity for her. It was streaking black around the corners of her eyes. She might have been crying. Not now, but earlier. Jane noticed him studying her. She smoothed her dress around her thighs.

"I didn't know what to wear. I hope this is okay."

She said it more to herself than Dab. Jane looked at her face in the mirror. She evened out the makeup around her eyes with her fingers. Then she turned back to Dab and scowled.

"You're going to have to change. I really thought I was going to catch you at home. I was trying to time it so Mom would be gone first."

"We leave at the same time," Dab said.

Jane looked at him sadly, as if she wished she still knew that. She pulled away from the curb and made a U-turn in the middle of the block. Dab wondered if he should ask her to call the school. They would call his mother. It would be a thing. Everyone would worry. Jane seemed to read his mind.

"I texted Mom," Jane said. "I told her I had you. Then I turned my phone off."

Jane laughed. Dab loved that sound. It infected him. Then he remembered he was mad at her.

"You didn't answer my texts," Dab said.

"I'm sorry," Jane said. "You knew I was camping. I had no coverage."

"You got home last night," Dab said, believing that won the argument.

Jane was quiet for a moment. She drove them through their familiar streets. But she looked lost to Dab. He thought she might start crying again.

"I know. I'm sorry. I just . . . it was a bad weekend."

"Yeah, it was," Dab said. "Mom went dark."

Jane looked at him. Dab felt some satisfaction at her surprised look.

"But she went to work this morning," Jane said.

"Yes," Dab said.

"Then she's fine. And you?"

"I dealt with it."

Jane smiled as they pulled into the driveway of their childhood home, past for her, current for him.

"You still fit into that suit you wore for Robert's wedding?" Jane said.

Dab nodded, confused.

"I wasn't sure. You look bigger than before."

"Why do I need to put on a suit?"

Jane bit her lip and stared straight ahead out the windshield.

"We're going to a funeral."

Dab spit out his follow-up question before it lodged in his throat.

"Who died?"

"Someone I wish you had met. A friend of mine."

Jane got out of the car and Dab followed. He changed clothes as quickly as he could. She helped him tie his tie. He half expected their mother to burst into the house, yelling at Jane for taking him out of school. But they got back to the car without being confronted. Jane pulled away from the house.

"He was supposed to be my camping buddy. He had never been camping either. Everyone else grew up doing this kind of thing with their families. Can you imagine Mom spending a weekend in the woods?"

Dab laughed. Their mother was perfectly happy in nature in small doses and daylight. She was not that fond of bugs or creatures that came out at night or sleeping on the ground or darkness and chaos in general.

"After he got shot, we decided that we were still going on the trip. He was still alive when we made that decision. And then he died and we were still going. We needed to be together to talk about him and to miss him and to cry together. So that's what we did. That's what camping is going to be for me forever."

Jane fiddled with the radio. She found a song she liked and started singing along quietly under her breath.

"What was his name?"

Jane turned to Dab. She seemed surprised he didn't know. But her expression faded into a sad smile. She ran the backs of her fingers over Dab's cheek, sending a tiny shiver through his small frame.

"His name was Malcolm," she said. "He reminded me of you sometimes. He was just . . . good."

*   *   *

They drove in silence for a while after that. Jane took them out of town and onto the highway. They were headed for the city. She continued to flip through stations, pausing now and then for snippets of music she liked.

After some time, she started to talk about Malcolm. Dab listened and asked no questions. Jane had met Malcolm in class. He wasn't living on campus like she was, so she'd introduced him to her friends, and he'd become part of their group. With every story she told, Dab liked him more and felt her loss deeper. And as she continued to talk, he wondered what she wasn't telling him. Wondered whether there was more to their relationship. Something developing. There was an emptiness in her voice at times, gaps that would never be filled, a loss of something that had yet to be found. And as they entered the city and started navigating the narrow streets, they didn't talk at all, letting the radio and the voice of the GPS app fill the void.

It wasn't until they got close that Dab realized they were headed for the cathedral. It was the biggest and oldest church in the city, the kind of place tourists visited. Normal people didn't have funerals there. It was a place for rich people and politicians.

"Was Malcolm famous?" Dab asked as Jane pulled into a spot a few blocks away from the cathedral.

"He wasn't," she said with a sigh. "None of this is really about Malcolm. They're calling him the Last Victim. Most people don't even know his name."

Dab had heard someone talking about the Last Victim on the news. He'd had no idea it was Jane's friend.

After walking the final blocks, they got into a line to get into the cathedral. Security checked Jane's purse and ran a wand over both of them. Jane showed them a piece of paper that seemed to be a ticket, but Dab thought it must be an invitation. But he doubted both options, not sure if funerals needed either.

Inside, someone handed them a program. The cathedral was magnificent. Light streamed through stories-high stained glass. The stone arches of the ceiling rippled above them. It made Dab a little dizzy to look up at them. Jane nodded and gave small waves to a few people scattered around the endless pews, which were filling up fast. They looked young, around her age, probably the classmates and friends from Jane's stories. But they all seemed to be with family members. Dab thought he might be the youngest person here, but then he saw more children, some younger than him toward the front, probably relatives of Malcolm's. Jane spotted two open seats off to the side and ushered them in.

As his sister zoned out, Dab opened the slim program. He scanned the list of speakers: Both of their senators. An actor whose name he recognized. Other people he had heard of. This looked like it was going to take a while. And then he stopped cold when he saw the last name.

"The president is here?"

Jane sighed. She shrugged. Dab looked around toward the pews in the front. There were a surprising number of familiar faces. People he recognized from the news. People he had seen on TV and in movies. He thought maybe that one man shaking hands in the front was a famous technology billionaire whose name he couldn't remember. Was that why Jane had brought him here? He didn't imagine he would ever see these people again. But it didn't seem like his sister to care about things like that or to want him to.

Dab felt himself relax when Jane took his hand. Usually her palm was warm, but it was a little cold, a little clammy right now.

"I really am sorry I didn't talk to you this weekend. When I got home, I tried to text you, but nothing I wrote sounded right. I should have called you. I'm sorry I didn't."

Jane paused. Dab turned toward his sister. She was gazing off into the distance.

"I brought you here because I'm selfish. I needed to be here, and I needed to not be worrying about you. And the only way I could figure out how to do that was to bring you with me."

"It's okay," Dab said. "I didn't really want to go to school anyway."

He meant it to sound like a joke, but it didn't. It felt like a confession. Or maybe a concession.

"I know you don't," Jane said. "But you have to be there. You need to learn and grow and thrive and become the amazing person you're going to become. And you can't let those kids stop you from doing that. They don't matter. Their bullying and their name-calling and their mean little comments are just them trying to make themselves matter. But they don't matter. Not to you. Not to me. You know what matters?

"You matter. Who you are. Who you want to be. Who you will become. That matters. And anyone who doesn't want to help you get there doesn't matter at all."

Dab wanted to believe her. But it was hard. Those kids were hard to ignore. They were stronger and more confident and better looking and happier. How could they not matter?

"You know I wasn't popular in middle school, right?" Jane said.

Dab had had no idea.

"Kids used to pick on me. They didn't like the way I dressed, and I let myself not like it either. I had acne and they called me names. They deflected from their own flaws by criticizing mine. And you know what? Some of those kids are now friending me. I'm not sure if they don't remember. Or maybe they will apologize someday at some reunion. But it doesn't matter. It doesn't matter if they want to apologize or if they don't remember. And these kids being mean to you won't matter someday. They didn't matter to me in high school. They don't matter to me in college. You won't ever forget the people who did this to you, but I hope you will realize they don't matter."

Dab felt himself tearing up. He didn't know how to not care about them and what they said.

"It's hard," Dab said, so softly he wasn't sure Jane heard him.

But then she was hugging him. Dab fell deep into her arms. Jane whispered in his ear.

"I know. Today is hard. Tomorrow will be hard. But that's okay. Because today will also be wonderful. And so will tomorrow. You aren't just here because I'm selfish. You're here because I needed you here. You are the most important person in my life, and I needed you here to help me get through this hard day. And I will need you tomorrow. And the next hard day. And the good day after that. Okay?"

They were both crying now. Dab knew he was getting the front of her dress wet and he knew Jane didn't care. He was even starting to believe that those kids at school didn't matter.

The two of them stayed like that right until the famous rapper and the even-more-famous singer opened the ceremony with a rendition of "Amazing Grace."

ANN

THIS MEMORIAL SERVICE had turned into a massive made-for-TV spectacle, and Ann knew it was entirely her fault.

She thought about this as she watched the two famous actors reenact one of their iconic scenes from one of Malcolm's favorite movies. The two men—the Oscar winner who had been slumming in the movie and the former athlete who was seeking legitimacy—played an FBI agent and a prisoner with a secret, respectively. They had also been brothers in the film, which was a ridiculous action-comedy that made hundreds of millions of dollars and spawned sequels.

Jake had made Ann go with him to see the movie when it first came out years ago. She hated that kind of film, the dialogue and characters seeming like nothing more than a breather between car chases and violent set pieces. As he always did, Jake sneered at her when she let her hand drift into the popcorn and hit her arm when something interesting happened on-screen.

Ann remembered this scene. The characters had just survived a harrowing plummet down an elevator shaft, escaping an explosion that had decimated the floor of the skyscraper they were previously on. It was the last dramatic scene before the climactic showdown with the bad guy. By all rights, the two characters should have been dead. Instead, they picked themselves up and each gave a soliloquy, two monologues about family and loyalty and brotherhood and respect and love, that turned into a conversation and finally a deeply felt hug.

When she first saw it, Ann thought that the dialogue and the sentiment was cheesy and hard to swallow. But here, in the cathedral, under the lofty ceiling and in the light of the delicate stained glass, before an assembled rapt audience of mourners, on the altar in front of a young man's coffin, the words transcended the source material. The two actors bellowed their lines. No need for microphones. And the passion and conviction of them flowed over the crowd. The two actors turned to each other and made the world believe that they were brothers, that family was more important to them than any differences in their past. As they finished, they cried, each putting one hand on Malcolm's coffin.

Ann stood along the far wall with the other staffers from the foundation and the tech billionaire's company who were working at the event. The woman next to her, from company PR, was trying to stifle her tears at the performance. Ann found herself nervously fingering the laminated badge that identified her as staff. When the performance ended, the crowd murmured its approval, wanting to applaud but realizing it was inappropriate.

The actors descended the stairs solemnly to the first row of pews, where they each embraced Malcolm's mother and grandmother, then together placed a hand on Malcolm's brother's shoulders and spoke some private words to him.

Ann's guilt was amplified when she watched Malcolm's brother, Marcus, slump back down into the pew. He didn't seem to be enthralled by the fame and power surrounding him, unlike most of the assembled mourners who barely knew the deceased.

The memorial service had all come together quickly, which wasn't unusual when the tech billionaire got an idea in his head. He had the money and the connections to make almost anything happen. But it was Ann who had started the ball rolling when the news broke on Saturday morning that the last person to die due to gun violence in the United States had been identified. It started as a local news story about a young man who had died of his wounds the same day the violence ended. It was picked up by one of the national news networks, which dubbed Malcolm "The Last Victim." Other news outlets must have been considering the same angle, because by midmorning there was a consensus that Malcolm was their symbol of the past. It was Ann who realized that this was the same client she had tried to reach the previous day.

There was some uncomfortable footage of reporters accosting Malcolm's mother on the street outside her building. Ann decided that the foundation could help by providing one or two people to run media interference for the family, digging into the general fund to pay for the funeral and other associated costs. After floating the idea with her supervisor, she was surprised to be told less than an hour later that the tech billionaire was on board. Ann was to run point with the family.

She had spent the weekend in their apartment, the only constant in an exponentially growing group of organizers and publicists. Malcolm's story had struck a chord with the world—the wayward poor teenager who had gone to prison but come out stronger and was putting his life back together when it was so unfairly snuffed out. Everyone who came to the apartment told the family that they were inspirations. The tech billionaire was particularly moved by Malcolm's tragic tale. So as Ann did her job, learning about Malcolm and his family, her discoveries became reality. Whenever Ann found out Malcolm's favorite singer or movie, that translated into a song or a dramatic reading in the program. Word trickled back to the apartment about this politician or that who had been added as a speaker. When the president decided to attend, Ann knew that any focus on the family would be lost. They had become the least important element at the funeral of their son and grandson and brother.

"That was so beautiful," the PR woman said, placing a hand on Ann's arm. "I can't wait for his next movie."

Ann just nodded. She didn't know if the woman meant the Oscar winner or the former athlete. They both had films coming out. Ann didn't want to see either one.

Another singer, more famous than the two before her, took the stage. She sang soulfully and as if there weren't a coffin behind her. Ann watched Marcus retreat further into the pew. He looked like a petulant teenager, like a kid who didn't want to be there. This funeral was being captured by TV crews and hundreds of cell phones. Ann already could identify the many moments that would go viral. She hoped that Marcus and his sour expression wouldn't be one of them. It would be so unfair for the world to turn him into a meme, but also typical of the modern age.

And it would be all her fault.

Ann knew her intentions had been good. She understood how expensive death could be for her clients and their families. All she'd wanted to do was defray the costs for Malcolm's family and help shield them from an unfamiliar spotlight. Instead, she had helped turn his funeral into a spectacle.

The singer finished. Again, unrealized applause hung in the air. The crowd was entertained. Ann felt most of them losing their interest in mourning. The politicians took their turns, each one twisting Malcolm's story into their own. After the mayor and the senator, Ann couldn't listen to any more. She needed to see the sun not filtered through stained glass, breathe the air not tainted by so much self-righteous self-congratulation.

Ann made her way toward the back of the sanctuary, toward the main doors. Whenever someone shot her a look that questioned her motives, she held up her badge, its laminated veneer an instant rejoinder to any accusations. She was on official business.

She felt relieved the moment she stepped out onto the majestic stone steps that led to the towering doors of the cathedral. The city continued to bustle around and below it. Not everyone had been frozen in time, rapt at the sacrifice of the Last Victim. Not everyone was as enthralled by the injustice and symbolism as those inside were.

Ann took a deep breath. She needed to shake this feeling before the end of the ceremony. It was her job to make sure the family navigated the exit from the cathedral. She needed to get them to the cemetery, where the foundation had gotten them a plot in a historic section normally reserved for city leaders and historical figures. The tech billionaire had designed a monument that would be placed on Malcolm's grave, but it thankfully wouldn't be installed for a month. The burial was for family and close friends only. No cameras. Just a coffin and a hole in the ground. Ann steadied herself again, banishing morbidity from her mind along with the other negativity.

She wandered aimlessly down a few stairs. A Secret Service agent stared her down. She flashed her badge, which seemed to satisfy him.

This was her fault, but it wasn't about her. Ann told herself that her own feelings were unimportant. But as she stood there, watching the cars drive by languidly on the distant streets that hadn't been blocked off, she knew her real guilt was because of her happiness. She had known when she left the house on Saturday that she wouldn't return until Monday. The foundation had found her a hotel about twenty minutes from Malcolm's family's apartment, though she hardly spent any time there. Ann slept in small bursts on the family's couch instead, power naps just long enough to keep her focused through the endless stream of phone calls and meetings. For two days, Ann had been both a help and a burden to Malcolm's family. But it had also been the first time she had spent a night away from Jake since they were married. She hadn't asked him. She had just told him that she had to go for work. She'd offered no explanation when he started yelling. She'd just walked out.

Those two days had been her happiest in years. As she helped these strangers, as she soaked in their grief, she secretly reveled in her own joy. For two days, she had not been scared. For two days, she had been free.

"Excuse me," a voice said behind her, deep and rich. "Are you the one who's been working with the family?"

Ann turned to find a man standing on the stair above her. He was looking at her intensely. Then she noticed a Secret Service agent in the distance giving her a concerned look. She held her hand up—*I'm okay*—and immediately felt shame for that. It wasn't an uncommon occurrence for someone to ask if she needed help when she was talking to a client on the street. The world worried about her and feared them. But her white hand could defuse a situation in a way their Black ones never could. The man standing above her was not a client, would never need to be, but he looked like them to the agent. Ann knew the man had noticed the exchange and was determined to ignore it.

"With Malcolm's family?" Ann said. "Yes, I'm with the foundation helping them."

The man stepped down to her level. She watched him dismiss his first response. Ann could sense that his reaction to the "help" from the foundation was similar to her own.

"So you've met Marcus?"

"I have," Ann said. "And how do you know the family?"

"I'm one of Malcolm's professors. He was a brilliant student."

The words hung in the air between them. In the distance, a siren wailed to life, moving away from the cathedral. Ann found herself wondering what types of emergencies still existed in the new world.

"Malcolm loved his brother more than anything," the professor said. "I've only spoken to Marcus a couple of times, but I feel like I know him through Malcolm. Did you know that the kid has taught himself to program in five different languages?"

"He writes computer programs?"

The professor looked at her sadly. Ann realized that she had found out so much about Malcolm over the weekend, and by extension his mother and grandmother, their lives, their problems. But she didn't know anything about Marcus, who had spent most of the weekend in his room, emerging only to have meals and when called by his mother to remind her of the name of this celebrity or that that his brother had liked.

"I think he's really good at it," the professor said. "Don't get me wrong. I appreciate what your foundation has done for the family. It is nice to be recognized and celebrated, even if this may be more about everyone else than Malcolm. He was never a victim, by the way, and even if that's how he's going to be remembered, he certainly won't be the last one."

"I'm sorry," Ann said.

She didn't even know what she was apologizing for. There were many possible reasons and all of them felt wrong.

"I don't need your apology," the professor said. "Neither does Marcus. But he does need your help.

Malcolm was so proud that his little brother hadn't made the same mistakes that he had. He felt that he had something to do with that, and he was probably right. But that anchor is gone now. Kids in places where Marcus live don't get a lot of chances. It's so easy for them to get lost."

The professor took out a business card and handed it to her. Ann quickly dug in her pocket for her own card. He took it with nod.

"All of this"—the professor waved his hand in the direction of the cathedral—"attention is going to disappear, maybe as soon as tomorrow. And Marcus is going to be in the same place he was before. But without his big brother. This is a bad day for him. But there will be many more. And it is going to be a very long summer for him."

Ann felt like she had been asked a favor, but she didn't understand what it was. The professor sighed and spelled it out for her.

"You work for one of the most important tech moguls in the world. Marcus is a smart kid who loves computers. Surely there must be something you can do to help get him through this summer."

Ann looked at the man's card, realizing she hadn't asked his name. Richard Davis.

"You're right, Professor Davis. I should be able to do something."

He smiled at her, satisfied. In the distance, the Secret Service suddenly moved toward their vehicles. The president must be done speaking. That meant the ceremony was over. Ann nodded one last time at Professor Davis, then hurried back to the doors of the cathedral. The mourners would be required to stay in their seats until the president had left through a side entrance. But then many of them would want to express their condolences to the family. Ann needed to be there to help them manage that and get them to the cemetery to bury Malcolm.

JULIAN

EVERY TIME THEY touched him, he felt himself becoming less clean.

The nurses here all had accents. Jamaican, Haitian, Filipino. They perverted the English language on their tongues, made it grate like sandpaper in his ears.

Except his mother. She spoke English right, sometimes whispering to him when they were alone. Sometimes to the other nurses, using names he recognized from when he used to live at home, when she would tell his father about her day at work.

You didn't kill anyone. It was the most common thing she whispered in his ear. She thought it would make him feel better. It made her feel better.

It only reminded Julian of his failure.

He still wanted to kill someone. Anyone.

Julian wanted to have hands that could strangle. Feet that could stomp a head into concrete. A penis that could fuck. He wanted to feel his elbows crack bones, his knees bruise stomachs.

He had all of those things—feet, hands, knees, elbows, a penis—but they might as well have belonged to someone else. Julian felt nothing from the neck down. There was sensation in his face. His cheeks ached. His chin itched. He knew that the back of his head rested on a pillow.

And he could swallow.

The Filipino nurse said he was lucky when she fed him. He could eat real food. Sort of. His diet ranged from liquid to mush, nothing that needed to be chewed. The Filipino woman spooned it into his mouth, having raised his bed just enough to let gravity help him. Still, he choked sometimes. It happened with his own saliva too on occasion. The nurse would sit patiently and wait. She smiled, and he wanted to bite her lips off and spit them in her face. Julian had teeth. He could feel them in his mouth. If he concentrated hard, he could click them together. But after a moment, the Filipino nurse would bring the spoon back to his lips, and he would want to deny her access, but he was hungry and his reflexes opened his mouth enough at the touch of the spoon for her to push through.

His mother was there every day, not that Julian could track time. He had trouble following words, linking them into sentences. His world had devolved into snippets, in the air, in his mind. Sometimes she was in her work scrubs, sometimes in normal clothes.

His father hadn't yet visited him. Not that he knew of. Not when he was awake.

The doctors and nurses and police officers who frequented his room didn't know if he could understand them. They talked around him, not to him.

His injuries were often described as traumatic. To his spine. To his brain.

His future was considered uncertain. The doctors said he wouldn't regain much use of his body. The question was whether he would live. The police officers had faded away as a presence, having been more prevalent in the first few hours or days or minutes. They'd questioned whether he would ever be charged or tried. They debated among themselves whether he was being punished enough.

His mother talked of taking him home, setting up his room to accommodate his new condition, taking him on outings in a special van they would buy. Then, she usually cried.

If he did go back home, his father would have to see him. Someday.

"The president is talking at that poor boy's funeral. Turn on the TV."

"Never seen so many people turn out for a black boy before."

"It's a new world."

There were two nurses in the room. The Jamaican, the Haitian. The TV was mounted near the ceiling. Julian could see if from where he lay. It was rarely on. Channels flipped by until finally landing on live news coverage of the president's eulogy.

"... *a world where men like Malcolm don't need to be afraid to walk home at night in their own neighborhoods...*"

"That man has never been to that boy's neighborhood."

The other nurse grunted her agreement. Then Julian's view of the TV was blocked.

"Good morning, Julian. Time for your bath."

She sounded cheerful, but it masked her real feelings. These women all knew his mother, so they were nice to him. But he knew they hated him as much as he hated them. Only Julian was being honest about it.

He could not speak—the truth or otherwise. When he tried, it just came out as guttural throat clearing that led to overenthusiastic praise from the nurses and his mother. Their false faces infuriated him.

The nurse removed the covers from his body. She pulled up his gown, letting it bunch up around his shoulders. Julian could feel the fabric tickle his cheek. He could glimpse the edges of his own nakedness. Otherwise he wouldn't have known that anything was happening. Her words didn't correspond to any sensation. He felt the wet from the sponge only when she ran it over his chest and droplets spritzed in her haste onto his nose and forehead.

"*The threat of violence has pervaded human society for our entire existence. We have always known that we needed to avoid it at all costs. Now we are given the opportunity to build a world where it is not even an option.*"

The nurse worked methodically and thoroughly, dragging the sponge over every inch of his body. No part any different than the other. She flopped his penis to one side, then the other, lifted his testicles to get underneath, always keeping one eye on the TV.

"Was that who I thought it was?"

"Yeah. All the famous people are here today."

"Julian. I'm going to roll you over now."

Her dirty hands did just that. All he could see was the wall now. Julian didn't even know if she was still cleaning him until he felt the sponge on the back of his neck. When he was returned to his back, she was carrying his bedpan to the bathroom. She came back with it empty and lifted his legs to slide it back under him.

"Malcolm did not die in vain. He will always be a reminder to us. He did not let his past define his future. He was in the process of changing his life when it was cut so cruelly short. But in his example we can all find our own way forward in this brave new world. Our past does not have to define our future."

The nurse pulled Julian's gown back down over his body. The sheets rose to cover him.

"That man speaks and says nothing."

"He don't care about that dead boy at all."

One of the nurses laughed. The other one *tsk*ed. Julian wanted to shoot them both and watch their splattered brains drip down the walls. The TV was turned off. He wanted to ask them to leave it on. The distraction was nice.

But the screen was dark now, reflecting the room back at him. Julian could see himself in there, tiny and prone, immobile, useless.

"You rest now, Julian. I'll check on you later."

He wanted to scream. He wanted to curse her. Call her names. His anger had no outlet. It rested in the bones of his cheeks, the tendons of his neck, his throbbing temples. Julian wanted her to understand.

Julian made a small clicking noise in the back of his throat. It sounded damp and uncomfortable. He pushed harder and the clicking became almost a gag. The nurse rushed up to him quickly. She grabbed his jaw with one rough hand and opened his mouth with the fat fingers on the other. She peered inside him, searching for a blockage in his airway. Keeping his mouth wide, like a dog about to get an unwanted pill, she grabbed a device next to the bed. The suction. Julian felt the long stick work its way around his tongue, his palate, the back of his throat. The roar of it filled his head.

When she was satisfied, the nurse replaced the device by the bed. Again she was smiling down at him. She wiped his face with a tissue, gently, like his mother used to do. Then she left without another word. After a few minutes, the overhead lights shut off, leaving him alone in his gray netherworld.

His mother was wrong. About many things, but one in particular. Julian had killed someone. Tanya was dead.

He heard people talking about her sometimes. Never the way she should be talked about. Debating whether he'd corrupted her or she him.

The president had spoken at the funeral of that dead black boy. Julian didn't know if Tanya had even been buried. He didn't know, would probably never know, where her body was.

And as his eyes closed, removing him from the world and into the limited recesses of his own mind, Julian felt nothing but rage.

MARCUS

NONE OF THESE people knew Malcolm. None of them.

"Don't be rude."

Marcus had heard his grandmother's voice in his head through the entire ceremony in the cathedral. And he did his best. He wanted to be rude, but he wasn't. He shook the president's hand. He let himself be hugged by the first lady. They were just two well-wishers in a long parade of hugs and gripped hands and people touching his shoulders, his forearm, his face, the back of his neck. There was no part of him they didn't think they owned. Women he didn't know kissed him. Men he didn't know cried in front of him.

But Marcus felt nothing in that place. He was as empty as the space between his seat and the lofty ceiling.

Both he and Malcolm were wearing their church suits. Marcus's didn't fit particularly well anymore. He had grown since they'd bought it. He probably would have gotten Malcolm's as a hand-me-down someday.

No one else could see how well it still fit Malcolm. Someone had decided that the casket in the front of the cathedral should remain closed. But Marcus had gotten to see his brother before the ceremony, before the pews filled up with hundreds of people he didn't know, who all knew who he was. At that moment, looking at his brother's closed eyes and his hands folded neatly over his tie, Marcus didn't feel Malcolm there. He could see his brother; he couldn't feel him. This wasn't the case in the apartment, in their room. There, Marcus felt the presence—and absence—of Malcolm acutely. But in this cathedral, throughout the speeches, he felt neither Malcolm's presence nor his absence. He felt nothing.

When he was getting dressed in his room alone, before he wandered out into the living room and that woman from the foundation, the one who had moved into their apartment, had helped him fix his tie, Marcus had considered bringing Malcolm's gun to the service. He'd assumed that the family of the dead wouldn't have to go through a metal detector, wouldn't be patted down. He had been wrong on both counts. He and his mother and his grandmother were checked the same as everyone else. Marcus hadn't wanted to bring the gun to hurt anyone. In fact, he knew he couldn't hurt anyone. But he did want them to be scared. He imagined standing on the pew, waving the gun, pointing it at the people pretending to mourn his brother, pulling the trigger, watching them scramble and duck away. When that scene played out in his mind, he did feel something, but it wasn't his brother.

After the ceremony, after the last of the celebrities and politicians told him he was going to be okay, that his brother hadn't died in vain, the woman from the foundation ushered them back to the limousine. Marcus didn't feel his brother there either. It wasn't a long ride to the cemetery. His grandmother held his hand while his mother cried softly across from them. The woman from the foundation sat quietly with them. She had spent most of the past few days telling them things—who was going to be there, what was going to happen—but now she was silent. There was nothing left to say.

At the gravesite, Malcolm returned to Marcus. He felt him when they carried the coffin over and placed it on the mechanism that would lower it into the earth. He felt him when he looked into the rectangular hole in the ground, just wide enough for the casket and a thin layer of dirt added to all sides. He felt him in the faces of the much smaller group that had been brought to witness, aunts and uncles, cousins, friends of his mother's, old women who knew his grandmother. People he rarely saw outside of today. Malcolm's professor stood off to the side, staring at his hands. There was also a small group of young men and women, mostly white, shifting nervously among themselves. They must be friends of Malcolm's from the college. Marcus wanted to talk to them but didn't know how, and they didn't approach him, though at one point a smallish boy who was probably older than he looked regarded him sadly as he hugged a tall girl who was crying.

They all stood around the open grave and the closed casket. The pastor from their church started a sermon. Marcus felt Malcolm shifting next to him, as uncomfortable and bored as he was. This should have happened in their church, just a few short blocks from their apartment. That was where Malcolm would have been sitting in the pew next to him, making little jokes under his breath, getting Marcus laughing while the pastor droned on and their mother shot them dirty looks. But here in this graveyard as the pastor spoke of passing to the next world and sloughing away the sins of this one, Marcus grew cold. A chill passed through him—Malcolm saying good-bye.

Marcus felt his chest constrict. He couldn't say good-bye, not here. He wasn't ready to watch that wood box lower into the damp ground. He lost the ability to breathe, thinking of the dirt being shoveled on top of it. Marcus turned to walk away, but he felt his mother's hand on his arm.

"Where are you going?" she whispered under her breath.

"I can't . . ."

"Let him go," his grandmother said.

His mother removed her hand and turned back to the open grave. Marcus walked away. He could feel the disapproval behind him as he stalked off toward the welcome hall at the entrance of the cemetery, the place where tourists stopped first to get their brochures. Marcus seethed at the idea that Malcolm would become part of their walking tour: *See the final resting place of the Last Victim*. They would forget his name and know him only that way. Marcus had seen a sketch of the monument they were going to put on top of Malcolm, all marble and imposing and solemn, nothing like his brother. He wondered if they would try to make him come back here when it was finished.

All of the foundation's vehicles, including the family's limo, were parked in the circular driveway by the welcome center. The foundation had promised transportation for all the mourners' trips home. It was the final kindness in a long day of charity. Marcus wanted to slash the tires. He wanted to break the windshields. The thought of getting back in that limousine made him queasy. He was pretty sure Malcolm had never been in a limo.

"Are you okay?"

The voice was tentative and familiar. Marcus turned to see the foundation woman behind him. She looked like she had been crying. His anger subsided a little—not that much, but enough for him to remember that she had told them she had spent time with Malcolm, for just a few visits, to ensure the program was working for him. This woman at least had a claim to know his brother.

"Sorry. That's a stupid question. Of course you're not okay. And you don't need to be."

Marcus considered the woman's face. He tried to remember her name. Maybe it was Amy.

"I just needed some air," Marcus said.

It was the kind of thing people said on TV and in movies. He felt dumb as soon as he said it. He had already been outside by his brother's grave. But it was true. There was no air there he could breathe. The foundation woman didn't seem to notice.

"I was talking to Professor Davis earlier," she said. "He told me that you're a very talented programmer."

It took Marcus a moment to remember that Davis was Malcolm's professor's name. The guy was a history teacher; how would he know Marcus was a good programmer? The woman was holding out a business card to him. Marcus took it. Her name was Ann.

"You know who I work for. I think there are a lot of opportunities for you. But only if you want them. Today is not the day to think about it. But tomorrow might be. You can call me or text me anytime."

Marcus could hear Malcolm's voice in his head. *Don't make my mistakes. Take your opportunities.*

But the voice was far away. Muffled. Being suffocated under a growing mound of dirt.

"I have to leave," Marcus said.

"Oh, all right," Ann said, looking around for a family member. "I can have a car take you somewhere."

"I'm going to walk."

Marcus had no idea how far he was from his apartment. But he had to leave and he didn't want to get in any of the cars. He wanted to walk forever, in a straight line, away from here. The woman looked panicked.

"It's at least a few miles home," she said. "It will take hours to get there. Your mom will be worried."

But Marcus was already walking away, backing toward the front gates. He locked eyes with Ann.

"Tell her not to worry," he said, knowing it wouldn't do any good. "No one can hurt me. Not anymore."

Outside the main gates to the cemetery, Marcus turned left onto the main road. He walked for many blocks before taking out his phone and mapping a route home. He had been headed in the wrong direction. He didn't care.

Marcus walked. Sometimes he followed the path on his phone. Sometimes he ignored it or deliberately turned the wrong way, forcing it to recalibrate the way home. He walked through countless neighborhoods, on large streets and small. Into parks, up hills, past shopping areas, through valleys of apartment buildings and prairies of manicured lawns and deserts of abandoned warehouses. He purposely routed himself through areas where just the previous week he would not have been safe. But any dangers that had lurked there barely registered now. Everywhere he saw people walking on the sidewalks, loitering in front of their homes, talking to their neighbors, not looking over their shoulders. In the wealthier neighborhoods he still got lingering looks, though less fearful and more curious. In the poorer ones, more nods and smiles than the vague threats and scowls he was used to. The city was exhaling a collective sigh, taking stock of itself anew.

Marcus walked for a long time. His path meandered but generally pointed toward home. He had started later than he'd thought and the sun set on him sooner than expected. The darkness, usually bringing more risks, instead found children playing on quiet streets and parents just home from work enjoying the warm evening on porches and stairs. The dinner hour brought out grills and coolers, another round of impromptu gatherings.

Everything grated at Marcus. Malcolm had never seemed scared on the streets around their neighborhood. He probably hadn't been afraid the night he was shot, right up until the moment he heard the gun go off, the instant he felt the bullet tear through him.

The surroundings became more familiar. This was the edge of his neighborhood. Only a few blocks before he was home.

His mind had wandered along the way. He thought about programs and code, losing himself in the language and the commands. He had written mainly games, but those were so trivial. They could do nothing to quell his anger. Nothing to ease his pain. Marcus had a red-hot smoldering inflammation inside him. It throbbed and called his name. It demanded retribution for Malcolm. But it had no outlet. There was no gun that could satisfy it, no bullet left to fire. But the foundation woman's words had gotten him thinking. He was talented. He could write a program that would decimate those who still lived. Those who could no longer be shot and killed. Those who were starting to feel invulnerable. Marcus could still hurt them. He had read about hackers, glossed over the damage they could do.

Marcus could write a virus. And as he approached his building, he considered his targets.

"Get out of my way!"

A wiry young white guy whom Marcus recognized as one of the itinerant junkies who frequented his building ran at the door, which was being blocked by two women with interlocked arms. The guy looked like he was going to crash through them to get inside, a messed-up version of red rover, but he pulled up when he got close, like a stunt plane making a sudden turn upward. The junkie stomped his feet and shook his fists at the woman, who were unmoved and held fast.

Marcus approached the building. The women noticed him and smiled.

"Hey, Marcus," one of them said.

"Your mom and grandma are already upstairs," the other said. "They'll be happy to see you."

The women were about to move and let him in the front door when the junkie attached himself to Marcus's side.

"This guy, he's a friend of mine," the junkie said. "We'll go in together."

The women closed ranks. Marcus moved away from the junkie. "You're no friend of mine."

The junkie looked genuinely hurt. Marcus envied the man's ability to believe his own lies so thoroughly. Marcus went and stood next to the women.

"It's okay," he said. "I don't need to go in yet. I can stay out here all night."

One of the women, the older one who sometimes came to the apartment and gossiped with his grandmother, patted his arm. Marcus glared at the junkie, who threw up his arms and stalked off down the street, looking for another place to score.

The women separated, allowing access to the front door. The younger one, who was still older than his mother, touched his cheek.

"Your brother is proud of you."

Marcus nodded and hurried inside. Malcolm would not have been proud of what he'd been thinking on the walk home. He shook that off and wondered if the world had been infected by its own virus, by a disruptive program that had shut down one of humanity's core functions. It might not have alleviated that junkie's cravings, but it made it harder for him to sate them. He turned the corner and found the dealer sitting on the stairs.

"Figures those bitches let you in," the dealer said. "They're doing a number killing my business."

The dealer laughed. There was no menace in it. He seemed to find the situation genuinely amusing. Marcus froze, staring at the man who sprawled languidly in front of him. The dealer seemed too relaxed, maybe having sampled some of the product he couldn't move. But he sat up a little straighter in the light of Marcus's glare.

"Whoa, man, ease up," the dealer said. "I'm not having a great day."

"Did you bury your brother?"

"Oh shit, right. I saw some of it on TV. Did you actually meet all those people?"

The dealer was definitely stoned. Marcus wanted to hit him but knew he couldn't. He thought about his virus. There was no way to infect this man directly. The one thing Marcus could do to hurt the world probably would have no effect on the dealer at all.

"Fuck you," Marcus said.

He walked past the dealer, his anger only growing with the proximity. Then he noticed the bullets, three frozen projectiles, still hanging above the stairs. Someone had tied brightly colored strands of ribbon to each one to keep people from walking into them. They hung down below, swaying slightly in an unseen breeze, like the tail plumage of tropical birds, the tentacles of a jellyfish. Marcus let one run over his hand as he passed by.

"You know, I saw you," the dealer said.

Marcus paused. The dealer pointed up the stairs.

"The other night. I saw you shoot at us. I really thought that was it for me. Then the bullets just stopped there. You know, when it first happened, they were still too hot to touch. Like little ovens that had been turned on."

Marcus didn't care.

"How many of them were meant for me?"

"All of them," Marcus said.

The dealer laughed. "Everyone's getting fierce suddenly. I wanted to go out and get some food. Worried those little old ladies wouldn't let me back in."

"They shouldn't."

Marcus looked back at the dealer, who slumped against the stairs. He was shaking his head, defeated.

"I always figured someone would kill me," the dealer said. "I didn't think it would be you. It's weird now, you know. Not always expecting to die."

The dealer snorted again.

"I'm thinking I should go to Utah," he said. "Looks like not much left for me here. I've got family out there. Black Mormons, if you can believe that shit. So I might just go to Salt Lake City for a while."

Marcus couldn't tell if the dealer was talking to him or himself. It didn't matter. There was nothing he could to the dealer now except refuse to listen to him. Marcus sprinted up the stairs to the first landing, ready to get away.

"Hey!" the dealer called after him. "I didn't kill your brother!"

Marcus stopped in his tracks. He refused to look back down the stairs.

"I just said that before . . . I don't know why. But I didn't do it. It was good for business, having people think I would shoot someone. But I never did."

Marcus faced the dealer. "Who did, then?"

"I don't know. But it wasn't me."

Marcus didn't know whether to believe the dealer. It didn't matter. He ran up the remaining stairs, all the way to his apartment door. He could smell dinner from the hallway. His mother and grandmother had been making Malcolm's favorite meals all weekend. He opened the apartment door and breathed it in. The kitchen smelled like his brother. His mother saw him first and rushed over to hug him. Marcus regretted walking away from the funeral but knew that it had been his only choice.

"Come eat," his grandmother said. "While it's still hot."

His mother let him go. She ran her fingers under his eyes, trying to wipe away tears that were actually on her cheeks.

"Be right there," Marcus said. "It smells great."

Like a divining rod, Marcus was drawn to his room, where his brother felt strongest. He looked at his computer as Malcolm watched him from the futon. He took out Ann's card from his pocket and put it on his keyboard. He wasn't going to write a virus. He could disrupt the world in other ways. He felt Malcolm approving behind him. Marcus would text Ann. Find out what she meant by opportunities.

Tomorrow. Right now it was time for dinner. Marcus realized he was starving.

RICHARD

After Marcus left, Richard wandered away too, heading in the other direction, deeper into the cemetery. The sobbing receded behind him along with the sound of the shovel retrieving dirt from the pile aboveground and depositing it onto the wood casket below. He wove through the field of gravestones, the stillness settling around him. Each slab of marble or granite represented a loss, the blocks rising to various heights, some adorned with elaborate carvings, a lion or an eagle, a bust of a man or woman, others plain with only some words etched in their facades. It was a forest after a fire had stripped the trees to charred trunks, merely a reminder of what had stood before.

This cemetery stretched for acres in all directions, the biggest and oldest in the city, one of the few places where all inhabitants, regardless of race, ethnicity, income, or religion, mingled together. Richard had come here today to mourn Malcolm, but he was also looking for his mother. He had not been to her grave for years, not since the boys were born, and looking out over the vast landscape of stone and dirt, he wasn't sure he would be able to find it.

An image flashed through his mind—Elijah holding the Nerf gun. Richard felt his own seven-year-old hand wrapped around the real gun that had killed his father. His mother had cocooned his small hand within her own and pried the weapon loose. Richard remembered seeing her take the gun just as he had, finger looped over the trigger, as if she was considering shooting the dead man again.

Richard didn't cry that night. He couldn't remember breathing, though he knew he did. But he listened as his mother told him that she had done it, not him. People didn't take kindly to Black boys with guns, no matter their age. Her son was not a murderer. They would not brand him a criminal, not her baby. She would not let them take him away and put him in a juvenile facility to be eaten alive or hardened forever. That would not happen. Richard had not killed this man. She'd killed him. And by the end of her speech, when she was on the phone with 911, Richard believed her. He knew it was their lie to share, and he believed it was true.

Seven years later, Richard began to wonder if it was time to tell the truth. He was fourteen. On the phone with his mother, he in the living room of his aunt's house, she in a hallway on a prison line, Richard told her that he had been accepted to a prestigious private high school. They had given him a full scholarship. It was the kind of place where every kid had a guaranteed future, safe and clean and rich. Richard would never feel welcome there, but he would take advantage of everything the school offered him. But there on the phone, he was telling his mother about the middle school graduation she would be missing and how much he wished she could be there. That was when it struck him. There was no reason she should be in prison. She hadn't killed anyone. Enough time had passed that he didn't consider himself to have killed anyone either. It was a seven-year-old version of himself that didn't exist anymore. Surely no one could prosecute a child that no longer existed. But when he tried to suggest that it was time to tell the truth, that maybe she could come home, the line went dead. Richard thought maybe her phone time was up. Sometimes they cut her off abruptly. But when he visited her two weeks later and made the same suggestion, she slapped the glass between them to silence him.

"This is the truth," she said. "I'm here and you're going to that school. You're an adult now. A teenager who does something like this ain't no child to them. You listen to me. You don't give anyone no crazy ideas. You go to that school. That's all you're gonna do. You go to that school."

Seven more years passed. Richard was a junior at a university far away. He was a successful student. Some of his friends knew that his dad was dead, that his mom was in jail. He had done exactly what she said. He had stayed in the first school and now was staying in the second. Richard had already started to consider the third school to come. But the idea of getting her out had never quite left his mind. The university had a law school, and the law school had a project. On a pro bono basis, the future lawyers and their professors dug through criminal records and convictions, looking to prove the innocence of those jailed wrongly.

Most of their cases revolved around a corrupt system framing the poor and the disenfranchised to maintain successful prosecution rates. Their tools were often DNA evidence that had been unavailable or ignored. It was detective work at the most basic level. But Richard knew he had an open-and-shut case. He knew who was innocent and he knew who the perpetrator was. He was on the verge of making an appointment with one of the professors to discuss his unusual case when he got the last phone call from the prison, a voice mail. His mother was dead.

You have our extended sympathy for your loss.

Richard heard the woman's voice in his head, the corrections officer reading off a script, sounding bored: *. . . the demise of your mother . . . please contact us for further information . . . two days to collect the remains . . .* Each phrase, rolling off the tongue of someone who had better things to do, sounded more obscene than the last.

The rest was a blur. Richard knew he'd called his aunts. He knew he'd flown home. He knew he'd attended a funeral at an unfamiliar church and stood over an open grave in this cemetery. Years later, he had tried to get his family members to tell him who had paid for the arrangements, but they'd waved him off.

Drifting through the tombstones now, Richard saw the open field in the distance, near the edge of the cemetery. That was where he was going. As he got nearer, it looked like an empty lot, the grass and weeds striving toward the sky, ankle and sometimes calf high. He crossed a paved path and stepped into the field, away from the better-groomed landscape around the more prominent headstones. His foot immediately bumped into a piece of rectangular granite, flush with the ground and hidden in the grass. He brushed over it with the sole of his shoe. A simple engraving listed a name and two dates, birth and death. It belonged to someone else. It was not his mother, but she was here among the others, buried in the weeds.

The markers here were laid out in a grid, side by side for maximum efficiency, each one distanced exactly the length and width of a simple pine coffin away from the others. Richard waded in, searching for his mother. He had only the vaguest memory of where she was but sensed that this area had no new occupants. It was full and forgotten, so his memory would not have to compete with a changed landscape. Static, so unlike the world around it.

Richard had spent many hours considering how the end of violence affected the world. Olivia had as well. He'd heard her on the phone with her law school classmates and professors, her clerkship judge, colleagues in other district attorney offices around the country. They were considering the implications of the new world. What it meant for parole and sentencing, how it would affect recidivism. They talked about what kinds of plea deals made sense now. Was anyone still a threat to society? What was the meaning of the word *threat*? The entire criminal justice system would have to change. So much of its harsh nature was based on the danger of the violent criminal. Protecting the law-abiding from the damaged and deranged, even when that determination was made on a wholly speculative basis. There was an excitement, a passion, in Olivia's animated conversations that he had not heard for a while regarding her work. He suspected that soon enough she would be moving on from being a prosecutor to engage this new reality. She was looking forward, into the future.

Meanwhile, Richard found himself mired in the past. Not a problematic place for a sociologist, but maybe also not a helpful one yet. Still, he found himself needing to reconstruct history with a lack of violence as a new variable. He wanted to write alternate histories. Richard wanted to radiate out not only from this moment but from all points in humanity's shared story, hoping that any extrapolation, fictional though it might be, could help prevent mistakes going forward. It was an amorphous project in his mind, but it was persistent. He wondered if there was anyone in the world today whose struggle had not changed, anyone in such dire straits as to have had the geography of their situation remain unshifted. Only the dead, he supposed.

Richard imagined his own life altered. What if the bullet hadn't found his father's head? If he hadn't been able to kill? If his mother hadn't taken the blame for what he'd done?

He continued to wander through the field of stones. Looking down on them, he could see that they were nestled within the green, not overgrown. He could read most of the names clearly. Only from a distance were they hidden.

It took time to find his mother. When he finally located her headstone, he looked around to see if anyone else had noticed. The only other person within sight was a grounds keeper, rolling slowly away on a cart laden with rakes and shovels.

Richard had spent the morning rehearsing speeches in his head. Monologues, lectures. Things he wanted to say to his mother. But now, standing over her grave, he had no voice. He realized it would be pointless to speak out loud. A slight breeze rustled through the grass. He no longer even knew if he was there to thank her or apologize. Neither. Both. He wanted to tell her about the kids, about their new home, his love for Olivia. But he wanted her to feel it, to experience it all, and that was impossible. There was nothing he could do or say to bring her back.

The field around him was a washed-out mix of greens and browns, inoffensive and bland. But looking down at his mother's name, he noticed a plant curling around its edges. A weed, but an ambitious one, had bloomed with a cluster of bright yellow blossoms. He looked around again, and now he saw other splashes of red and violet, yellow and orange, scattered around the field, subtle and inconsistent.

Richard knew he didn't have to say anything. And maybe someday he would bring the boys and Olivia here. They wouldn't have to say anything either. In silence, he dropped to his hands and knees and began to clear the weeds away from the perimeter of his mother's gravestone. He left the yellow flowers intact.

ANN

JUST INSIDE THE front door to her house, Ann almost took off her shoes, but she decided to leave them on. It had been a long day spent mainly on her feet. A long three days working with Malcolm's family. She was exhausted. All she wanted to do was collapse on the couch with someone who would rub her feet and bring her a drink. A hypothetical husband who wasn't Jake.

She had seen lights on in the house from the car. He was home. Ann hadn't spoken to Jake, hadn't texted him, since she'd left Saturday morning. She had no idea what he'd done all weekend. She assumed he'd gone to work today. Ann hadn't thought much about him. Some, but not much. And she had been happy, as guilty as that made her feel.

Shoes on, Ann turned the corner to peer into the kitchen. Jake was not there. No sign that anyone had been cooking, that any meals had been eaten there. Ann had been expecting a pile of dishes waiting for her. A few steps away, she looked into the family room. The TV was off. No one was on the couch.

The dread had risen in her the moment she pulled into the driveway. Ann realized that it was something she had learned to ignore in her daily routine. It was just part of the rhythm of her day: Growing relief as she drove away in the morning. The satisfaction of working a full day helping people at an organization she loved. Mounting uneasiness as late afternoon faded into early evening and she approached her home. But after a couple days away, she had lost some of the detachment she had developed over the years. She felt the prickly nausea in the base of her throat, the queasiness deeper in her stomach. Jake was here, lurking, and she didn't want to be. The fact that the world had changed meant little in this forgotten corner.

He can't hurt you, Ann thought. *Not anymore.*

She didn't believe herself. Down the hall, she could see a light on in their bedroom.

Ann had spent the day directing politicians and celebrities, fielding media requests and deflecting over-eager attention seekers. When it was done, she had been personally commended by her boss, one of the richest men in the world. But here she found herself frozen in the hallway, terrified to walk to her own bedroom.

In another world, in another house, she would have called Jake's name from the front door. He would have been eager to see her, excited to hear about her brush with being at the center of the universe.

Instead, Ann found her tongue dried to a piece of bark in her mouth. She went back to the kitchen and poured herself a glass of water, drained it, and refilled it from the sink. He probably heard the water running. He probably had seen the headlights in the driveway. He probably knew she was there.

Ann went back to the front door and retrieved her suitcase. Bag in one hand, glass of water in the other, she walked down the hall to their bedroom.

Jake sat on their bed. He had been watching the door. He knew that Ann was coming, and he had been waiting for her. In his hand, a pair of scissors. The bed was covered with colorful strips of cloth, and at first Ann thought he had been engaged in an uncharacteristic crafting project, maybe sewing a quilt, until she realized that he had been cutting her clothing up. He was surrounded by the tatters of her wardrobe, dresses, blouses, pants, all reduced to shreds.

Jake watched her realize what he had done. His smile widened. He pointed the scissors at her.

"I watched your funeral on TV today," he said.

Ann saw herself ignoring his comment. She saw herself putting her suitcase on top of the dresser and unpacking it in silence while he watched, placing the unworn clothes into drawers and taking the toiletries back to the bathroom. Ann saw herself gathering the remnants of her clothing off the bed, stuffing them into a garbage bag, which she stowed in the back of her closet instead of taking it out for the trash. She saw herself rushing home every day to make him dinner, night after night, year after year. Ann felt him stab her with the scissors, though she knew the sharp edge could no longer cut her flesh by his hand. She, too, saw her own funeral.

As the visions spooled in her mind, Ann stood by the door, suitcase still in one hand, clutching the glass of water in the other. Then the glass was gone, flying through the air. Ann had thrown it at his head. She wanted it to smash against his temple, embed itself in his skull. She wanted Jake to bleed in front of her. She wanted to hurt him.

Her aim was good. The glass was on target. But at the last moment, instead of impacting Jake's cheek, it swerved. Water showered over the room, soaking the bed and the floor, as the glass orbited his head, boomeranging back around in Ann's direction before taking an abrupt turn toward the floor. It shattered on the ground. Jake looked down in shock at his bare feet, which were now surrounded by shards of glass.

Ann wanted to watch him stand up and try to avoid cutting his feet. She wanted to see him wince when he failed.

She stopped to catch her breath. Jake looked so small and helpless on the bed, trying to figure out what to do next. The scissors hung limply in his hand. He seemed more like a child caught after a stupid impulse than her husband. Or had he become her, sitting there waiting for the next punishment? And she him, looming over her, ready to deal it out?

Ann didn't want to be either of them. She resisted her urge to get on her hands and knees and clear the glass away from his feet. She tamped down the desire to gloat at his plight. There was no one in this house she wanted to be. All the roles belonged to someone else.

Still holding her suitcase, Ann turned and left the room. She walked down the hall to the front door.

"Where are you going?"

Jake's voice called after her, angry and desperate.

Ann wasn't sure where she was going, but a list was already forming in her head. People who would take her in for the night, maybe longer. Just until she got her feet back under her.

"Ann!"

She didn't stop. Ann walked out the front door and left it open behind her. She drove away and didn't look back.

SYMPOSIUM

THE EMPTY
SHELL

THE EMPTY SHELL loved to fly. In the decade since his country had changed, since its citizens had been allowed to travel outside its borders again and return without consequences, he had been to many places around the world, but he'd enjoyed few of them as much as the flights to get there. It thrilled him every time they took off. The otherworldliness of it—defying gravity, looking down on the clouds, the constant roar inside the cabin—made him light-headed and even giddy, though he didn't show it. The Empty Shell particularly enjoyed turbulence, just what they called light chop, when the plane swayed and rolled, even the sudden dips that made his fellow passengers gasp and grab the armrests. He wondered if that was what a roller coaster was like. He had never been on one, or any amusement park ride. Most of the countries he had visited had them, but he had been accorded a certain level of dignity among his countrymen and the rest of the word that prevented him from doing things that seemed undignified, such as screaming with wild abandon as he dropped straight down while sitting in a tram car. He likened his fate to that of the Queen of England, whom he had met once and also didn't seem to be afforded the opportunity to have much fun.

The seat belt light went on. A voice came over the loudspeaker. The Empty Shell hurried to put his earbuds back in so that the universal translator on his phone could interpret for him. The voice in his ear was the same as the one on the loudspeaker, explaining that they would be landing in San Francisco soon. The announcement would be made in Korean next, but the Empty Shell enjoyed using the translator when he could. It was a marvel of technology, now available on every phone, tablet, computer, and miscellaneous device worldwide. There was never a language barrier anywhere anymore. The speaker talked in their language, and the listener heard the same words in theirs. Even more amazing, the translated words in the listener's ears were always in the voice of the original speaker.

The Empty Shell took his earbuds out again when the Korean started. He smiled. He was flying to America for the first time in his life to meet one of the three men who had invented the translation software.

He had received many invitations to America before but had always turned them down. He had met many billionaires as well, but he was particularly intrigued to meet Marcus Wright. There was no shortage of interesting origin stories among the wealthy and self-made, but Marcus's was particularly compelling to him. The Empty Shell sometimes felt that he had become more of a symbol in his country than a person. Marcus's brother Malcolm, the Last Victim, suffered from a similar categorization. So he felt it necessary to go to America as the first speaker in a lecture series about the end of violence that bore Malcolm's name.

The Empty Shell enjoyed flying, but he also did not sleep on airplanes. As the descent into California began, he hoped that his jet lag wouldn't interfere with his demeanor. Dignity was imposed on him, but he wasn't always dignified when tired. He looked around the first-class cabin. He had insisted on being in coach as he always did, but the Americans ignored him, and when he got to the airport he discovered he had a first-class ticket on a fully booked plane. This was typical of the Americans. Even after the change, they still believed that they were always right, and the rest of the world still let them get away with it.

There was some research showing that the United States had been one of the least affected by the end of violence, along with most European countries. A study by a group of Harvard professors had ranked every country in the world by the aggregate effect on its citizens. It turned out that there were countries in the world where violence had not been a daily part of most people's lives. Despite the United States' love affair with guns, that had been the case there. The Empty Shell's country had been the number-one most changed in the study.

This had not surprised the Empty Shell or anyone else. Those countries that had been ruled by fear and the threat of violence found themselves upended overnight. It didn't take long for the people to realize that they were no longer in imminent physical danger from their own governments. It took a lot longer to figure out what that meant. In some countries, such as the Empty Shell's, the ruling class took great measures to try to maintain the status quo. The Dear Leader ordered the food supply sequestered and unleashed a propaganda barrage on all State media denying that anything had changed. But the Dear Leader and his top generals and the political elite soon discovered that they did nothing but give orders and they had lost their ability to compel anyone to follow them. Their drivers stopped showing up to chauffeur them, and their cooks did not prepare any more meals. Their toilets weren't cleaned and their children weren't cared for. Those inconveniences were only the first things they noticed before the general strikes began. The electricity to their homes was cut off. The water filtration systems malfunctioned. Their communications and their satellite feeds were disrupted. The Dear Leader could suddenly no longer communicate with his military on the front lines or watch his favorite sitcoms. And while it started with workers not showing up at factories, soon it was also their supervisors. In the army, it started with the soldiers and quickly spread to the brass. Those at the bottom were used to being hungry and going without basic services. Those at the top were not and no longer had any recourse to force the masses to serve them.

The generals had turned to the Empty Shell for assistance. In their wisdom, they had televised the failed final execution, forcing the entire nation to watch. But instead of proving that they could still kill with impunity, they'd shown that they were helpless. The entire country had seen the Empty Shell stand up in that square. In that moment, he had become all of them, and they had all stood up or sat down or spoke out.

The generals had a plan. They would announce the end of the Dear Leader's reign and install the Empty Shell as the new president. There would be only chaos without control, they said. He could prevent a disaster from occurring. They smiled when the Empty Shell agreed to give a speech at the same square where he had stood up, from the same podium where the Dear Leader had spoken, to a crowd of thousands who had taken up residence there to wait for change and the millions more who would see his remarks on television.

The generals wrote his speech for him. And when the Empty Shell stepped up to the microphone, he ignored it.

His speech was simple. Their country was at a crossroads. The people needed to choose new leaders. They needed to write a constitution and create new laws. They needed to be free, as were so many others in the world. The people could choose any leader they wanted, with two exceptions: they could not pick the Dear Leader, and they could not choose him.

The generals wanted to turn off his microphone and cut the TV feed, but they didn't know how. They wanted to force him off the stage, but they couldn't move him.

The generals had been right. There was some chaos in the weeks and months that followed, but it was also intoxicating. Here, as in many other countries that had suffered too long under dictators and through brutal wars, the people emerged and took control.

The Empty Shell played his role—the one he felt comfortable with, not the one others wanted him to embody. He had now been the face of two pivotal moments in the young history of their new nation. Some wanted him to be their Father. Some their new deity. Most wanted him to lead. The Empty Shell knew they didn't need the first two—the Dear Leaders had cast themselves in those parts for decades. But he did lead as best he could, considering himself an ambassador. Foreign leaders and rich investors from every country wanted to meet him. And he did his ceremonial duties, encouraging them to help his country grow and thrive. But he let others set the policies and handle the politics, stepping in only when they strayed too much toward the past, such as when they were considering subsuming his country into their southern neighbor through reunification. When the first president was elected, the Empty Shell attended the inauguration. When the first congress was sworn in, he read the words that they repeated back to him.

Mainly, though, he returned to what he enjoyed most. He wrote. Novels, essays, poems. He was happy when people read them. And he was happy when they didn't.

The bump of the tires on the runway jolted the Empty Shell, prompting him to look out the window. As the plane taxied to the gate, he marveled at how much the tarmac looked like every other airport he had seen, how similar they all were and how little some things had changed.

MARCUS

"**T**HEY BUILT A statue of me," Sang-hun Pak said. "They put it up in the main square in the same spot that had previously been occupied by our first dictator. It made me nauseous to see myself standing there in his place."

The man the world knew as the Empty Shell stood next to Marcus in the cemetery. Together they considered the marble obelisk that sat on top of Malcolm's grave. Marcus understood how Pak felt. This abomination had never reminded him of his brother, and it made him queasy that it was the world's impression of him.

Pak took a step forward and picked up a bullet that had been left on one of the monument's ledges.

"They do the same thing at my doppelganger," Pak said. "They leave bullets. Shells."

Marcus nodded. It had become a tradition at the cemetery to leave a bullet at the gravesite of the Last Victim. Many tourists and pilgrims brought their own. For those who didn't have their own, the gift shop sold bullets that could be placed at the grave, which then were retrieved at the end of the day by staff to be resold the next day.

"I wish people would leave flowers," Marcus said. "I hate this thing."

He motioned at the marble slab. When it had gone up, he'd still been only seventeen. His voice had meant nothing to those who erected it. Not that he had used his voice then. He hadn't even known how to complain to anyone but his mother and grandmother. And they'd worried that his anger would jeopardize the opportunity he had been given by the tech billionaire. So, even though no one in the family particularly liked the monument, they were silent on the subject.

What Marcus wished wasn't actually that people brought flowers. He wished no one visited at all. His brother had become a tourist attraction. The words *Last Victim* were etched into his gravestone. That was why he rarely visited this place. His brother was with him every day, in everything he did. Malcolm felt furthest away here.

There were tourists in the cemetery today. They lingered around Marcus and Pak, keeping their distance. But Marcus knew that it wouldn't be long before someone broke the invisible barrier and approached them. Both he and Pak were recognizable faces, the billionaire and the dissident. Their stories inspired people, and people who were inspired could be bold and annoying.

Pak had bowed his head and closed his eyes. Marcus couldn't be sure whether he was praying or just lost in his own thoughts. Pak had taken his earbuds out and held them in his hand. Marcus did the same.

They would put them back in next time they needed to talk. But for now, Marcus appreciated the silence.

Marcus remembered back a decade. The day after Malcolm's funeral, he had texted Ann. Then, she was just the woman from the foundation. He remembered thinking about the long summer before him, how he had nothing to do. Ann had texted back immediately. And a week later, he was wearing his church suit again, taking a series of buses to get to the other side of the bay to meet with the tech billionaire. He walked into the offices of the billionaire's company and found himself in a sea of T-shirts and shorts and flip-flops. The young woman who fetched him from the front atrium told him that only the lawyers wore ties.

It turned out that there was no summer program available for Marcus. So the billionaire had offered him a job instead. Marcus found himself working for the summer with the company's speech recognition team. He loved it. He had always found computer languages a natural extension of his own thoughts, but now he saw the possibilities of allowing computers to talk to everyone. It felt natural for him to be that translator between two worlds. So when he was admitted to Stanford the following year with a full scholarship from the foundation, he continued the work he had started. But it was a fateful meeting with a fellow freshman from China, his eventual cofounder, that led him to shift from translating between people and computers to using computers to provide flawless translation between people.

Pak was saying something to him. Marcus rarely took his earbuds out when he was with foreign visitors, of which there was a constant stream in his orbit.

He had grown used to never being unable to understand what was being said to him. So now to hear the Korean untranslated was jarring. He quickly put his earbuds back in. Pak smiled and started over.

"I would love to see your foundation, if we have time," Pak said.

He gestured toward the crowd that was starting to gather nearby. Marcus sensed that he wasn't interested in being approached any more than Marcus was. Although at least Pak was unlikely to be pitched investment ideas. Marcus nodded, and together they walked back toward their driver.

Marcus's foundation was housed in the apartment building he used to live in. He had bought or financed most of the surrounding neighborhood. Many things had changed in the wake of the end of violence. Many things had not. The climate had continued to deteriorate. Companies continued to get preferential treatment in Congress. There were still Democrats and Republicans, and their disagreements hadn't shifted much. Gun sales in America had increased after the change, the only country where that had occurred. Thousands still died from gun-related suicides and accidents. There was still persistent poverty. There was still racism and xenophobia. People were no longer able to kill each other over their differences, but it didn't stop them from hating each other.

Those were the things that Marcus used his foundation to counter. He still had trouble fathoming how much money he actually had. The company he and Zhang had founded had truly revolutionized the world. Every device had a translator now. And his company had used the strides they'd made in speech recognition and pattern identification to transform countless other fields. But persistent problems of inequality didn't need his programming skills. They needed his money and resources.

Pak and Marcus made it back to the car before the gawkers around them screwed up their courage. Marcus told the driver where they were going. He was relieved to be heading to his neighborhood. Some claimed he had turned it into a laboratory for his foundation's experiments. But he was satisfied with the results. He wanted to gentrify without displacing any residents. He had a vision, and three years ago he had tracked down Ann to run his foundation and make it a reality.

The car pulled away, heading out of the cemetery. Pak looked out the window. He seemed serene, comfortable with silences. Marcus had told him earlier about the challenges his foundation was tackling. Pak had said that his country now faced some of the same issues, but he said it with a smile that suggested he was happy to have such problems compared to those of the past. It made Marcus think of something he had just read by the Empty Shell.

Your fiction is our reality. Your reality is our dream.

Then Marcus remembered the book he had in his bag. He had to go into the boxes from the old apartment to find it, opening up ones labeled *Malcolm* that he hadn't looked at in years. He dug into his bag and pulled out Malcolm's copy of *The Collected Works of the Empty Shell*. He handed it to Pak.

"It was part of the curriculum for one of my brother's classes," Marcus said. "He read me one of your poems the night he was shot."

"Which one?" Pak asked.

Marcus took the book back and paged through it until he found the poem. He read it once to himself, then handed it back to Pak, who nodded as he read it to himself. Marcus was wondering if he remembered writing it. He would ask him about it later. But now, Marcus thought of his brother as the Empty Shell leafed wistfully through the early archive of his own words.

DAB

"Is that seat taken?"

A gray-haired woman in a blue jacket was pointing to the open seat next to Dab. She was already motioning to those sitting between her and him to stand up so she could pass by. Dab waved his hands to stop anyone from moving, creating a standoff. The woman stared him down, which made him shift uncomfortably.

"My friend is sitting here," Dab said. "She'll be right back."

The woman scowled. She looked to others in the row for confirmation that no one was coming back because no one had ever been there. But she just got shrugs and avoidance in return. Finally, she skulked off up the aisle in search of another seat.

The auditorium was full. It had that buzz about it that happened at the college when a famous or notorious speaker was on campus. Dab's missing friend had forced him to attend this lecture. She had chastised him for not realizing that the dissident he was about to hear was firmly lodged in the first category. Dab had never been much for international politics. She had laughed at him and called him provincial.

Dab checked his phone. No messages. He scrolled to their earlier text. Wright Hall, Main Auditorium. He was in the right place. She was late again. She was always late, but Dab could never be mad at her. Dab swiveled his head around to look up the aisle. She wasn't there, but the gray-haired lady was harassing another group of students.

"Who are you looking for?"

He turned toward the familiar voice. Cristela was making her way to the open seat from the other aisle. Dab stood up to let her pass, and she kissed him on both cheeks before dropping into her seat. Her flowered skirt fanned out around her.

"I've had a day," Cristela said.

"I'm sure," Dab said. "What happened other than having to get out of bed?"

Cristela gave him her patented raised eyebrow, his favorite look.

"Isn't that enough?"

Cristela let out a big sigh and threw her hand across her forehead in a mock swoon. Dab laughed. Whatever annoyance had been lingering inside him blew away.

Dab and Cristela had met on their first day at the college. Their rooms were on the same hall, two doors away from each other. Neither of them much liked their freshman-year roommates, so they spent endless hours in the common room, avoiding homework and eating pizza.

Cristela sat up suddenly and turned to Dab. When she focused her intensity, it could burn a hole right through you.

"How about you? Did you have a good time on your date?"

"It wasn't a date exactly," Dab said.

"Oh, really?" Cristela scoffed. "Did you and Henry go to dinner alone?"

"Well, yes . . ."

"And what happened after that?"

"We went back to his room . . ."

Cristela squealed. Dab held his hands up defensively as people around them looked their way.

". . . and talked. That's all."

"Until when?"

Dab answered sheepishly. "Two in the morning."

Cristela hit him on the shoulder.

"That is most definitely one hundred percent a date. Are you going out again?"

"Tomorrow night."

"Slow down, Casanova! And during finals!"

Dab laughed. He had told her at first that he didn't have time to come to this talk because he was stressed over finals week. She had guilted him into both last night's date and today's lecture. Dab could always count on Cristela to force him out of his naturally monastic ways, to drag him out of his room to go on whatever adventure she was planning.

When they had met, it hadn't taken long for Cristela and Dab to share first-day stories: *Where were you when the violence ended?* Dab had gone first. He'd told her about his bully and the slurs that spread

through the school after the kid realized he couldn't
beat Dab up. As end-of-violence stories went, Dab's
was better than average. Most people, at least in a college like theirs, talked about their reactions to seeing
the news on TV. Dab usually closed his by slipping in
that his sister had known the Last Victim and that he
had attended the funeral.

Cristela's story was far more compelling. In that
common room during freshman year, Dab realized
that it was amazing that she was even there. She had
fled her country because of violence, unaware that she
was fleeing something that had just become impossible. On the journey north, she and her sister had
learned that they couldn't be shot or stabbed or raped,
but it was possible to drown.

Cristela had been the first new friend Dab introduced to Jane, who worked in the city at a nonprofit
dedicated to poverty alleviation. Everyone loved Jane
and everyone loved Cristela, so of course they loved
each other. A couple of days later, Cristela had told
Dab that she was jealous that he could see his sister
anytime he wanted to. Her sister had gone back to El
Salvador, something Cristela still couldn't understand.
He told her that she could borrow his sister anytime
she needed her.

"Who is this guy again?" Dab said, gesturing
toward the front of the auditorium.

Cristela narrowed her eyes and grunted at him.

"I showed you that video of him standing up in
the square after they tried to execute him."

Dab remembered watching a video of two cats
walking back and forth on their owner's outstretched
arms while he danced a little jig. He still wasn't

convinced that hadn't been doctored. No one could be that strong. But he only vaguely remembered some guy standing up.

"You're impossible," Cristela said. "Did you read any of the book I gave you? All of his writing from before?"

Sheepishly, Dab shook his head. Cristela crossed her arms and looked stern.

"Did you read the book I gave you?" Dab said.

"I started it. It has elves in it. I don't read books about elves."

"I like books with elves."

"I know you do," Cristela said in her most pitying tone.

"Elves are better than people," Dab said.

Cristela flashed him her biggest smile.

"Not all people. Not better than Henry."

"Stop it."

But he didn't mean it. Dab slumped in his seat, turning red, as Cristela continued to tease him. He enjoyed every second of it as they waited for the speaker to arrive.

She was right. Not all people.

ANN

"Sweetie, Daddy makes chicken nuggets just as good as I do. I promise. Now put him back on the phone, please."

Ann's four-year-old had become a fierce negotiator. But Ann had not realized until right now that her maternal style of microwaving chicken nuggets was anything special. From her position just offstage, she peered out into the audience at the Wright auditorium. She could feel their anticipation for the Empty Shell and, of course, her boss, Marcus. Ann chided herself for not using the full name of the auditorium, even if only in her head: the Malcolm Wright Memorial Auditorium.

"I'm so sorry. I didn't think she was going to tell you about my failure."

It was Charlie, her husband of six years. They had met at a donors conference when she still worked for the other foundation.

"You couldn't really have messed up chicken nuggets," Ann said, barely stifling her laugh.

Across the stage, hidden on the other side, Marcus and the Empty Shell were talking to the president of the college. Marcus was one of their top donors. In addition to this building and two more on campus, he had recently endowed the first chair in post-violence studies to Professor Davis. Ann regularly fielded phone calls from pissed-off Stanford administrators who didn't understand why Marcus gave money to their competitor across the Bay instead of his own alma mater. Usually Ann politely reminded them that Marcus did not have a Stanford degree, having left school after junior year to focus on his company.

"Um, yeah, so I was supposed to do it for only twenty seconds," Charlie said. "I accidentally did two minutes. And then I was chasing after the other one—you know we have two children, right?—who had taken off his diaper, and well . . . I made chicken nugget hockey pucks."

Ann couldn't hold the laugh back anymore. She heard Charlie echo her on the other end of the line. Her daughter was in the background saying it was not funny in her most indignant voice. Marcus heard Ann laughing from the other end of the stage. He smiled and strode out to the podium to start his introduction of the featured speaker.

"So just get some more out of the fridge," Ann said.

"Those were the last of them," Charlie said.

"I really need to get better childcare," Ann said.

Charlie laughed again. Ann could live inside that laugh.

"I'll let that slide this time. But only because it's your birthday."

Charlie and the kids had made her breakfast in bed this morning. After taking an extra twenty minutes in the shower to get the syrup out of her hair, she'd declared a moratorium on all future meals in bed. Still, it made her smile thinking of the three of them trooping in with a tray, the biggest smiles on their faces.

"Ann, come on out here," Marcus said.

Ann took a moment to realize that she was being called out from behind the curtain. She usually stayed behind the scenes when Marcus was around, stepping out only when she needed to represent him. Of course, on a daily basis, she was front and center, making his vision for the foundation run smoothly.

"I have to go," Ann said to Charlie. "The speech is starting."

"Okay, have fun tonight. We love you. Say, 'Happy birthday, Mommy.'"

Two tiny perfect voices screamed it at the same time.

After the speech, Ann had plans to go out with some friends. But first she had to figure out what Marcus was up to. She stepped onto the stage to the applause of the crowd.

"All together now," Marcus said.

Then he led the crowd, at least two hundred strong, in singing "Happy Birthday." Ann felt every part of her blush. When they finished, Marcus came over and gave her a hug.

"I'll get you back for this," Ann whispered.

"I look forward to it," Marcus said with a wink.

As she retreated back out of the spotlight, Marcus continued with his formal introduction of the speaker.

For the first few years after Malcolm's death, Ann had kept tabs on Marcus. She had used the success of the funeral to ask the tech billionaire for a favor. She hadn't expected him to give Marcus a summer job but was thrilled when it happened. Ann also made sure the foundation would find the money for Marcus's tuition if he got himself into Stanford, which he did. Of course, she had actually done a favor for the tech billionaire, who was an early investor in Marcus's company and made a boatload of money. What she hadn't realized until a few years later was that Marcus had also been keeping tabs on her. So when he came to her with the idea for the foundation and the outline of what he wanted to accomplish, she had been taken by surprise. With a baby at home, she wasn't sure she could run a new foundation. But the offer was too good to pass up.

It was the best decision she'd ever made. In only a few short years, they had put forward a new approach to rejuvenating neighborhoods, bringing companies and governments together to ensure that services were available and no current residents were forced out by rising costs. It certainly helped that every neighborhood was now a safe neighborhood after the change. They also worked closely with community policing programs as law enforcement continued to evolve in the new world.

"So please welcome Sang-hun Pak," Marcus said.

Marcus bowed as the Empty Shell took the stage. He backed off toward Ann and left it to him. Marcus stopped next to Ann and patted her arm.

"Some days are good days," Marcus said. "Happy birthday."

Ann smiled and nodded. She put her earbuds in to get the translation.

"You probably know me better as the Empty Shell," Pak said. "On the day the violence ended, I was in a prison cell waiting for my first beating."

Ann thought back to when she realized that the violence had ended. She was also expecting a beating. There had been many good days since then. Thinking of the night ahead, dinner with friends and then home to Charlie and the kids, she knew that today was undoubtedly one of them.

GABRIELA

CRISTELA STILL HADN'T forgiven Gabriela for her decision to leave the United States and return to El Salvador after finishing law school. For Gabriela, America had never felt like home. Not like it did for Cristela. Gabriela had always felt like a foreigner, like an outsider. When chided by Cristela, she'd admitted that she had gotten quite a bit from her adopted country. But it didn't change the fact that she'd always wanted to return home.

When Gabriela graduated from law school, she'd had choices. She had done well. There were multiple offers from law firms. She was on a path, a successful one. Both she and Cristela had recently become citizens. The future seemed certain for both of them. But Gabriela was focused on another opportunity. Like most countries of the world, El Salvador had started a process to account for all of its unsolved murders, one last push to lay the past to rest. The UN had created a global framework for such efforts called the Truth and Reconciliation Project. El Salvador had more accounting to do than many other nations, having suffered through many years of horrific violent crime before the change. They desperately needed lawyers to help bring closure to those dark times. Gabriela felt she had no choice but to answer the call to serve.

"What are you thinking about?" Enrique said.

"Nothing much," Gabriela said.

Gabriela had been driving on autopilot. She checked her mirrors and scanned the road in front of her before glancing over at her husband. It was still strange to use that word. *Husband.* They had been married for only three days, having gone to the court-house for a brief ceremony with little fanfare. They had already started planning for another wedding, in a church, with his family and hers, sooner rather than later, but they figured their other news would go down easier with her mother and her abuela if they were husband and wife.

Gabriela reached out and squeezed Enrique's hand before returning her grip on the wheel. She pulled onto the highway from San Salvador to Jucuapa, where her mother had been living with her abuela for the past decade.

It still amazed her how fascinated Enrique was with her. She reveled in his interest, his attention. They had met a few weeks after she had returned to her country at a dinner hosted by her new boss on the commission. It had been a heady whirlwind for her. The world had changed, but the chaos of the capital's streets had not. The sights, the smells, the sounds—everything was so much more vivid than in the sanitized world of America. Gabriela was dizzy from trying to absorb it all and square it with the memories from her childhood. She couldn't sleep and would go walking at two in the morning, down dark streets and alleyways, around crowded bars emptying out, just to get a sense of how little and how much had changed. She was thrilled and exhausted. The dinner party, in a secluded complex that reminded her of Tio Isaac's home, was a welcome breather.

At the party, Enrique had made fun of her Spanish, which had been bowdlerized by years in the States. He claimed to have studied English in college, but when she forced him to speak to her, it was so disjointed that she couldn't help but laugh. They spent the whole night talking in two languages, one foreign to him and both belonging to her.

Gabriela glanced at Enrique again as they reached a cruising speed on the highway. His eyelids were already drooping. Enrique was a very predictable man. If he wasn't driving, the motion of a car inevitably put him to sleep. Gabriela watched him drift off, then returned to her own thoughts.

The work at the commission was grueling. El Salvador had thousands of unresolved deaths to work through. The UN had given guidelines to countries, but each nation set their own rules. El Salvador had opted for the most inclusive and most forgiving. The rules were simple: any confession would be met with mercy. The process was streamlined. Confessions were recorded and made available to the public through an extensive archive. The crimes were subject to a trial. The perpetrators were convicted and then pardoned. Justice without retribution. Truth without vengeance.

Gabriela, like many of the other lawyers at the commission, had her own past to reconcile. Most of the lawyers, like the entire country, had both victims and murderers in their close orbit. The country was small. No one had escaped the shroud of death. So Gabriela had waited for the day when it would catch up with her in her work.

That day had been a week ago. The lawyers all knew the names of each other's ghosts. All were on the lookout for their colleagues. So when one of her coworkers stood in the door of her office, Gabriela recognized the look on his face. She herself had stood in the doorways of others wearing the same expression. Gabriela's father's killer had come in to confess.

Gabriela had waited to watch it until she was at home that night with Enrique in the small apartment they shared. The confession was brief. That was what they were encouraged to elicit—just the facts, as devoid of emotion as possible. The man on the video looked old to her, worn down and haggard, but she knew he could be any age. He described how he had killed her father. Then he moved on to his next victim. He had five confessions. Gabriela watched only one.

She had not cried that night. Or the next. She had been preoccupied with how to tell her mother and her abuela. She had decided to wait until this weekend when they were together.

But now, driving toward her mother's childhood home, to the town where her abuela had been born, she doubted that decision. How could she possibly share such news? They were going for a celebration, after all, her abuela's seventy-fifth birthday, just a small gathering of friends and family. How could she bring the specter of past tragedy into the joy of the present? Not to mention the announcements about the future. Her marriage to Enrique. The baby.

Gabriela rested her hand on her growing belly. She was just starting to show. It had not been planned. For the future, certainly, but not now. But she was pregnant. She had told Cristela, which had sealed the deal on her sister coming to visit over the summer. Gabriela would take a few days off. They would go to the beach. She would need a maternity bathing suit.

Another hour and a half to Jucuapa. Enrique snored softly next to her. The road was straight and clear ahead. Gabriela drifted further into the past.

Thinking of Oscar, her last ghost.

Gabriela remembered waking up on the muddy banks of the Rio Grande a decade earlier, soaked and shivering. The air had rushed into her lungs in a sudden inhalation. She wondered if she had stopped breathing. She wondered if she was actually dead. Cristela was still cradled in her arms, unconscious but breathing. They were both alive. Gabriela looked up at the dark sky. She wondered which side of the river they were on, which country this mud belonged to. The expanse above her looked the same from both sides. Then the lights had approached, bouncing around them, slicing through the night. The two men shined the flashlights in her eyes and spoke to her in a language she didn't understand but could identify as English. They had made it to America.

But when they stood her up, started to move her toward some nearby vehicles, Gabriela had looked desperately around for Oscar. It came back to her, the last memory of him, his head bobbing above the churn, receding into the distance, until finally it was consumed by the black water. Oscar was not on this side of the river with them. They were alone with the agents.

Later, when she joined the commission, Gabriela had access to hundreds of databases from countries around the world, including Mexico. She searched for Oscar. Scoured every death registry she could find from the days and weeks after her arrival in the United States. Gabriela came up empty. Maybe he had survived. Maybe he had been dragged to shore and saved. She liked to think so.

* * *

Gabriela felt something move inside her. She considered the feeling, reasonably sure that it was too soon in the pregnancy to feel the baby kick. She was hungry. Someday soon, she figured, she would be able to tell the difference between movement in her intestines and in her uterus, between a new life and gas. She grinned at the thought. That was another conversation to have with her mother and her abuela.

That first night in America, on cots in the detention center, Gabriela could never have imagined where she would be today. It was there that she'd first learned about the changes in the world. The other migrants around her were cheered at the thought that those they had left behind were no longer in danger and mourned those already lost. The conferred in hushed whispers about what it meant for their future in this country. Gabriela listened to the voices around her and held her sister, who had woken up but had remained strangely silent. Only after Cristela had fallen asleep and the large room had gone still did

Gabriela cry softly into her pillow, not for her father or the other dead from her past. She drifted off in a sea of tears for Oscar.

A decade later, back in El Salvador, she'd again wondered what had become of Oscar and searched again for him, scouring photos of men with his name to see if he had lived. But then one night, as she stared at her computer screen, Enrique asleep beside her, Gabriela realized that she would never know what had happened to him. Even in the new world, so much was still uncertain.

On the road to Jucuapa, Gabriela pulled over into the right lane, drifting away from the city and into the relative calm of the countryside. She rubbed her stomach and thought about the feast that awaited her, her mother and abuela undoubtedly cooking and singing in their kitchen with the random relatives who had been enlisted to help. She realized she didn't know when she would tell them about her father, but it would come after she told them about their grandchild, their great-grandchild. She might not even have to say a word. Her mother and her abuela would take one look at her and they would know.

ACKNOWLEDGMENTS

THANK YOU TO my editors, Ben LeRoy and Sara Henry, for your guidance and hard work that made this a better book at every step of the process. Also thanks to Matt Martz and the entire team at Crooked Lane, particularly Rebecca Nelson, Madeline Rathle, Melissa Rechter, and Rema Badwan, for making the road to publication so smooth and enjoyable.

I truly don't have enough ways to express my appreciation to my agent, Stacy Testa, who has been a tenacious and tireless champion for my quirky little novels, giving me the encouragement I need to improve them draft by draft and finding them perfect homes when we decide to set them upon the world. Also, huge thanks to Michelle Kroes, Berni Barta, and all the folks at CAA for helping to take my work from page to screen.

No writer can be successful without the people who read their work-in-progress and tell them the unvarnished truth about it. So thanks to my friends and first readers—Elana Tyrangiel, Todd Carter, Vivienne Azarcon, Sarah Leavitt, Mark Thurber, and others—who are willing to take on my unpolished early drafts and let me down gently (more or less) about their glaring flaws.

It has been a challenging couple of years, and the unflagging support of all our friends and family have carried us through it. There are too many people to thank, so consider this an inadequate blanket appreciation to all of you who have helped keep us standing through the hard times.

Finally, I wouldn't be a writer if not for my parents, who always allowed me the space and freedom to believe I could follow my dreams. I hope that I can do the same for my kids, Allie and Maya, who are inspirations to me as they make their way into the world with more confidence and ability than I ever had. And, of course, I would be nothing I am today if not for Gillian, the strongest, bravest, smartest, kindest, and generally most awesome person I know. The day I moved into that apartment on the outskirts of Tokyo next door to you was the luckiest day of my life.